KAREN CLARKE is a Yorkshire-born writer living in Buckinghamshire with her husband and three grown-up children. As well as her previous five psychological suspense novels, Karen has written several series of romantic-comedies and co-written three thrillers with author Amanda Brittany.

Also by Karen Clarke

Your Life for Mine
And Then She Ran
My Sister's Child
My Husband's Secret
My Best Friend's Secret

Books by Karen Clarke and Amanda Brittany
The Secret Sister
The Perfect Nanny

The Mother's Secret

KAREN CLARKE

ONE PLACE. MANY STORIES

This novel is entirely a work of fiction. The names, characters and incidents portrayed in it are the work of the author's imagination. Any resemblance to actual persons, living or dead, events or localities is entirely coincidental.

HQ
An imprint of HarperCollins*Publishers* Ltd
1 London Bridge Street
London SE1 9GF

www.harpercollins.co.uk

HarperCollins*Publishers*
Macken House, 39/40 Mayor Street Upper,
Dublin 1 D01 C9W8

This paperback edition 2025

1
First published in Great Britain by
HQ, an imprint of HarperCollins*Publishers* Ltd 2025

Copyright © Karen Clarke 2025

Karen Clarke asserts the moral right to be
identified as the author of this work.
A catalogue record for this book is
available from the British Library.

ISBN: 9780008607593

This book contains FSC™ certified paper and other controlled
sources to ensure responsible forest management.

For more information visit: www.harpercollins.co.uk/green

Printed and bound in the UK using 100%
Renewable Electricity at CPI Group (UK) Ltd

All rights reserved. No part of this publication may be reproduced, stored in a retrieval system, or transmitted, in any form or by any means, electronic, mechanical, photocopying, recording or otherwise, without the prior permission of the publishers.

This book is sold subject to the condition that it shall not, by way of trade or otherwise, be lent, re-sold, hired out or otherwise circulated without the publisher's prior consent in any form of binding or cover other than that in which it is published and without a similar condition including this condition being imposed on the subsequent purchaser.

For Tim, with love

Prologue

Thirty years ago

If only the baby would stop screaming. My head is pounding, my nerve endings raw and exposed.

It's the hottest day of the year but despite throwing open all the windows and doors, I can smell the sweat on my body. When did I last have a shower?

It's a wonder the neighbours can't hear her bawling. They're probably at work, or too polite to complain about the noise. I don't know my neighbours, and that's the way I like it. Did like it. Now, I'd give anything for one of them to come and take control, because I'm not up to this. Hard to believe I had a job once, a good one, yet here I am, undone in two weeks by a seven-pound baby I was never sure I wanted in the first place. I kept it to please him, *but then he didn't come back.*

As the screaming intensifies, I grab the Moses basket and march out of the kitchen to dump it in the living room. I stumble upstairs to my bedroom, every part of me aching as though I have the flu. I slam the door and lean against it for a moment, the wood warm through my thin nightdress. I thrust my hands over my ears, tears soaking my cheeks. The sound of crying still bites at my edges, but at least it's further away.

I drop my hands and sit on the edge of my unmade bed, skin crawling as if there are ants underneath. Adoption, that's the answer. I don't want to be a mother without him. I can't do it on my own.

Minutes crawl past and it takes a moment to realise the screaming has stopped. The tension across my shoulders instantly eases. She must have cried herself to sleep.

For a second, I think I hear a movement downstairs, and remember all the doors are open. But I'm so tired and the thought of her waking up and going through it all again is like a weight, pressing me to the bed.

Despite the stifling heat, I crawl beneath the crumpled duvet and let sleep swallow me whole.

Chapter 1

Kate

'What's wrong?' I ask Dan, trying to hide my irritation as he pushes aside his uneaten cereal with a sigh. It's such a beautiful morning – the sunniest July on record – and I want to enjoy my last three weeks of pregnancy, not tiptoe around my husband's delicate feelings.

'Nothing.' He gives a ghost of a grin. His brown, rock-star hair flops forward as he stares into his coffee mug. 'Just a bit tired.'

There are clues to his state of mind: the three-day stubble, red-rimmed eyes and the ancient sweater with fraying cuffs he's started wearing around the house, like a comfort blanket.

'Are *you* OK?' He passes the question like a baton, aiming a nervy glance at my mid-section as if worried I might explode. I feel a pang for the old Dan, the one who would swing me around and dance me up and down the kitchen or throw me on the bed and tickle me until I begged for mercy. The new Dan treats me like a piece of china he's frightened of breaking.

'I'm fine,' I say, on a sigh. 'I'm pregnant, not ill.'

We don't talk properly anymore. We have solicitous exchanges, interspersed with an occasional outburst from me, followed by a hurt silence from him. The pregnancy wasn't planned. We'd gone away for a weekend and I forgot to take my pill, but Dan said not to worry, 'Whatever will be, will be.' I'd taken that to mean he'd be thrilled when I found out I was pregnant, but instead he's slowly retreated and I've got to the stage where I'm not sure I care anymore. I feel stronger with a baby inside me, as if I can take anything, like my mum did with me. Us two against the world. Maybe that's the problem.

'He'll come around once the baby's born,' Mum had said, when I confided my worries to her, but she didn't sound convinced. 'Maybe he feels a bit threatened.'

'By a foetus?' I'd wondered if she was right but couldn't bring myself to ask him. Perhaps I didn't want to hear the answer.

'You should have come to the scan,' I say now to Dan. 'It looked like a proper baby this time, sucking its thumb.' I bite into my thickly buttered toast and close my eyes. I could eat all day long and have to restrain myself. 'You could almost imagine cuddling it,' I add for effect.

'I know, I've seen the photo,' he says but has the grace to flush. His excuse for not coming was an appointment with a client he didn't want to let down. He's become obsessed with work, insisting we need a steady income for when I'm on maternity leave. I know it's his way of looking after us, but I'd have preferred him to be more involved with the baby. He managed a couple of antenatal classes but was so uncomfortable with the matey camaraderie of the other dads-to-be, all cracking jokes that wound up the health visitor, that we didn't go back.

Perhaps I've taken too much for granted. We never really discussed becoming parents. I just accepted it would happen one day, like I'd known the night I met Dan he was the man I wanted to marry.

He's the eldest of five. His parents Rory and Cass are bohemian types, who believe in free expression, and Dan was often left in charge of his younger siblings growing up. He's such a naturally caring person, I assumed he'd want children of his own one day, but now it's a reality he seems to be rebelling, as if his childhood experiences have put him off.

I wait for him to say something else, but he keeps staring into his mug, as if looking for answers, so I leave the kitchen and heave myself upstairs, cradling my swollen belly as if it might fall off. My back hurts, but that's nothing new at the moment.

I flop on the bed and stare at the floral wallpaper that's been here since we moved in a few years ago. I'd been planning to replace it with something less fussy but as work has got busier, it hasn't left me with enough time for home improvements.

I'm not a crier, but tears cluster in my eyes. Forcing them back, I think about phoning Mum, but she'll only start trying to talk me into giving up work.

'You're an interior designer, not a brain surgeon, Kate. Can't Saskia manage the showroom without you?' Or, 'Why don't you put your feet up? Think of the baby.' As if it might slip out if I move about too much. I sometimes think she's forgotten what it's like being pregnant.

She's proud of me but has never fully understood my love of interior design, the buzz I get from meeting clients and creating beautiful rooms for them. She always hoped I'd be an accountant, earn a good salary, have a pension plan. She's a bit better since I opened the showroom in Marlow and took on more clients, but I know she worries about me being my own boss, the responsibility and pressure it brings.

Even though it's Saturday, I'd normally be on my way to work by now, but Saskia's going in early to change the window display and won't mind opening up. She's keen to show off her own design flair and will relish the opportunity to be in charge. She keeps telling me to take it easy too, but in a half-hearted way. She knows I love my job.

When my phone – charging on the bedside table – rings, I

shoot to my feet and snatch it up, not bothering to look at the screen to see who's calling.

'Mum? I was just about to ring you.'

There's silence at the other end.

'Saskia?'

More silence.

I glance through the bedroom window at a gossamer wisp of cloud in the pale-blue sky and wonder vaguely whether I'm going to end up being a single mother like Mum was. I'd have to worry about that later.

'Hello?' I say again. I walk round the bed, smoothing a hand down my stretchy T-shirt dress, pressing the phone hard to my ear. 'Hello?'

'Kate Burgess?' The voice is female, small and breathless, as if the owner's been running.

'Who is this?'

She clears her throat – a fussy little sound. 'Magda Trent,' she says with more confidence. 'We talked the other day, at your showroom. About you redesigning some of the rooms in my cottage. I gave you my details and said I'd be in touch.'

'Yes. Yes, of course, I remember.' I spring into professional mode. I'm not going to turn a new client away, whatever else is going on in my life. 'You mentioned you were hoping to open a guesthouse and we discussed me staying overnight.' It was a service I'd started offering to customers with guesthouses or B&Bs, so I could get a better feel for the place before beginning my design ideas. 'Bear with me a moment.'

As I reach for my iPad and scroll through for Magda's details, I recall a round woman with soft, dark eyes and greying hair scooped up in a tidy bun. She'd seemed nervous, glancing shyly around, and after she'd gone, I commented to Saskia that she wasn't our usual customer, that she didn't look like she cared about interior design.

'Talk about stereotyping.' Saskia had grinned. She'd been out the back, unpacking a consignment of fabric. 'They're not all bored trophy wives, or yummy mummies spending hubby's cash.'

I find Magda's details. 'Bluebell Cottage, near Lexminster?'

'That's the one.' Another pause, as if she's weighing up her words. 'I wondered if it would be convenient for you to come over and give me a quote.'

'Today?'

'If possible.'

I mentally run through my diary. I have a consultation this afternoon, but Saskia can deal with it. I'll have to relinquish control at some point. 'I could be there within the hour,' I say, hoping I can find her cottage. My sense of direction is terrible. Mum always jokes that I could get lost turning out of our garden gate.

'It's a bit off the beaten track, I'm afraid,' Magda says, as if she's read my mind.

'Maybe you could give me your postcode for my satnav.'

'How about I meet you halfway,' she suggests. 'There's a lay-by on the bypass, just outside Marlow. You could follow me from there.'

I think quickly. It makes sense. I don't want to waste time driving around and end up getting lost. 'Fine,' I say. 'If you're sure you don't mind?'

'Not at all.' Her voice is warmer. 'I'll be in a silver Vauxhall Corsa,' she says. 'See you there in, say, twenty minutes?'

'Look forward to it.'

She takes a breath, as if she's going to add something else. 'Bye then,' she murmurs.

The line goes dead.

I put my phone back on charge and check my reflection, deciding against getting changed. T-shirt dresses are forgiving and it's the comfiest thing I've got. Plus, it's shaping up to be a blisteringly hot day and keeping cool is a priority.

I slick on a light layer of make-up and brush my hair; its

coppery hue pleasantly burnished thanks to the pregnancy hormones. Saskia jokes that it would be worth getting pregnant, if it would turn her fine hair thick and glossy.

As I pass Dan on my way out, he looks at me round the fridge door. 'Where are you going?' he says, appraising me with moss-green eyes. 'You're wearing lipstick.'

'I'm meeting a client,' I tell him, grabbing the overnight bag I keep ready for such occasions, and pushing my laptop inside my tote bag. I avoid his outstretched hand. We've got out of the habit of touching lately.

'Kate, just a minute . . .'

I catch his worried gaze. His eyes have always expressed his feelings, but all I can see when I look at him these days is the panic he couldn't disguise when I told him I was pregnant. It's never quite gone away.

'I'm staying overnight so I'll see you tomorrow.' Ignoring a twinge in my lower back, I rush outside before he can respond and manoeuvre myself into my Nissan. Revving the engine, I back the car out of the drive and onto the road, pretending I haven't seen Dan coming after me.

I don't bother returning his wave as I drive away, and his hand drops to his side. He cuts a forlorn figure in my rear-view mirror and as he recedes to a dot, I feel a pang of sadness and regret for childishly ignoring him.

Chapter 2

By the time I reach the main road, my spirits have lifted. The sun cuts through the windscreen, warming my bare arms, and I turn up the radio and shoulder-dance to some cheesy pop music.

Away from the house, I can pretend everything's fine with my marriage. I'm a healthy, pregnant woman on her way to meet a potential new client and what Dan chooses to do with his Saturday is up to him. He's supposed to be finishing a table for one of my customers, but he's got a wedding gig tonight. Band practice will take priority over furniture making. Not that I begrudge him. He's been a musician for as long as I've known him, but I wonder, sometimes, how it's going to fit in with being a parent.

The sheep-dotted fields of the Chilterns flash by as I leave Marlow behind and head for the bypass. The satnav assures me in a smug monotone that it's ten miles away in a straight line. Even I can manage that.

When 'Mamma Mia' comes on I sing along, smiling as I remember taking Mum to see the show in London last year for her fiftieth birthday. I was astonished when she said she'd like to see it. She's a creature of habit and rarely goes out in the evenings, but it was worth the effort of getting her to London to see her smiling goofily, eyes shining like marbles as she clapped along.

She'd seemed younger in a way that had made my chest ache.

She reverted to her usual self on the way home, worrying about being mugged on the Underground, telling me to close my bag or my purse would be stolen, with the pinched expression she wore when she was anxious. I'd struggled to hold back my frustration, telling myself as I always did that she couldn't help being that way. For all I know, she's never been any different. There's no one I can ask. Her sister, my Auntie Cath, lost touch after moving to Australia, and their parents died long before I was born.

'No wonder she's like she is,' Dan had said, after I introduced him to Mum, when he was being generous and giving her the benefit of the doubt. She'd fluttered around him, asking what his parents did for a living, as if we were living in Victorian times. 'What with her parents dying, and her sister moving to the other side of the world and being a single parent.' I'd explained to him by then that my father hadn't stuck around when Mum fell pregnant with me. She never saw him again and won't talk about him. All I knew was that he'd been married to someone else. 'I suppose it's enough to make anyone paranoid,' Dan had added.

'She's not paranoid.' I'd been moved to defend her, knowing she only had my best interests at heart. 'She's just careful.'

Dan had looked like he wanted to say more, but I changed the subject, relieved to have got the introductions out of the way, satisfied Mum had accepted our relationship was serious.

Too late, I notice the lay-by approaching and pull the car in, without indicating. A lorry swerves past, horn blaring. The driver's face is twisted with anger as he flicks a V-sign out of his window.

Heart hammering, I wrench on the hand brake.

'It's OK,' I murmur, placing a hand on my belly. The baby squirms powerfully, as if he's just woken up, and I take a deep breath through my nose, and release it in a whoosh, as advised by my 'Pregnancy Yoga' book. I've had a feeling for weeks now my baby's a boy. Mum says it must be a girl because I'm 'carrying at the front', which made Dan laugh. *Where else would you be carrying it?*

I've opted not to be told, despite Saskia's pleas to find out so she can start buying appropriately coloured Babygros or organise a gender reveal party. But I like the mystery of wondering and mulling over names. I fancy Charlie, which was my grandfather's name, or Samuel, after Dan's grandfather. Charlotte if it turns out to be a girl.

Dan says he doesn't mind either way. Maybe he doesn't care.

It's hot in the car. I buzz the window down and take a lungful of warm air. I need to let Saskia know where I am, ask her to do this afternoon's consult. I rummage in my bag for my phone.

'Shit,' I mutter, remembering I left it charging in the bedroom. I rummage a bit more, as if it might magically appear, then look through the window, willing a phone-box to materialise. Do they even exist anymore?

I toss my bag aside and drop my head on the steering wheel. I must talk to Saskia, or she'll wonder where I am. I can't let this afternoon's client down, but I can't turn back because she will be on her way. And if Saskia calls Dan, he won't know where I am either.

I let out a groan. I can't call Mum, and she panics if I don't check in with her every day. I don't know why, because I've had a textbook pregnancy, but then she liked me to check in with her regularly even before I was pregnant. It drives Dan a bit mad. Maybe I can ask Magda Trent if I can borrow her phone.

I'm swearing under my breath when a silver car glides past and pulls up in front of me. My heart gives a funny little leap, as though I'm meeting a lover instead of a client.

I close the car window and prepare to climb out, then pause. I imagine what Mum would say. *Wait for the other driver to get out first. It could be anyone.* The lay-by is quiet, set against a grassy slope leading to a bank of trees.

Narrowing my gaze, I peer through the back window of the Vauxhall in an attempt to see the driver. I realise she's looking right at me in her rear-view mirror, and as our eyes lock, a jolt of energy shoots though me. I lift my hand in a wave, and Magda responds. Her gaze slips away, and for a split-second I feel as if I've been cut adrift.

Another deep breath and I clamber out of the car, feeling somehow exposed. 'Magda! Lovely to see you again,' I call brightly.

She's standing by her open car door, round and upright like a bird. Her previously greying hair has been coloured a reddish-gold and is twisted into a neat coil at the nape of her neck.

As I approach, I see that she's probably in her late fifties, taller than me, and was a beauty once, with barely lined skin, and chestnut-brown eyes that give me a direct look. The shapeless clothes she'd worn to the showroom have been replaced with a light-blue belted shirt-dress, revealing her plump calves, while her feet are encased in navy canvas deck shoes.

I'm horribly aware of my sandal straps digging into my puffy ankles.

'Thank you for coming,' she says formally, and I detect a faint northern accent I hadn't been aware of before. Her gaze fixes on my belly, and blotches of red stain her cheeks.

I wait for the pregnancy conversation: the one complete strangers feel compelled to start that usually end in a gruesome birth story, but she remains silent.

'Sure you're happy to lead the way?' I chirp, reminding myself it's my job to put her at ease. 'Lovely car,' I add, foolishly. What I know about cars could be written on the back of a stamp.

She turns and stares at the bodywork, gleaming under the sun, as if surprised to see it. 'The cottage isn't far from here,' she says, and when she smiles a dimple forms in her cheek. 'Shall we go?'

'OK.' I nod, keeping my smile in place. She's obviously keen to get on. 'I'll follow you then, shall I?' I say, mentally kicking myself. Isn't that what we'd already agreed? I don't know why I'm on edge. 'After you.'

Magda nods, and after fumbling with the door catch, she gets back in her car, and I return to mine.

She drives carefully, which suits me. I'm like Mum in that I've always been a cautious driver, and more so now I'm pregnant.

A couple of miles down the bypass, Magda takes a left turn, indicating well in advance. I relax a fraction. She's obviously being considerate of me.

We're in a different county, one I don't know well. I've been hoping to expand my client base and look around me with interest. The streets are wide and tree-lined, the houses double-fronted and well maintained.

At the end of the road, Magda turns right, then takes a sharp left, and another right, until we've exchanged the leafy streets for a country road full of twists and turns.

As the miles flash by, I catch snatches of fields, a sparkle of a stream, some dense woodland, more hills. We pass through a few villages with pretty names: Kimble, Crestwood, and a couple I instantly forget.

Eventually, we slow behind a tractor, and I glance at the clock on the dashboard. With a shock I realise we've been driving for half an hour. I'm thirsty but daren't take my eye off Magda's car to reach for my bottle of water. We must be nearly there now.

The tractor finally turns, but my relief is short-lived when I realise that Magda is turning too. The road narrows to a dusty ribbon, cutting between high, spiky hedges, and a canopy of overhanging trees blocks out most of the sunlight.

She wasn't joking when she said she lives in the back of beyond.

Perspiration speckles my brow, and my seatbelt digs into my shoulder. I flex my hands, which ache from gripping the steering wheel too hard. All the windows are down, as the car's air-conditioning has stopped working, but there's barely enough breeze coming in to ruffle my hair. It strikes me I know nothing about the woman I'm following and probably wouldn't have come had the client been male. Then I tell myself off for thinking like my mother. I'm the one who placates and reassures, when she imagines danger round every corner.

All the same, I jump and swerve as a pheasant darts in front of the car and shoots into the hedgerow opposite. On my left, a tree looms, with a white wooden sign fixed to its trunk. CHERRY TREE FARM is painted on it in blue letters, and the tractor bumps through an open gate into the mouth of a field.

Magda keeps on driving.

I peer around for signs of life but can't see any houses through occasional gaps in the hedgerows. I suddenly want to stop, or turn the car round, and the realisation that I might not be able to find my way back to the main road makes my armpits prickle.

Perhaps this is a short-cut, and we're about to emerge into a suburb. The thought seems ridiculous, but I can't imagine how anyone living out here could be interested in interior design. The landscape is for farmers or recluses, or old people who've lived in the same house all their lives.

I hear Saskia's voice in my head, mocking me for stereotyping, and mentally shake myself.

All the same, I'm on the verge of stopping to at least have a swig of water, when Magda indicates right. Her brake lights come on, and she swings the car through a concealed gateway set into the hedge.

I follow carefully, trying not to scratch the car.

'Thank God,' I mutter, when I've pulled safely through and stopped on a gravelled area outside a pretty, two-storey building. My eyes widen as I take in the honey-coloured walls and steep, moss-covered roof. With sparkly windows that look like smiling eyes, and an arched front door frilled with pink summer roses, the cottage could have leaped from the pages of a lifestyle magazine. There's an air of comfortable certainty about it, as if it's been standing for centuries, and perhaps it's my hormones, or the relief of arriving, but my eyes fill with tears.

I switch off the engine, remove my seatbelt and lever myself out of the car. I suddenly can't wait to get inside and plan how to design the interior.

Chapter 3

Dan

'What's up, mate?'

Dan raised a shoulder and continued strumming his guitar. He wasn't sure how to respond to his friend's concern. 'Nothing,' he lied when the silence became uncomfortable.

After Kate had roared off to meet her client, failing to spot him waving, and leaving him feeling guilty and resentful, Eric phoned. He'd asked if Dan could manage a practice session before their gig that night.

'Late mornings are best because the neighbours are out. Less chance of anyone complaining.'

Glad of a reprieve, Dan had ignored the plates in the sink and the shopping list Kate had written the night before and pushed to the back of his mind the unfinished coffee table in his shed-cum-studio that should have been completed yesterday.

Instead, he ran upstairs to change out of his old jumper into a T-shirt and noticed Kate's phone on charge. He felt a spasm of alarm that she wouldn't be able to contact him. What if she went into labour? He didn't think she should still be working so hard this far into her pregnancy, but there was no point saying so. His opinions didn't count for much these days.

He grabbed his keys, jammed on his helmet, and revved his motorbike out of the garage. Opening the throttle he sped across town, the muffled roar of the engine drowning out his thoughts. Increasingly when he was out on his bike, he felt like riding on to somewhere nobody knew him.

Not that he could tell Kate. He felt terrible even thinking it, though he had a feeling she knew. He'd never been good at hiding his feelings from her. Had never wanted to, until lately.

'Dan?'

Eric's voice snapped him back to the moment.

'He's thinking that he's going to be a daddy soon, and he won't be able to perform for much longer because wifey will need him at home,' said Zoe, with uncanny accuracy, in her transatlantic twang. She was tall, with long, tanned limbs, her mane of liquorice-black hair dyed ice blonde at the tips. She picked her way like a cat through the cables snaking across the floor. 'Isn't that true, Danny-boy?'

'Not at all,' he said, laying down his guitar. Raising his head, he found himself trapped in the beam of her silvery eyes. He read mockery in their depths, but knew it was a disguise. Since joining Skinny Rivers as their lead singer six months ago, Zoe had made it clear she wanted him, married or not. Her tight white jeans outlined her endless legs, and he quickly looked away.

'So, what is it then?'

'I was thinking about tonight's playlist, that's all.' His cheeks stung with tell-tale colour and he was glad of the dingy lighting. Eric didn't believe in opening the blinds, favouring a pub-at-night atmosphere in his converted warehouse-studio.

Zoe caught her full lower lip between her teeth and slid her hand into his. She pulled closer, her small breasts brushing his chest.

He'd already noted she was braless beneath her long-sleeved

top and couldn't help comparing her figure to Kate's. Not that it was a fair comparison. Zoe was his wife's opposite – dark where Kate was light, hard-edged to Kate's soft curves. Not his type he would have said, if anyone had asked, although in the eleven years he'd been with Kate – six of them married – he'd rarely looked at other women.

'Leave him alone, Zoe,' Eric said amiably, rolling a cigarette.

Zoe slid him a look of wry amusement. She dropped Dan's hand and moved to the old leather sofa beneath the window. Flopping down, she fanned herself with a leaflet.

'It's boiling in here,' she complained with a pout. 'When are you guys going to get air-conditioning?' She'd grown up in America, and probably couldn't understand why the humid heat didn't bother them.

'You pay for it; I'll get it.' Eric grinned, and expertly ducked the cushion she tossed at his head. 'We don't usually have summers like this in the UK.'

Calum, the drummer, pushed back his tangle of straw-blond hair and threw Dan a quizzical look. 'How come you've managed to escape?' He smirked. 'Get written permission?'

'Don't you bloody start,' Dan said, anger blossoming. He plucked a bottle of beer from the ice-box by his feet and took a lengthy swig. The cool liquid tasted like nectar. 'I came because Eric asked if I was free, and I was. Unusually, since I'm the only one here with a proper job,' he added, though he knew Calum was scornful of his carpentry work. 'Who are you, bloody Jesus?' he'd laughed, the first time Dan mentioned it. 'Kate's meeting a client today, and . . .'

'Hey, have you met any of these yummy mummies she decorates for?' Calum interrupted. His beady eyes gleamed.

Dan had never been keen on him, even at university where he and Eric and Dan had met as students, forming the band during their second year. With his rosy cheeks, blond curls and cherubic face, Calum looked like a vicar's son, but drank too much and held questionable views about women.

Eric had a sense of loyalty to him, but Dan secretly blamed Calum for their failure to hit the big-time. If he hadn't turned up late and wasted to their one and only meeting with a major record label, nine years ago, they might have been signed. Things weren't the same after that. They'd gone their separate ways for a while, drifting back together when Calum and Eric failed to find regular work. Nowadays, the music was more of a hobby – at least to Dan. Gigs in pubs and clubs, and the occasional wedding booking, like tonight. He suspected the others still harboured hopes of being discovered, especially since Calum had drunkenly suggested they apply to go on *Britain's Got Talent*. He claimed later he was joking, but Dan wasn't so sure.

'They're not all yummy mummies, you tosser,' he said, and Zoe let out a throaty laugh. 'Often it's a business she's working for.'

Eric blew out a series of smoke rings. 'Can't imagine her up a ladder in her condition,' he joked, brown eyes crinkling at the edges. He was starting to look his age, Dan thought, his black hair too long and streaked with grey. He supposed they all were, especially Calum, with his watery, bloodshot eyes. He was thirty but looked a decade older.

'I wouldn't mind an introduction,' he was saying, not remotely offended. 'They could probably do with a bit of Calum magic.' He made a pumping gesture with his arm, then kissed his stringy biceps. He was sitting on a stool behind his drum kit, baggy shorts riding up his skinny thighs.

Dan caught a glimpse of his balls and glanced away, aware of Zoe's gaze. She had a way of watching him intently, as though studying him for an exam. Under her gaze he felt skewered, like a butterfly, there to be admired, with no consideration for his life beyond the band.

What was he doing here? he wondered, suddenly irritable. Kate would be upset if he didn't finish that coffee table and there was hardly any food in the house.

He thought of the wooden cradle he'd started making for the baby, intending it to be a surprise. Kate had been superstitious about bringing anything into the house before she'd reached six months, but at this rate it would never be finished.

'Can I have a drink?' Zoe said, interrupting his thoughts.

He felt a sag of resignation. 'Sure.' He picked out a bottle, glistening with condensation, and threw it to her. She caught it easily and rolled it along her collarbone, making an ecstatic face. He smiled, in spite of himself.

Kate hadn't met Zoe. He'd mentioned they'd taken on a new singer, but she hadn't been to one of their gigs for ages, which was probably just as well, though Kate wasn't the jealous sort.

A flash of annoyance rose, that he couldn't relax and enjoy himself for five minutes without feeling guilty. He couldn't blame Kate; it wasn't her fault, but he wished they'd properly discussed having a baby in the first place, and that he hadn't been so glib about her forgetting her pill. He should have told her how he really felt: that the thought of being a father terrified him. That he was worried he might turn out like his old man.

He hadn't really known until Kate blurted out the words 'I'm pregnant' – on his birthday of all days – that he wasn't ready to be a parent. Maybe never would be.

It had thrown him how excited Kate was from the start. She'd seemed so set on building up her business, to the point where she was working ridiculous hours, and had never even mentioned wanting a baby. As it was, they were the only couple in their crowd to be married with sensible jobs, and with a foot on the property ladder thanks to some money Dan had inherited from his grandfather.

He'd scaled down practising with the band to concentrate on his sideline carpentry business, scared he wouldn't be able to provide for his family otherwise, the way his own family hadn't cared about providing for Dan and his younger brothers and sister. Carpentry was one of the few useful things his father had taught him, and something he'd always loved, but the thought of making a living from it suddenly seemed set in stone. Or wood, he thought, rather grimly.

Calum threw his drumsticks on the floor, jolting Dan out of his reverie. 'I'm bored, man.' He got up and bounced on his toes like a boxer, jabbing the air with his fists. His grubby vest revealed a selection of dubious tattoos.

Eric stubbed out his cigarette, lit another and yawned, eyelids drooping. 'I could do with a nap,' he said. He was sitting on the floor, head lolling against the wall.

Zoe narrowed her eyes at Dan, like a sniper. She made a show of moistening her top lip with her tongue. The heat and beer were making him drowsy, softening his edges, but he looked away. He and Kate hadn't had sex in ages. She was worried it might harm the baby, and he hadn't pursued it.

Slowly, as though the pockets of her jeans were weighted with stones, Zoe moved over and dropped next to Dan on the sofa. She snaked an arm around his neck and rested her head on his shoulder. Trying to empty his mind, he breathed in her scent, which was surprisingly innocent and soapy.

With her free hand, Zoe dug her iPhone into a speaker on the arm of the sofa and switched it on. Music filled the room, one of their songs, about good times, and being on the road, being free. Zoe's vocals were low and mellow, oozing out like honey. Normally, Dan was critical of his musical abilities but conceded that he sounded pretty good on this track.

He remembered serenading Kate on their wedding day and how she'd cried, not caring that it was cheesy, or that her mascara had smudged.

From their first meeting, at a university gig she'd attended with a couple of girlfriends, he'd been drawn to her calm exterior. She'd been more mature than the girls he'd met up until then, her attitude a welcome contrast to the chaos of his upbringing, her creative streak a sexy surprise. He'd liked the way she turned to him for advice and took him seriously. And if he was honest, he'd liked that she didn't need looking after, unlike his previous girlfriend who had turned out to be clingy, unwilling to do anything or go anywhere without Dan.

'What are you thinking?' Zoe lifted her head and ran a hand through his hair. The drag of her nails on his scalp gave him goosebumps and he moved away slightly. Eric glanced over, his forehead furrowed, as though their closeness bothered him. He'd been Dan's best man at his wedding and was fond of Kate.

'Nothing much,' he said to Zoe, shifting further away.

She leaned over and pressed her lips to his ear. 'Shall we go for a walk down by the river?' Her breath was warm and damp. 'I know a place where it's pretty secluded.'

He didn't like to ask how she knew. There was a lot he didn't know about Zoe and didn't want to know.

He pulled out his phone, playing for time. He glanced at the screen, then remembered Kate hadn't got her mobile with her. He felt a wriggle of worry, remembering how she'd pressed her hands into the small of her back earlier. Then he thought of her unforgiving face as she left the house, and how she'd ignored him when he went after her. She probably hadn't given him a thought all morning.

'Sure, why not,' he said to Zoe.

He avoided looking at Eric, smiling instead into Zoe's triumphant eyes. 'Great,' she said. 'Let's go.'

Chapter 4

Kate

As Magda manoeuvres her Vauxhall inside the garage attached to the side of the cottage, I get out of my car and stretch. It's quiet, with only a twitter of birdsong and the distant drone of a tractor to break the silence.

The sun pours down, releasing mingled scents of rose and lavender from the garden, and as I inhale their perfume some of the tension leaves my shoulders.

I stoop into the passenger seat for my bag, glimpsing my reflection in the wing mirror. My make-up has melted, exposing a shiny forehead and the dusting of freckles on my cheeks. My eyes – normally a pale, clear grey – are bloodshot, as if I've been crying, and my lipstick's vanished.

I quickly renew it, then hunt for a band to tie back my hair but can't find one. The slam of Magda's car door makes me jump. I grab my bags, straighten and move to the porch, aware of my lumbering gait. Pregnancy has made me ungraceful, and my ankles are spilling over my sandals like dough.

'It's beautiful,' I say, out of breath, hoisting my tote bag onto my shoulder, my overnight bag in my other hand. It weighs a ton, as if I've stuffed it with bricks.

'Thank you,' says Magda, a smile on her lips. 'As I said, I want to turn it into a guesthouse.'

'It's a great idea.' I can see at once that it's perfect, even if it seems a long way from civilisation. 'How long have you lived here?'

'Not long.' She fumbles with her keys, almost dropping them. Up close, I notice a fine fretwork of lines fanning out from her eyes. Her skin is very pale, almost translucent, as though she takes care to stay out of the sun or uses a high-factor cream. 'I'm new to the area,' she adds.

'You're from Yorkshire,' I say, finally recognising the lilt.

Her gaze catches mine. 'You can tell?'

'Only slightly.' I sense a faint rebuke and heat sweeps up my face. Perhaps I've been overfamiliar, or she's trying to forget her roots and be 'posh'. I like an accent. Dan still has his Irish brogue, despite living in England for years, and I love it.

'The garden's wonderful,' I say, changing the subject and looking around. 'It must be a lot of work.' I can't quite picture her with a spade and guess it's her husband's domain. There's a thin gold band on her wedding finger, and I try to visualise what he looks like. Bald and jolly, I decide, with a bristling white moustache.

'I'm afraid the house isn't in such good shape.' She jabs her key in the front door lock and turns it, wiggling it slightly as though it sticks – a bit like ours at home. I keep meaning to give it a squirt with some WD40.

'I'm banking on that, or I wouldn't be here,' I say, in a jocular tone. I'm finding it hard to act naturally for some reason and blame it on my hormones.

'I'm so glad you are.' A brilliant smile illuminates Magda's face, like the sun bursting through a raincloud.

'Oh!' I say, flustered. I've never had a client be quite so effusive about my presence, but before I can comment, she pushes open the door and steps inside.

'Come in, come in,' she beckons, standing to one side and flourishing her arm. 'I'll get us a drink,' she adds, teeth flashing white in another smile. 'I made some lemonade this morning.'

At once, saliva rushes to my mouth. I'm so thirsty I can almost taste it: cold, and tangy and delicious. 'Sounds lovely.'

'We can take it out on the patio at the back of the cottage,' she says, sounding pleased.

As I edge past her my belly brushes her arm. 'Sorry,' I murmur, cheeks buzzing with colour. I still haven't quite adjusted to my new dimensions. It's like driving a bigger car than I'm used to, but Magda doesn't react.

'I'll show you around after we've had a drink,' she says, closing the door and pressing it into the frame. She drops the latch and slides two bolts across. 'Old habits die hard,' she says as she turns, perhaps reading something in my face. 'I lived in a rough neighbourhood for a while.'

My curiosity is piqued. How has she come from somewhere like that to this? Looking about me, I take in the tobacco-coloured wallpaper, and a low ceiling criss-crossed with wooden beams. The floor in the hall is uneven and dips in the middle and is covered in a carpet so faded it's impossible to determine its original colour. It was probably put down in the seventies.

'It's . . . got a lot of potential,' I say, trying to ignore a tightening in my belly, which has happened a few times lately. I've been told it's due to Braxton Hicks contractions – a sort of practice run for the real thing. 'I can show you some pictures of a nineteenth-century guesthouse I redesigned last year to give you some ideas,' I add, when Magda doesn't reply. 'A new front door with a stained-glass pane would let more light in here,' I continue, running a hand along the wall. I can't detect any dampness, which is a good sign, and I recall what she told me at the showroom: that the property was built over a hundred years ago, and although the decor left a lot to be desired, the structure of the building was sound. When I asked what sort of look she had in mind, she'd suggested something homely, which made a change from the usual remit of 'minimalist meets vintage' or 'rustic with a modern twist' or 'farmhouse chic' or 'we want to feel like we're living in Morocco, but on a budget'. ('You should tell them to go and *live* in Morocco,' Dan had joked, and I remembered his words when I visited the couple's apartment and had to smother a giggle.)

'Come through to the kitchen,' Magda says, and I follow her down the narrow passageway, careful of the floor dip, noticing that the patch of carpet had a faded pattern of swirls. On my right is a steep, wooden staircase, sunshine filtering down from a window on the landing, highlighting brighter patches on the walls where pictures must have once hung.

To my left are a couple of wood-panelled doors, one of them slightly open. I glimpse a smallish room, empty apart from a mole-coloured sofa in the middle of the hardwood floor and a television perched on top of an old-fashioned glass cabinet. It's obvious Magda hasn't lived here long. There's no real sense of her, not like at Mum's, with all the things she collects – books and easy-care plants, mostly – neatly arranged on shelves, pairs of reading glasses resting on various surfaces and a scent of ironing in the air.

The interior of the cottage smells musty and my nostrils prickle. I bite back a sneeze and my eyes water. I wonder if I have any tissues in my bag, but before I can check, Magda opens the door at the end of the hall and ushers me through it.

'It's quite nice in here,' she says, bustling forward. She plucks a flowery apron from the back of a chair and ties it around her waist, and I'm reminded of mothers in the Enid Blyton books I'd read as a child. As if to reinforce the image, there's a sweet smell of baking in the air, and a sponge cake filled with buttercream and strawberry jam resting on the side.

The kitchen itself is old-fashioned but cosy with a flagstone floor and a dark red Aga against the far wall, an inglenook fireplace opposite, hung with copper pans. Completing the picture-book feel is a tortoiseshell cat, sitting on a stripy mat in front of the fireplace, manically washing its paws.

'That's Arthur,' says Magda, stooping to stroke his glossy fur. He lifts his head to her touch, purring loudly. 'He appeared one day and hasn't left.'

'Hello, Arthur.' He ignores me, as if sensing I'm nervous of cats after being badly scratched by a neighbour's tabby as a child. Mum had insisted on taking me to the doctor to get it checked, murmuring about gangrene and sepsis and I'd been wary ever since.

'He's a bit shy,' Magda says, as if I might be offended by Arthur's ambivalence.

'He's cute,' I say politely, my gaze travelling to an open sash window above the butler sink, framed by red gingham curtains. There's a view of fields beyond the garden, which is surrounded by a high wall that looks centuries old and is partially covered with ivy, a scented breeze floating in.

'Sit down, my love,' says Magda, her manner much more relaxed as she indicates the oak table in the centre of the kitchen, a bowl of rosy-skinned apples in the centre. 'It's a bit cooler in here at the moment, before the sun moves round.'

I cross over and pull out a spindle-backed chair. 'This is lovely,' I say, while Magda opens the fridge and takes out a glass jug. I watch her stir the cloudy liquid with a long-handled spoon and smile at how much she resembles a cartoonist's idea of a farmer's wife, right down to wisps of hair escaping their coil and floating around her cheeks. I can just imagine her in charge of a guesthouse.

I lower myself gingerly onto the chair like a pensioner with arthritic knees, but as soon as I sit there's pressure on my bladder and I want to stand up again. 'Sorry to ask, but can I use your loo?'

Magda gives me a concerned look. 'Of course,' she says, nodding to a door leading off the kitchen, and I quickly relieve myself in the tiny toilet room. There isn't even a window, just a dusty extractor fan high on the wall, and I quickly wash my hands at the miniature sink, glad to get out.

'Better?' Magda greets me, taking two tumblers from a cabinet and filling them with cloudy lemonade.

'Yes, thank you,' I say. 'I may need to borrow your phone too, if that's OK,' I add. 'I'm afraid I left mine at home.'

'Of course,' she says as I take the proffered glass and inhale. It smells how I imagine a lemon grove would smell, and I take a few sips. 'It's delicious.'

I can't imagine Mum making lemonade. She's tried her hardest in the kitchen over the years but isn't a natural. I spent many mealtimes pushing her burned or tasteless food around my plate, pretending I wasn't hungry, until I learned to cook at school and found I loved it.

'So, you think you can do something with the old place?' Magda's shiny brown eyes glance over the room.

'I'll need to have a good look round, but I'm sure I can.' Excitement stirs. I want her to hire me.

'Money's no object.' She leans forward, her tone warm and confiding. 'You can do whatever you want, my dear.'

My heart flips. If she wants almost every room in the cottage redesigning, the fee will tide us over for the coming months. Although Dan has plenty of work lined up, his customers rarely pay on time. It would be nice to not have to worry for a while. The timing isn't the best with the baby due, but there's still a lot I can do.

Money's the least of your problems, a little voice pipes up. I ignore it, giving Magda my brightest smile. 'I can't wait to get started.'

She pours some more lemonade, and we chink glasses. 'Me neither,' she says, and we take long swigs.

The mood feels quite celebratory.

'I must give you a quote first, of course.'

'Of course,' Magda agrees, but I have the impression she doesn't care about money and wonder what she does for a living. It's hard to visualise her in a job, somehow. Maybe she's inherited the cottage, or her husband is wealthy.

'Have you run a guesthouse before?'

'No, this will be a first,' she says, eyebrows lifting, as though my question has taken her by surprise. 'I've been thinking of a new name and I'm pretty settled on Honeysuckle Cottage if that doesn't sound too cheesy. There's plenty of honeysuckle in the garden.'

'That sounds lovely,' I said. 'And it's just you?' I add carefully.

'Just me,' she says. 'But I'm not afraid of hard work.'

I've drained my glass again. I can't seem to quench my thirst, and hope it's the hot weather and not diabetes, which I've read can develop in the latter stages of pregnancy.

'I've a vision of each bedroom having a theme,' Magda says, pouring me the last of the lemonade. 'Maybe a different colour scheme in each, thick curtains and carpets. There are bare boards up there that have seen better days.'

'I'm sure we can come up with something suitable,' I say, stifling a sudden urge to yawn.

'Now, can I get you something to eat?'

I shake my head, remembering my gloomy breakfast conversation with Dan, his bowl of uneaten cereal. 'No, I'm fine, thank you.'

Magda's expression grows concerned again. 'Is everything OK, dear?'

Absurdly, tears spring to my eyes. 'Pregnancy hormones.' I flap my hand in front of my face. 'I'm so sorry.'

'I can see you've not long to go.' Her sympathetic gaze drops to my enormous belly. 'A month?'

'Just under three weeks.' I pluck a tissue out of my bag and dab beneath my eyes. 'I'm sorry,' I repeat. 'I'm not usually this unprofessional. I don't know what's wrong with me.'

'Don't be so silly.' She reaches out and covers my hand with hers. It's large and warm and surprisingly comforting. The urge to cry grows stronger. 'I remember what it was like to be pregnant.'

'You do?' Her face swims in front of me through a haze of tears.

She nods. Her eyes lock with mine and there's such sadness in their depths, my breath catches in my throat.

Oh God. Maybe her baby died.

Before I can speak, she asks, 'Do you have a husband?'

I blink and swallow, words clogging my throat. This is ridiculous. 'I do,' I manage to squeeze out.

'Problems?' She says it with such compassion, I feel an impulse to tell her everything – all the worries I've kept from Mum over the past few months, knowing she'd go into panic mode and make everything worse.

'Dan – that's my husband – he's finding it a little difficult to adjust, that's all,' I say, sniffing. I pull my hand from hers and blow my nose, knowing I must look a sight. My face was already shiny, and now my eyes feel puffy. 'He'll be fine once he sees the baby.' I attempt a watery laugh. 'At least, I hope so.' *Get a grip, Kate.*

Magda's eyes are gentle. 'Men can be fools,' she says, with such quiet conviction I wonder what her story is. Not a happy one, by the sound of things. I'm guessing that if there isn't a husband, there are no children either. Maybe running a guesthouse is a substitute for both.

I make an effort to get back on track. 'So, what about this patio you were going to show me?' I say brightly. 'I'd love to see it now.' I stand up too quickly. The room lurches, as though I'm on a boat and I grip the edge of the table to steady myself.

'Of course,' says Magda, a smile in her voice.

My vision clears and the room stops moving.

'Are you OK?' Spots of scarlet brighten Magda's cheekbones, and her eyes shine with concern as I sink back down, head spinning slightly.

'Just a bit light-headed.'

Glancing round, I catch sight of a mobile plugged into a charger near the kettle. 'Would it be OK to use your phone first?

I really need to speak to my colleague.' I point at it, feeling faintly ludicrous. So much for being businesslike. 'I'm sorry to ask.'

'No, no, it's fine.' Her face relaxes. 'Of course you can.'

I push my hair back. It feels too heavy, weighing my head down, reverting to the thick curls I usually straighten each morning.

Magda rises and unplugs the phone. It's an ancient model, with big keys and a tiny screen. 'The signal's patchy, I'm afraid,' she says as she hands it over. 'Maybe stand by the window.' She eases herself up. 'I'll wait outside and give you some privacy.'

I'm about to tell her she doesn't have to, but she's already opened the back door and is heading into the garden, closely followed by Arthur.

I tap in the number for Inspired Interiors, relieved I have it memorised; my fingers fumble a little, more used to the touch-screen of my iPhone.

Saskia picks up right away. 'Kate, where are you?' She sounds mildly alarmed. 'I was expecting you in ages ago.'

'I know,' I say, voice lowered. 'I forgot my phone and couldn't call you. I'm with a client. She rang the house this morning and asked me to come out and give her a quote.'

'Couldn't she have waited until Monday?'

'I don't mind,' I say. 'You might remember her; she came in last Tuesday.'

There's a silence, and I imagine Saskia's looking her up on the system. 'Magda Trent?'

'That's her.' I glance through the window but can only see varying shades of green and blue outside. 'She's turning the place into a guesthouse, so I'm staying overnight.'

'Are you sure that's wise, in your condition?' Saskia sounds concerned.

'The baby's not due for a few weeks; I'll be fine,' I said, injecting my voice with reassurance. 'It'll be worth it. I've a feeling she wants me to go ahead as soon as possible.'

There's a warning throb in my temples. I've had a couple of

migraines since being pregnant and hope one isn't coming. 'It's not that big, but has loads of potential,' I say. 'I think she wants me to do all the rooms, apart from the kitchen.'

'That's great.' Saskia's words are followed by a gulp. Her brick-coloured tea addiction is legendary. She gets through at least eight mugs a day. I picture her at the computer, hair curtaining her heart-shaped face, fingernails painted her favourite colour of the week – currently, Essie's Ballet Slippers, a shade of pink so pale I joke that she might as well not bother. 'She lives near Lexminster?'

'Yes,' I say. 'Although it must be on the outskirts. We were driving for about forty minutes from the bypass and it's quite remote.'

'You're not really selling it as a guesthouse,' Saskia says drily.

'Well, maybe not *that* remote. There's a farm nearby. Cherry Field or something.'

'Er, cherries don't grow in fields.'

'Don't they?' I rub my temple, willing away the pain building behind my left eye. 'Remind me to never try to grow them.'

Saskia laughs. 'Staying there's a bit drastic at this stage of your pregnancy,' she says, sounding suddenly doubtful. 'What if the baby comes early?'

'It won't,' I say, firmly. 'I was nearly a fortnight late, according to Mum, and I've a feeling this one's going to be too. And it's only for the night. It'll be good, actually.' I hesitate. 'Dan and I . . .' I stop as a shadow passes in front of the open window.

'I know things aren't too good at the moment,' says Saskia, filling the gap with her trademark diplomacy. 'You're welcome to crash at mine, any time.'

'I know. Thanks.' I'm grateful, but Saskia's just moved her six-foot-five, rugby-playing boyfriend into her tiny apartment and I'd feel like a gooseberry. A heavily pregnant gooseberry. Plus, I'm technically her boss and although we're friends too, it would feel like crossing a line to take my problems into her home. 'Listen, can you do the consult this afternoon?'

'Ooh, yes, please,' she says at once. 'Sure you trust me?'

'Of course I do.' Saskia's great with the customers and has seen me in action enough times to know how it goes. 'The details are in the diary,' I say. 'And I've left a mood board in the office.'

'Fantastic.'

'I'll speak to you soon.'

As I ring off, Magda slips back in and closes the door. Her expression is neutral, but I wonder if she's overheard. Not that it matters. I was hardly discussing state secrets. 'I'll just give my husband a call and let him know where I am,' I say, dialling his number.

She nods and crosses to the fridge. 'I'll make us some lunch,' she says. 'I don't know about you, but I'm starving.' She turns and wags a finger. 'I won't take no for an answer.'

I smile, willing Dan to pick up, and feel a wave of annoyance when his voicemail kicks in. What if I'd gone into labour, or my car had broken down? He's probably turned his phone off if he's at Eric's.

'As you know, I won't be home tonight,' I chirp, keeping my tone light for Magda's sake, though I long to say something cutting. 'I'm staying at Bluebell Cottage, near Lexminster.' Anxious suddenly that he might worry, I add, 'It's all good, I'm fine. And Saskia knows all about it.' I pause then say brightly, 'Could you let Mum know if she calls? Speak soon!' before ringing off and replacing the phone on the work surface. 'Thanks, Magda.'

As I turn to sit down, I'm seized with nausea. Saliva rushes to my mouth and I think I'm going to be sick.

'You're hungry,' says Magda, inspecting my face, which feels as if all the colour's been drained away. 'Stay there and I'll cook some eggs, and we can have some cake afterwards. I made it earlier.' She nods at the Victoria sponge on the side, and I swallow hard and sit down. She's probably right. I'd got home too late the night before to cook, and made do with a couple of bananas, and my earlier breakfast of toast seems a long time ago. I breathe deeply, one hand on my belly, and the sick feeling subsides.

Magda moves around the kitchen, humming softly.

The cat, back on the mat, stops licking himself and sits motionless, watching a bee suspended by the window.

Magda turns and catches my eye, her pupils large and dark, and for the strangest moment I sense something out of balance – not as it should be. Then she breaks into a smile and the moment passes. 'Won't be long now,' she says.

Chapter 5

After finishing a plate of scrambled eggs with ham, my stomach settles.

'That was delicious,' I say, pushing aside my plate. 'Thank you.' I stifle a yawn. I feel tired, my eyelids heavy.

'Everything looks better on a full stomach.' Magda lays down her knife and fork and dabs her mouth with a sheet of kitchen roll. 'At least that's what my grandmother used to say.' Smiling, she clears the table and fills the sink with water, then flicks on the kettle.

'Tea?'

'Coffee, please, if you have it.' I went off coffee at the start of my pregnancy but need a jolt of something to keep me awake. Mum would tell me off for drinking caffeine, which she'd read was bad for the baby, but Mum worries that everything is bad for the baby, even though I've done everything I am supposed to. 'White with one sugar,' I add.

'Coming up.' Magda spoons instant granules into two white mugs, pours on boiling water and adds a splash of milk. 'Here you are.' She places the steaming drink in front of me, and although I prefer real coffee, the aromatic scent helps clear the woolliness in my head.

'Thanks.' I sip the hot liquid, feeling guilty that I'm letting her wait on me. Mum's the same whenever I visit, rushing about in her precise way, refusing to let me lift a finger with a sort of grim determination.

'It's my job, Kate; I'm your mother,' she says when I object, in a tone that brooks no argument.

Magda seems to be genuinely enjoying herself, her movements brisk, her eyes bright, and I wonder if she's lonely out here on her own. 'Just brushing up on my hostess skills,' she jokes, returning to the sink. 'So, how long have you been an interior designer?'

'It's all I ever really wanted to do,' I find myself saying. 'Even as a teenager I was doing up rooms for friends, and I designed a bedroom for one of my mother's work colleagues when I was sixteen. She was so thrilled, she told all her friends. It made me feel good.' I'm not sure why I'm telling her this. 'I was going to be an accountant but changed my mind halfway through the course.' It was actually Dan who changed my mind. Sometimes, I forget about that. If he hadn't encouraged me to follow my heart, I could be doing the accounts for some dreary company right now.

Magda nods for me to continue.

'I worked part-time through university, to get some experience, and after I left, I started a business online. I got some customers through word of mouth, and gradually built up good contacts in the building trade. Last year, I opened the showroom with a friend, and I'm hoping to expand into hotels.'

'Very enterprising.' Magda sounds so admiring, I bask in her approval, recalling Mum's disquiet when I ignored her advice about a 'proper' career. She was worried I was on the road to financial ruin.

'Do it as a sideline, not a living,' she'd pleaded, practically wringing her hands. 'What if you go bust? You'll never have any job security.'

'No one has job security anymore, Mum.'

'I do.'

She's done office work for years, first at my primary school, so she could be around during the holidays, and then for a firm of solicitors when I was older. She seems happy. Mum has never been ambitious for herself.

The cat yowls, startling me out of my reverie. It stretches, then stalks to a cat flap in the back door and leaps through it. Sunshine streams through, bouncing off a copper pan, creating a rainbow effect on the ceiling.

With an effort, I pick up my bag and pull out my laptop. 'I'll show you some pictures of the house I redesigned last summer,' I say. 'It's one I'm particularly proud of.'

'I'm afraid there's no broadband or Wi-Fi.' Magda turns, flashing a grimace. 'Haven't got round to setting it up yet.'

'Oh.' I close the lid, wondering for the first time how she came across Inspired Interiors.

'How did you find us?' I probed.

For a second her face goes blank, then she says quickly, 'Oh, I simply googled "interior designers in Buckinghamshire" on my phone and your name came up. I had a look at your website and liked what I saw.'

I feel a flash of relief. She wouldn't have contacted me if she hadn't been impressed by what she'd seen online.

'I've got my portfolio in the car,' I say. 'We can have a look through that when you're ready.'

'No rush.' She rinses the plates and stacks them on the wooden draining board to dry.

I open my mouth, intending to offer to help, and am overtaken by another enormous yawn.

Magda watches, a smile playing round her lips. She dries her hands on a tea towel and tucks it into the waistband of her apron. 'Someone's tired,' she says lightly.

'I'm so sorry.' I blink at her, eyes watering. 'It must be this heat.' My upper lip feels damp with perspiration.

'Maybe you should have a nap before we do any more work?

I can show you to your room.'

'Thanks, but I'm fine, honestly.' I smother another yawn. Agreeing to an overnight stay is one thing. Taking an afternoon nap is a step too far. 'I'll go and get my portfolio,' I say, blinking too much. I haven't felt this sleepy since the early weeks of my pregnancy.

'I got a pretty good idea of what you can offer from looking around your showroom,' Magda says, with the same slight air of rebuke I'd noted when I mentioned her accent.

'I've got some fabric swatches and wallpaper samples in the boot too.' I fumble about in my handbag. 'Let me just find my keys.'

Magda comes over and pulls a chair close to mine. She sits so our knees almost touch. I look up. The brightness from the window is behind her, casting her face into shadow. A mass of frizzy tendrils has escaped at her temples, creating a halo effect.

'My dear girl,' she says softly. Her hand reaches out and covers mine, trapping it mid-rummage. 'You really have no idea, do you?'

'Sorry?' Confusion swirls through me. I think she must be talking about my keys and attempt to remove my hand. 'They'll be in my bag somewhere,' I say. 'Just let me have another look.'

Her grip moves to my wrist and tightens like a cuff. 'It's time to come clean.'

I look up again to see her watching me intently. 'I'm sorry for bringing you here under false pretences,' she says.

My head feels stuffed with cotton wool. 'What do you mean?'

'Has your mother ever talked to you about the circumstances of your birth?'

What? Her face swims in and out of focus. 'What's my mother got to do with anything?'

The sun shifts, slanting across Magda's face. I catch a shimmer of tears in her eyes.

'What is it?' A panicky feeling rises in my ribcage. Why is she talking about Mum?

'Oh, Lexi.' *Lexi?* Chair legs scrape the floor as Magda shuffles nearer. Her face is so close to mine I smell coffee on her breath.

'Magda, what's going on?'

She grasps my upper arm with her other hand. For a moment I think she's going to draw me into a hug. 'Can't you guess at all?' she says, a little breathless.

'Guess what?' My voice is an octave higher than usual. 'What are you talking about?'

The air between us shifts and I have a dizzying sensation of falling. I try to pull away, but her grip tightens.

'I've imagined this for a long time,' she says, so quietly I barely catch her words.

I attempt a laugh. 'You're scaring me now.'

'My darling, there's no need to be scared.'

Darling? 'Who's Lexi?'

Her face folds into a smile and her dimples reappear. '*You* are.' She nods for emphasis, as though I'm a child she's trying to convince to be good, her tone cajoling.

I wonder if she's having a psychotic breakdown. 'You're not making any sense. My name is Kate,' I say, as forcefully as I can. 'Now please let go of me.'

Her eyes close, and when they snap open, they're as soft as silk, and she's gazing at me as if I'm the most precious thing in the world. 'I'm just going to come out and say it,' she says at last, her thumb stroking my wrist in a hypnotic gesture. 'The woman you think of as your mother . . . she isn't.' Each syllable is so clearly defined it's as if I can see the words floating in front of me. '*I'm* your mother. *Me.*' She removes her hand at last and clenches it against her chest. 'You're my daughter, Lexi.'

As her words sink in, my heart plummets and time seems to freeze.

Chapter 6

Dan

It was cooler by the river, a light breeze ruffling its surface. Ducks circled the water's edge, searching for stray crumbs, while the towpath swarmed with tourists dressed for summer.

Zoe led Dan up a grassy track shaded by tall trees.

'Lovely, isn't it?' she said. She'd pushed her hair back with her sunglasses and her eyes were shining with mischief.

Dan couldn't help smiling. 'Better than being cooped up in that apartment.' He felt a stab of treachery. Glances had shot between Eric and Calum when Zoe announced her intention to whisk Dan off to the river for a breath of fresh air.

Eric had hauled him to one side while she was 'freshening up' in the bathroom. 'What are you doing, mate?' His eyes were dark with concern.

'We're going for a stroll by the river,' he'd said but couldn't hold his friend's gaze. Unlike Calum, Eric had never smoked anything stronger than cigarettes, preferring to keep a clear head, and often gave the impression he could read Dan's mind.

'Be careful with her. You know she's a bit messed up?' he

warned in an undertone, eyes shifting to the bathroom and back. 'She apparently had some sort of breakdown when she came to England. She doesn't talk about it much, but . . .'

'I thought you took her on because she has a great voice, not because you felt sorry for her.' Dan's attempt at a joke fell flat. 'How messed up is she?'

'I don't know, she wasn't forthcoming with many details. Tough childhood, I think.' Eric pulled a face. 'Just be careful.'

'You don't need to worry about me.'

'You know we envy you? Cal and me.'

Dan's stomach had curdled. 'What do you mean?'

'You and Kate.' Eric let go of Dan's arm and spread his hands. 'The baby coming. The nice house. Being your own boss. You've got it all.' He spoke in the estuary accent he sometimes affected to disguise the fact that he was from Surrey, privately educated, the son of a wealthy property developer. 'Don't screw it up, Danny-boy.'

Dan had checked to see if Eric was being ironic, but his face was stiff with sincerity. 'Easy for you to say.' It was like being reprimanded by his father. Hell, even his dad wouldn't have come on that strong, despite his firm belief that Dan had married too young.

'I thought it was what you wanted,' Eric had persisted, his face close to Dan's. He smelled of beer and cigarettes, and a trace of the aftershave he'd worn for years, bought by an ex-girlfriend he'd never quite got over. 'You said when you met Kate you knew she was the one and there was no point hanging around.' He released a half-laugh, remembering. 'I admired that. How definite you were.'

Dan remembered it too. 'I still am,' he'd said, prickling with annoyance. What did Eric know? He had no responsibilities, his path through life smoothed by family money. And anyway, Dan was only going for a walk with Zoe, not planning to run off with her.

'I wouldn't mind living in one of those houses.' Her voice

drew him back to the present, low and raspy – a smoker's voice, although she didn't smoke, claimed to find it disgusting. She was pointing to a row of expensive-looking, red-brick buildings on the opposite side of the river, with meandering gardens leading down to the water. Most of them had brightly coloured boats moored nearby.

'I'd worry if I had kids,' Dan said. 'All that water, and no fences.'

His youngest sister Rosie had nearly drowned one summer, when Dan was ten. He'd been kicking a ball about at the time, with some of the boys from the commune where they were living, and later learned that a father, picnicking nearby with his family, had jumped in the lake and saved her.

Dan had been badly shaken by the episode, had had nightmares for ages afterwards, imagining Rosie's face, eyes wide and staring, floating beneath the surface of the glass-like lake, but his parents were frustratingly cavalier about the episode.

'She won't try swimming in there again,' his dad had said as he cuddled Rosie, who was tightly wrapped in a blanket in front of the campfire, basking in her parents' undivided attention.

Had it been a front? Dan had wondered later. He thought he'd heard his mum crying that night and arguing with his dad, but things were back to normal the following day, and he decided he must have imagined it.

'Children need rules and boundaries,' Kate had said, bug-eyed with shock when he recounted this incident early in their relationship, when they lay awake into the small hours, sharing and comparing life histories, but he'd privately thought she'd had a few too many. She'd led a pretty sheltered childhood, as far as he could tell, just her mum and herself, no wider family, not even grandparents, and Helen could be overprotective.

Dan wasn't well-travelled either, but that was more to do with his parents' beliefs about saving the environment than anything else. They'd certainly moved around Ireland a lot, but instead of giving him a sense of freedom, it had left Dan yearning for stability.

He'd made sure he attended school regularly – unlike his younger brothers – and had achieved good grades. He couldn't wait to escape his nomadic lifestyle, and as soon as he was sixteen had gone to live with his grandfather in his big old house in Killarney. From there, he'd fled to England, having secured a place at the University College in London to study History of Art – mostly to annoy his parents, who couldn't see the point. To be fair to them, he hadn't done anything with his degree, but he liked having it. And he'd loved being at university. His friends there had become his family, and he'd loved feeling part of something constant. He particularly liked having his own room in the house he'd shared with some fellow students and had enjoyed a couple of relationships during his three years there.

'Too much, too soon, mate,' Eric had warned at the time. He'd taken Dan under his wing from week one, perhaps sensing he was a little out of his depth. 'You come on too strong, Danny-boy. Maintain some mystery, for God's sake, the girls love that shit.'

But he couldn't be like Eric, or Calum, who'd been in his prime at nineteen. Dan tended to wear his heart on his sleeve and had his heart broken a couple of times and broken a couple, too. But nothing came close to the feeling he'd had meeting Kate when she came to see one of their gigs with some friends.

She later expressed astonishment that he'd felt so strongly. She claimed she wasn't the kind of girl to inspire passion, which had only made him love her even more. He quickly realised she had no idea how beautiful she was, with her wild red hair, dove-grey eyes and wide, generous smile.

He was appalled when she told him she was studying accounts and finance at a nearby university because it was an easy commute from Buckinghamshire, not too far from home, because her mother thought she should aim for a 'safe' career.

'But I thought you loved interior design.' They'd got chatting properly at the party they'd gone to after the gig, once her drunk friend had been safely put to bed, and afterwards went to a café where they'd laughed and talked until it closed, both aware that something special was happening.

'But design's a hobby, not a job,' she'd argued, clearly parroting her mother. Her face had clouded then, as if realising she was on the wrong career path but couldn't do anything about it.

'Look at the difference you've made to this place,' he said later still, brandishing an arm around the flat she'd transformed in the few months they'd lived together. It was tiny and cheap, but with clever use of paint, quirky pieces of art, and some strategically placed rugs and knick-knacks, she'd turned it into a home. 'You could definitely do this for a living.'

He still considered it his proudest moment, convincing her to switch courses, and hadn't regretted it for a minute. He'd helped her become the woman she was meant to be. Kate's words, not his, though it hadn't helped relations with her mother, who turned frosty with him after that – and she hadn't been particularly friendly before. Bad enough he and Kate were living together, only visiting Helen every other weekend, and only then because Kate insisted. She sometimes went alone because Dan couldn't bear the stilted conversation and awkward silences.

'I used to swim competitively when I was a teenager,' Zoe was saying, bringing him back to the moment once again. She linked her arm through his, her skin surprisingly hot. 'You couldn't get me out of the water back then.'

He banished a mental image of her in a bikini.

'Anyone fancy a boat trip?' said a voice behind them.

They turned to see Eric, red-faced and breathless, beads of perspiration on his forehead.

Dan quickly drew away from Zoe.

'What the hell, Eric?' She gave an amazed laugh. 'You look like you're about to have a heart attack.'

'What about an ice cream?' Eric doubled over and rested his hands on his knees, drawing air into his lungs. 'There's a van over near the park,' he said, gasping.

Guessing he'd run after them because he was worried about him being alone with Zoe, Dan felt an uneasy mix of emotions. Surely, he knew Dan would never cheat on his wife?

'*What about an ice cream?*' Zoe mocked Eric, rolling her eyes. 'I think it'll take more than an ice cream to cool me down,' she said, winking at Dan. Her eyelashes were so long and thick, he thought they couldn't be real.

'I'll have a Mr Whippy with sprinkles,' he said, to disguise the fact that he didn't know how to respond, and Zoe laughed as if he'd said something hilarious.

Straightening, Eric observed them, his expression beneath his battered old baseball cap as disapproving as a maiden aunt's. Dan suddenly understood: why hadn't he seen it before? It was obvious Eric was attracted to Zoe himself and couldn't understand why she preferred to be with Dan.

'Oh, go on, make that two Mr Whippys with sprinkles,' said Zoe, adopting an indulgent tone. 'Good idea to get rid of him,' she whispered to Dan.

It was clear Eric now regretted his suggestion but couldn't think how to back down. He removed his cap, scratched his head, then put it back on. 'You gonna come with me?'

'I'm sure you can manage on your own.' Zoe's voice was airy. 'It's not that far.'

'We'll be over there.' Dan nodded towards a clearing set back from the river, self-consciously pulling away from Zoe's fingers tracing a pattern up his arm.

Eric looked like he wanted to say more. He opened his mouth and closed it again. 'OK,' he said at last. 'I won't be long.' He dug his hand into his jeans pocket and pulled out a ten-pound note, looking surprised to see it. None of them carried much cash now everything was contactless. 'Don't do anything I wouldn't.' There was an edge to his voice, and when neither of them responded, he turned and set off in the direction of the ice-cream van, throwing

Dan a grim look over his shoulder.

'Probably the most exercise he's had in ages,' Zoe said, watching Eric's retreating back. 'I've never seen him move that fast.'

As his friend broke into a jog, Dan squashed a stab of guilt. He knew Eric had his best interests at heart, which was probably more than Zoe did. When she slipped her warm hand into his and tugged him after her, he found he couldn't let go. She led him to the clearing and flung herself down in a patch of long grass, stretching her legs out and tilting her face toward the sun.

She studied him through narrowed eyes, her hair sweeping the grass behind her head. 'Aren't you going to join me?' She gave a sultry pout. Dan thought of Kate, working on a Saturday while he was out here with another woman.

Sounds of laughter floated across from the park, and there was a blast of music from one of the big houses opposite, quickly turned down. A boat packed with tourists thrummed past and water slapped the bank, forcing several ducks to take off with squawks of outrage.

Zoe patted the ground beside her, and Dan lowered himself a little distance away, batting at a wasp. He leaned back on his elbows, willing himself to relax, but the effect of the beer was starting to wear off and he felt a headache brewing.

Zoe inched closer, stroking his wrist with her thumb. 'You smell good,' she whispered. The heat of her lips seared through his T-shirt as she kissed his shoulder. Her hair had fallen to one side, and his mind did a little shift. He recalled waking up with Kate the morning after they slept together for the first time, the way she'd tied her hair up, and the surprise of her long, slender neck. He'd felt such tenderness towards her and knew in that moment he wanted to be part of her life forever. When he said as much, she took his hand and kissed his fingers, and said lightly, 'Wait until you know me properly, you'll soon change your mind.'

But he'd known he wouldn't.

'What is it, Dan?' Zoe's look was quizzical, one thick dark

eyebrow raised. She'd plucked a blade of grass and was trailing it along his chest in a languid movement.

'I'm happily married,' he reminded her. He closed his eyes, the pounding in his temples increasing. *My wife is pregnant. I'm going to be a father.* He repeated the words in his head, trying to feel them. Zoe pulled closer still, her breath like a warm breeze on his cheek.

'I don't mind,' she whispered.

He felt as though he was sinking into a deep sleep.

'Here we are, guys.'

Dan's eyes flew open. Eric was back, his forehead dripping sweat. In one hand were three ice-cream cones, while the other flapped to indicate an oxygen mask might be required. 'Sorry,' he panted. 'They've melted a bit.'

Dan jolted upright, relieved at the interruption.

'Thanks,' he said, grasping a sticky cone. He sank his teeth into the mound of ice cream, wincing as pain lanced through his gums to his brain.

Zoe accepted her proffered ice cream graciously enough, but he could tell by the way her face folded up that she was annoyed by Eric's presence.

'So, a few weeks from now you'll be a dad,' he said pointedly. He'd flopped on the grass in front of them and devoured his ice cream in a few greedy bites, licking his fingers afterwards, then wiping them on his half-unbuttoned shirt, which revealed a swirl of dark chest hair.

'Subtle,' murmured Zoe. Her tongue darted in and out like a cat's, lapping her creamy concoction.

'Yep.' Dan injected his voice with an appropriate amount of enthusiasm. 'If the baby doesn't come early. Or late.' *Sooner rather than later. Better late than never. It's never too late. Least said, soonest mended.* Whenever he thought about the baby being born, thoughts like this would crowd his head and flutter like starlings, until he couldn't picture it at all. Instead, he experienced a dropping sensation, like being in a falling lift. The thought of being responsible for a tiny human scared the life out of him.

He couldn't tell Kate. She'd embraced every aspect of her pregnancy, even carrying around a Tupperware container filled with sliced carrot, cucumber and celery to snack on in case she felt sick. He was ashamed even now to think how much it had unnerved him, seeing this new side of her.

Maybe she was right, and if he'd gone to the last scan with her, he'd have felt differently, but he'd struggled to feel what he was supposed to feel at the first one, no matter how hard he'd tried.

He'd studied the ultrasound photo afterwards, which Kate had stuck on the fridge, trying to imagine the fuzzy image as a living, breathing baby, part of himself and Kate, but he couldn't quite make it real. He imagined the love stored inside him, and the sight of his son or daughter releasing it, like a river breaking its banks.

He was sure it would happen. *But what if it doesn't?* He'd wondered if there was something wrong with him, had even thought about talking to someone, a doctor, but could imagine how it would sound – selfish and pathetic, confirming every joke and assumption made about men being total pricks.

He'd always been able to talk to Kate if something was bothering him, but this . . . he wouldn't know where to start. Better to focus on work, on being a provider – not that she needed him for that. In fact, Kate increasingly gave the impression she could manage perfectly well without him.

He thought of her driving off that morning, angry and distant, without her phone, and wished his mind would stop racing. It was as if the ice cream had triggered more guilt, as well as accelerating his headache.

Zoe's leg pressed against his, her long hair brushing his arm as she finished her ice cream. She pulled a tissue out of the canvas bag she'd brought and dabbed at her lips and fingers.

'Have you thought any more about making me a godfather?' Eric was persistent; he'd give him that.

Zoe let out an exasperated snort. 'Why don't you just ring his wife and tell her you're worried I'm going to shag her husband?' Storm clouds gathered on her brow. 'He's a grown man, Eric. Get off his case.'

A flush crept up Eric's neck. 'I was just making conversation,' he said darkly. 'Which is more than you were doing.'

'Sometimes, it's nice not to talk.' She didn't bother to hide her sarcasm. 'There are more interesting things to do.'

'Maybe you should go and do them with someone else.'

'Haven't you got somewhere you'd rather be?'

'Not really.' Eric lay back and locked his fingers behind his head. 'I might have a little nap, actually.'

'Probably with one eye open, you pervert,' Zoe shot back.

As Dan realised properly what she'd had in mind when she asked him to come for a walk, he felt ashamed that he'd gone along with it so readily. He was wrong to have assumed she'd respect the fact he was married and wouldn't try to take things further.

Before he could tell the pair of them to shut up, his pocket vibrated. He tugged out his phone with tacky fingers, and his heart gave a thud when he saw there was a voicemail. How hadn't he heard it ringing? It might be the hospital. Kate might be about to have their baby.

Zoe glanced over and scowled as Dan tapped in the voicemail number. She grabbed a handful of grass, crawled over to Eric, and sprinkled it on his face.

He sneezed and sat up. 'What the fuck?'

Dan crammed the phone to his ear. The connection was terrible, but he could just about make out Kate's voice, bright and friendly – a complete contrast from her tone that morning, saying she'd arrived safely and would see him tomorrow and that she'd spoken to Saskia to let her know where she was. Could he tell her mum, if she phoned? She was fine, no need to worry.

Her words had the opposite effect and unease crept along his nerve endings. With her due date only three weeks away, he'd rather she came home tonight. He stood up too quickly and stumbled, light-headed.

'What is it, Dan?' Zoe's voice was sharp.

He looked at her and saw that she cared about him more than he'd realised.

'I've got to go,' he said, his mind zeroing in on the one thing that was important. His wife and their unborn baby.

Chapter 7

Kate

She's crazy, I think, her words ricocheting around my head. *I'm your mother, Lexi.*

But Magda doesn't look crazy. Her face is earnest and hopeful. She nods, as if encouraging me to do the same and make her words come true. I try to speak, but every coherent thought has fled my brain.

'It must be a shock,' she goes on when I don't respond. 'I probably shouldn't have come out with it like that, but I couldn't think of a better way to tell you.' Her voice seems to reach me from a distant corner of the kitchen. 'I've rehearsed our meeting so many times in my head, but once you were in front of me, it was different.'

'I don't know what you're talking about.' My voice sounds odd, as if someone's got a finger on my windpipe. 'I have to go.' I reach for my laptop and jam it in my bag with shaking hands.

'No!' Magda's eyes grow wide, as if she hasn't envisaged this outcome. 'Stay, please,' she urges. 'Just hear me out.'

I remember her sliding the bolts across the front door and am gripped with sudden fear.

'I called you Lexi after my grandmother, Alexandra,' she says in a rush. 'She was a wonderful woman; you'd have liked her.'

'My name is Kate.' I emphasise each word, cheeks tingling with heat. I want to stand up but feel incapable of rising.

'I was hoping she might have confessed.' Magda reaches her hand towards me once more, her expression moist and pleading. 'That she wasn't your biological mother, I mean.'

'This is silly.' I try a laugh, but it doesn't come out right. 'You must have got me mixed up with someone else. My mother's called . . .'

'Jane.'

I catch my breath. 'Helen Fletcher, actually.' *But her middle name is Jane.*

'Ah.' Magda's face clears. 'Explains why I couldn't find her. She was Jane Goodwin when I knew her.'

Oh God. My great-aunt – the woman we'd lived with for a while when I was little – was called Maria Goodwin. That *can't* be a coincidence. 'OK, so how do you know my mother?' I say, not sounding like myself.

'Does that matter right now?' A tear tips over and spills down her cheek. She brushes it away with her fingers. 'I just want to get to know you, my darling girl.'

'Of *course* it matters!' My heart's clattering and my mouth's bone dry, my mind reeling. 'Tell me how you know Mum.'

She mumbles something I can't quite hear.

'Sorry?'

'She took you from me.' Her voice is louder, her chin quivering. Her whole face starts twitching with emotion, as if the impact of her words is only now sinking in. 'She took you and I let her.'

'You mean she kidnapped me?' Blood is roaring in my ears.

'No, no. Not kidnapped.' Magda bites her bottom lip with small white teeth, her hand hovering near mine. 'It's more complicated than that.'

I stare at her, feeling slow-witted and stupid. 'I don't understand any of what you're saying.'

'Oh, Lexi.' Her voice breaks. She bows her head, hands rising to cover her face, and tears leak through her fingers. 'I want us to get to know each other,' she says, the words muffled by her hands. 'I want . . .' She shakes her head, as though what she wants is impossible to articulate. Her distress is so acute, my own eyes brim with tears. *This can't be happening.*

'Is this why you brought me here?' My head swims. 'You weren't really looking for an interior designer, were you?'

'You can see this place needs a facelift,' Magda manages, dropping her hands into her lap. 'But yes, it's mainly why I brought you here. Your job made it convenient, that's all. I'm sorry.'

I squash a hand to my mouth. She'd planned this: leading me to her remote cottage.

'Please don't look at me like that,' she beseeches, dropping to a crouch in front of me and placing a hand on my knee. 'My intention isn't to hurt you.'

The heat of her touch burns through my leg. 'Why do you think you're . . .?' I can't bring myself to say 'my mother'. 'That I'm your daughter?'

'I don't think it; I know it.' She says it with such conviction, it's clear she believes her own words.

The drilling in my temples increases. 'Can I have some water?'

'Of course.' She straightens at once. Wiping the sides of her hands across her face, she crosses the kitchen. 'You need a moment to let it sink in.'

As she fills a glass, exhaustion crashes over me, reducing my ability to think. She hands me the water and I take a couple of sips.

'I was in the park,' Magda says softly. 'I can't even remember how I got there. I'd been walking in the rain, trying to stop you crying. You were just a couple of weeks old at the time. Jane and I got chatting.'

I clatter the glass onto the table. 'Which park?'

'In Leeds, where I lived at the time.'

My spine freezes over. Mum grew up in Leeds. *I was born in Leeds.*

I press my fingertips to my forehead and massage the skin, my breathing shallow.

'She admired your red hair.' Magda's eyes move over my head in a way that makes me feel slithery inside. 'She said she'd had a miscarriage and that she'd always wanted a little girl.'

A flashback. I'm six years old, asking Mum for a baby brother because my best friend Josie had one.

Mum's eyes had turned pink and watery. 'I lost a baby before you came along, Katie, and had an operation in my tummy after you were born,' she'd said in a funny voice. 'I can't have any more babies, love. That's why you're so special.'

Had it been an elaborate lie? *Oh God, oh God.* I should get up, go to the door, but no sooner has the thought filled my head than it's gone.

Watching me, Magda's face flickers with annoyance. 'I thought you'd be . . .' She stops, gives a little shake of her head. 'No, I'm sorry. Of course, it's a lot to take in.'

'But why would my mother take your baby?'

'It was for the best at that time.' Magda's gaze has turned inward as if she's seeing the past. 'I wasn't coping. She wanted to help.'

'So . . . what, she just took your baby?'

'I prefer to think she was helping me out, but later, I got better.' Magda refocuses. 'I wanted you back,' she says. 'You were all I had left of Patrick. I wanted my family back.'

'Patrick?' My head spins.

'I wanted you back,' she repeats. 'But you'd gone.'

My hands move to my stomach. I think of my baby tucked inside and try to imagine not wanting him, letting someone else raise him. I attempt to picture Mum, taking another woman's baby, but it's ludicrous. She's never had so much as a parking fine in her life.

'I have a birth certificate,' I blurt out. 'Birth certificates can't lie.'

'Can't they?' Magda sits down, calmer now. She folds her hands on the table and studies me, a head teacher with a difficult pupil. 'Are you sure?'

Another memory. A skiing trip to France at secondary school. All my friends were going, and I wanted to too. I'd never been abroad and needed a passport, but Mum couldn't find my birth certificate, said it must have got lost when we moved south. 'Do you have to go, love? It'll take ages for a passport to come through.'

I'd made a big fuss, unwilling to let go of my dream of gliding down a ski slope alongside my best friend and Will Logan, the boy I'd fancied all term.

Mum flapped, tutted, protested, but I got my passport in the end, as I knew I would. I went on the trip and fell out with my friend when I caught her snogging Will Logan outside our chalet.

Mum didn't want me to go because that's the way she was – she didn't like me being out of her sight for long; that was all, nothing to do with this woman's story. *So why am I covered in goosebumps?*

'If I'd registered your birth, I'd have proof,' Magda says. 'But I didn't, because . . . like I said, I wasn't coping and I didn't get that far.' She looks briefly stricken. 'It's made everything *so* much harder.'

'So, what have you been doing for the past thirty years?'

'Trying to get on with my life, working here and there. My father left me his house when he died, which I sold, and plenty of money, and I thought about hiring a private detective to find you, but it was pointless because I had no details to go on, had no idea of your new name, or where in the country you might be. It was torture.'

I try to think past the pounding in my skull, sifting through her words. 'Tell me something about my mother that no one else would know.'

Magda scratches her elbow, where the skin looks red and

inflamed. She smooths stray hairs behind her ears and glances upwards, thinking. 'Her parents died in a car crash when she was fifteen. She has an older sister who lives in Australia.' Her voice is almost robotic. 'She worked in an office; she liked it there. There was a great-aunt who lived down south on her father's side. She was lonely.'

Acid burns my throat. Mum's not on social media, and even if she was, she wouldn't reveal details like that. Magda could only have got that information directly from her.

Images swirl through my brain, but they're grainy, like an old film. Had Mum really decided to raise someone else's child – to keep a baby that didn't belong to her?

If only I wasn't so tired. It's a struggle to keep my eyes open.

'I know those things about Jane because she told me.'

It's as if Magda's read my mind. Dazed, I glance at my belly. *There are no photos of Mum when she was pregnant with me.*

The thought settles in my head like cement.

'There was no one around to take a picture,' she said once when I asked. I'd thought it sad, even though she was smiling her bright determined smile when she said it.

How can she not be my mum?

'I have to go.'

Magda sags back in her chair, chest lifting in a sigh. 'I'm not going to stop you,' she says gently. 'You're free to leave if you want to.'

My head's throbbing in earnest, the beat expanding. 'This is so hard to believe.'

'Is it really?' There's a gentle reproach in her voice, as if it's obvious that no one would go to these lengths unless they were telling the truth.

Of course it's hard to believe, I want to scream. *You're telling me that my life is a lie.* The words dissolve before they reach my lips.

The sun disappears, plunging the kitchen into gloom. Through the window, the view has lost definition and I have the unsettling feeling I could be anywhere.

Magda's watching me closely, as if trying to decipher my reaction, and I'm about to rise when my mind flies back to my birth certificate – the gap where my father's name should have been – and a thought emerges through the fog in my brain.

'So, if you're my mother, who's my father?'

'His name is Patrick Gilmore.' Magda presses her lips together as if stemming a surge of emotion. 'A man I loved very much,' she says in a rush. Her eyes catch mine and there's a fierce light in their depths. 'Still love. He'll be so happy to know I've found you.'

My father.

The words wrap around me like a spell, and I know in that instant I can't leave until Magda's told me more.

Chapter 8

Dan

Dan tried returning Kate's call, but either the phone was switched off or there was no signal and it didn't connect.

He carried on walking, back to the apartment block where his bike was parked, the sun hot on his neck. There was nothing much he could do now but return home.

About to enter the building to pick up his helmet, his phone rang. He answered immediately, expecting it to be Kate.

It was his mum.

'Hey, Danny, just wondering how you were,' she said in her soft Irish brogue. 'Not long now till the baby comes.' Dan's parents had seemed pleased at the news they were going to be grandparents for the first time but warned that they wouldn't be hands on, though Dan had a feeling his mum would change her mind once the baby arrived. They didn't fully approve of Dan and Kate's stable, suburban lifestyle and still enjoyed communal living, even in their late sixties. But his mum had to be more excited than she'd let on, as she'd been phoning more over the last few months than Dan could ever remember, wanting updates, asking to speak to Kate.

'I'm fine,' he said, deciding not to mention he didn't exactly know his wife's whereabouts. 'Kate's fine too.'

'Are you sure about that, love?'

His mum had always had a knack for reading between the lines where Dan was concerned. She claimed it was because he was her firstborn, whereas his father took everything at face value, never digging far beneath the surface. A free spirit, he liked to call himself, which, when Dan grew old enough to understand, meant he could be a hands-off father, leaving his wife to deal with the day-to-day running of their large family.

'I'm fine,' he said again, not wanting to worry her.

'If you say so, Danny. Rosie sends her love, and the boys are raring to come over and meet their nephew.'

Dan had stayed close to his little sister but had never had much in common with his younger brothers, just a year between each, all alpha males, always competing when they were growing up.

'Well, it won't be long now.'

'Is Kate still working?'

'She is.'

Unsure what else to say without giving away that they'd parted on bad terms that morning, he said he had to get to work too as he had a job to finish.

'Don't forget to keep us posted.'

'I won't.'

As Dan ended the call, he entered the building and took the stairs to Eric's apartment where he found Calum spreadeagled on the sofa smoking a joint.

'Want a drag?' He held it out to Dan.

'No thanks,' Dan said shortly. Calum knew he wasn't into drugs of any sort and liked to tease him about it, or suggest it was Kate's influence and that he was 'under the thumb'.

'Have a nice time by the river?' Calum wiggled his eyebrows suggestively. 'What have you done with Zoe?'

'She's coming back with Eric, I expect.' Dan was determined not to rise to Calum's insinuations.

'Shame it's not him she's into; he really likes her,' Calum continued. 'They'd make a good couple.'

'I wish she liked him too.' He picked his guitar up and strummed a few chords, then put it down again. The others would be back soon and he didn't want to be here when they were.

'I'm off,' he said to Calum, grabbing his helmet off the kitchen counter. 'See you later.'

'Lucky you,' Calum called after him as he left.

It was cool in the stairwell and the heat outside felt oppressive.

He put on his helmet and climbed onto his bike, backing slowly out of the space. As he turned to head home, he spotted Zoe and Eric walking back. They didn't seem to be talking, Zoe no doubt still annoyed with Eric for gatecrashing. Dan sighed. He didn't need this kind of complication in his life but had no idea what to do about it. As she lifted her hand in a wave, he pretended not to notice and roared away.

Chapter 9

Kate

My father. I think of the space where he should have been over the years. The man I'd imagined so many times, but rarely asked about.

'Aren't I enough for you?' Mum had said, before I was old enough to know when to keep my mouth shut. 'I didn't know at first, but he was already married to someone else and had a family. I never saw him after I fell pregnant and I've no idea where he is. We don't need him, Katie.' She only called me Katie when she was upset or trying to placate me. 'We have enough love, don't we? We don't need a man in our lives.'

When I was older, I wondered if she was ashamed of her affair, because even then I knew it was out of character for her – that she wasn't the type to have a casual fling, so she must have really loved him – but I didn't ask.

Mum didn't have boyfriends, and there were no male relatives, so my best friend Josie's dad had been my role model, growing up. He'd taught me to ride a bike and included me in family jokes. Sometimes, I'd feel an ache inside, watching him piggyback

Josie around the garden, or pick her up from a birthday party, but mostly I was used to having only one parent and didn't mind. When anyone asked about my dad, I'd say he was dead. It seemed easier that way.

I'd felt his absence most strongly on my wedding day. Seeing Dan being hugged by his father, Rory – ill at ease in a too-tight suit – I'd longed for that special relationship, not just for myself, but for Mum. Having a partner might have deflected some of her love for me, which came in bursts and was often too intense. At times, she'd cradle my face between her hands, eyes burning with emotion, her voice too passionate. 'You know how much I love you, don't you, Kate?' Or her eyes would follow me hungrily, as if trying to pin me in one place and keep me there.

My father.

A sudden urge to vomit brings me to my feet. I lurch to the sink and retch, but nothing comes up.

'Kate . . .' I sense Magda approaching, perhaps to offer comfort. Something is lodged in the plug-hole – a chunk of cat food – and the sight of it makes my stomach heave again.

The moment passes, and I pull a shaking hand across my mouth. Thrusting my hair back, I look at Magda. 'Sorry,' I mutter. 'I'm not normally sick.'

Her hand touches the air near my back. 'I'm the one who's sorry, Kate.' Thank God she's not calling me Lexi anymore. 'Please don't be angry with me.'

'I'm not angry, I'm . . .' I don't know what I am. My heart's galloping, and I can't work out if it's the shock of what she's told me, or the scrambled eggs and lemonade roiling in my stomach.

'The last thing I want to do is make you sick.' Magda gives me a faint smile. 'If you'll let me explain, it will all make sense, I promise you.'

'So, my father's name is Patrick?'

Something flares in her eyes at the mention of his name. 'Yes,' she said. 'Patrick Gilmore.'

It's a nice name. Strong. I turn it over in my mind.

'Come and sit down,' she coaxes. 'I have some photos to show you.'

I obey, as though in a trance. The baby jabs my ribs and I press my hands on the sides of my belly as Magda pulls a folder from a drawer and flips it opens.

'This is him.' She slips me a photo, not looking at it, as though the image is already seared on her brain.

I examine it, a muscle throbbing in my throat. It looks vintage and faded, as if it's stood in sunlight for years, a head and shoulders shot, taken outdoors. A young man, his expression caught between amusement and annoyance. He's clean shaven with fine bone structure, and his light-brown hair is tousled. Light eyes are crinkled at the edges, almost smiling. I scour his features for a likeness and imagine it's there in his jaw line and high forehead. I don't look anything like Magda, but then I don't look like Mum either.

A spinning sensation consumes me, and I blink to clear my vision. 'He looks nice.' I wait for a flash of recognition, something to tell me for certain this man is my father. Nothing happens. But how can I feel anything from looking at a picture? 'It's too much,' I say, panic rising in my chest.

Magda retrieves the picture carefully, as if it's made from spun gold. 'There's plenty of time.' Her voice buffets me like a breeze, calm now, no hint of tears. 'We've hours to talk, and I'm happy to answer all of your questions.'

She hands me another photo of two young women this time, smiling into the camera. One recedes into the background with her androgynous clothes, plain face and slight frame. The other is curvy, with a creamy complexion and wavy fair hair bouncing around her shoulders.

The plainer of the two is unmistakeably Mum. It's her smile that draws me in and makes my throat constrict: wide and somehow innocent. I've wondered what Mum was like before she had me and have studied the few old pictures she has, looking for clues. She looks happy here, ordinary. Filled with hope for the future, no doubt. No sign of the anxiety I've come to accept as part of her, like her blue eyes.

Her face swims out of focus as tears blur my vision.

The other woman is Magda. She's attractive in a wholesome way and looks well groomed in a cream high-necked blouse, while Mum is sporting a plain white T-shirt, arms folded across her narrow chest.

I think how she hates having her picture taken, claiming they never capture a flattering likeness. 'I don't look like me.'

Because she's not who she says she is.

Stop it! I chide myself. *Think sensibly. If Mum took a baby and Magda wanted it back, the police would have got involved. She wouldn't have got away with it.*

My gaze switches to the other photo. In it, Magda's holding a baby, tightly wrapped in a lemon-yellow blanket.

I try to speak, but my tongue feels too big.

'Is that me?' I manage, pointing at the bundle in her arms.

'Yes,' she says simply, and her words have the ring of truth.

With a shock, I recognise the busily patterned wallpaper in both pictures, from my grandparents' house in Leeds, where Mum and I had lived until we moved away.

Magda was in Mum's home. Eyes flicking from picture to picture, I'm in no doubt she's telling the truth. She really knows my mum. And if she's right about that . . .

I pore over the photos until my eyes feel sore from staring.

'Kate?'

With an effort, I lift my gaze.

Some kind of battle is taking place on Magda's face. Her hand tightens over mine. 'We were friends once,' she says, her voice laden with sadness. 'It should never have ended the way it did.'

This is really happening.

'Patrick shouldn't have left me either, but he did.' Her voice softens further. 'If he'd been patient, things would have got better.'

'What things?' I try to concentrate, but my eyes are dragging down, the lids like lead weights.

Magda exhales slowly. 'He didn't think I could be a midwife *and* have a baby. I didn't think so either, not at first.'

'You're a midwife?'

'Was,' she says, absently. 'A long time ago. In the end, it was all too much for him. *I* was too much for him. He couldn't cope so he left. He went abroad.'

'Sounds like you are better off without him.' The words stay in my mind. Everything's muffled, as though someone's thrown a blanket over me. I try to catch my thoughts, but everything's slipping away.

The floor comes towards me and the photos slide from my hand.

I want them back.

My hands scrabble.

'Kate?' Magda's voice sounds far away, but her palm is warm on my forehead.

Mum. I want my mum.

'My darling, you're feverish.' Magda's voice is full of tenderness. 'You need to lie down.' Gentle hands lift me as I try to walk.

My baby. Be careful of my baby.

'Let me show you to your room. You mustn't worry, Lexi. It's going to be fine now; you'll see. We'll talk again later.'

The last thing I see, before blackness descends, are her narrowed eyes on my face. Like the wolf, in *Little Red Riding Hood*.

Chapter 10

Dan

Dan's spirits rose at the sight of home: a converted post office on the corner of a quiet street in Bisham, just outside Marlow. It was the sort of home he'd dreamed of when growing up. It had a tall chimney, cream-painted walls, small leaded windows, and a green front door with a shiny brass knocker. They would never have been able to afford it without the money his grandfather had left him, and while sometimes that bothered him, mostly he was grateful.

Inside, the house was too quiet, and the air smelled stale.

He opened a window and flicked on the radio for company. He put away the shopping he'd picked up on the way home and loaded the dishwasher, then stood for a moment, looking round.

Kate was everywhere: in the row of glass jelly moulds on the windowsill catching the light; the thirties-style enamel bread bin; the mismatched collection of colanders, ladles, milk jugs and canisters – items that had to be looked after to stop them rusting. Would they have time once the baby arrived?

There was a familiar tight, panicky feeling in his chest, and not for the first time, he wondered if he'd also inherited his grandfather's heart condition.

He made a ham and cheese sandwich and ate it, crumbs falling onto the kitchen table where he'd sat with Kate that morning. He tried to remember the last time they'd spent a night apart. It was about two months ago when she stayed at a boutique hotel that needed a makeover. He'd missed her, didn't enjoy having the bed to himself.

Moving to the living room, the Victorian fireplace faced him like an accusation. Kate had wanted it opened up, envisaging cosy fires during the winter months.

'I've sat in front of enough fires to last me a lifetime,' he'd said, conveniently forgetting how enjoyable some of those times had been, his mum playing guitar and his dad cooking sausages while his younger siblings played tag. 'I'd have given anything for central heating, especially in that freezing squat.'

Living in the squat had been a low point in his life. The shame and embarrassment of knowing they shouldn't be there – no matter how hard his father tried to justify it – had taken a long time to fade.

'You're a twat,' he said now to his reflection in the speckled mirror above the mantelpiece. He looked like shit, as if he hadn't slept for days, his hair sticking out at odd angles. Not how a father-to-be should look.

As he turned away, his gaze snagged on a photo propped on the 1950s sideboard Kate had found on eBay. It was a black-and-white shot of them on their wedding day, emerging from the registry office, Kate radiant in a vintage ivory dress. His arms were looped round her waist, hers around his shoulders. Their noses were touching, their faces creased with laughter.

He couldn't recall what had been so funny – probably something Eric had said – but the image filled him with longing. With a leap of intuition, he knew he was worried a baby would upset the domestic familiarity of the life they'd built together.

'Knob,' he muttered, fighting a wave of shame.

He picked up one of the design magazines Kate subscribed to and flicked through it; perfect homes for perfect lives. Scrubbed, smiling families, beaming out from minimalist rooms and kitchens that looked like operating theatres.

Kate wasn't a fan of the clinical look. Their living room seemed full up with a bouncy sofa, two plump armchairs, tall wooden bookshelves, a thick, patterned rug on the floorboards and traditional paintings on the walls. There were lamps and throws scattered around, so stepping inside was like entering Aladdin's cave.

'It's sort of womb-like,' she'd said, eyes gleaming as she led him around when she'd finished painting the walls Cranberry Crush.

'If wombs had fairy lights,' he said, catching her around the waist, thinking he never wanted to live anywhere else.

Some of the pictures and pages were missing from the magazine, ripped or cut out for the mood boards Kate put together. The jagged spaces unsettled him. He threw it down and ran upstairs, tugging his T-shirt off. He stayed in the shower, lemon-scented steam rising around him, until he felt restored. Deciding to let his stubble grow to a beard, he resisted shaving and brushed his teeth vigorously, avoiding his eyes in the mirror.

After pulling on a clean T-shirt and jeans, he headed downstairs, muscles clenching with shock when the phone shrilled. The sound was too loud in the hallway, cutting across the cheesy ballad warbling from the radio.

No one called the landline these days apart from cold callers, selling insurance or loft insulation. He picked up the handset, thumb hovering over the answer button then let the call ring out.

He made a mug of black coffee and took it outside. Clouds had obliterated the sun for the first time in days, casting the garden into shade. He headed for the converted shed at the bottom of the garden, which he used as a studio and workshop, and snapped the light on inside. Inhaling the comforting smell of wood shavings toppled his mind back to his dad, teaching him how to whittle small wooden animals.

It hadn't occurred to Dan then to wonder how his father could afford his materials, or the van he drove, or the rent for the market stall where he sold his well-crafted pieces. He hadn't known that his father's family was wealthy, that his dad's lifestyle choice was a protest against an extravagantly opulent upbringing; though he wasn't averse to asking for handouts when it suited him.

For a moment, Dan stared at his mess of tools and planks of wood and the half-finished cradle in the corner, covered with a blanket so Kate wouldn't see it. He crossed to his work bench, pulled on his safety goggles and face mask, and plugged in his router. All he had to do was cut a lip round the edge of the coffee table to hold a sheet of glass, and the job for Kate's client would be done.

As always, once he started working, he remembered everything he loved about woodworking, how completely the sounds, smells and rhythms absorbed him. It was similar to playing the guitar but required a different level of concentration and he let his mind drift free of everything else.

He began treating the wood with polish to protect it before putting the glass in, pushing back his hair with his forearm. He was so engrossed he wasn't aware that someone was tapping on the door until it grew louder, and he heard his name being called.

'Dan? Are you in there?'

Helen, his mother-in-law. What the hell was she doing here? He threw down his cloth and wiped his hands down his jeans.

'Dan!'

His stomach tightened. 'I'm coming,' he called, stumbling across the concrete floor, swearing as he stubbed his toe. Why couldn't she just come in like a normal person, instead of acting as though he was hiding from her?

He pulled open the door and shielded his eyes with his hand. The sun had reappeared, backlighting Helen's slight figure with a fuzzy glow.

'Hello, Helen,' he said, trying not to show his impatience. 'Kate's not here at the moment.' He was under no illusion that she'd come to see him.

'I know she isn't. I tried her phone and she's not answering, I rang your landline and no one picked up and neither did anyone when I called the shop.' Helen's voice had a snap to it that surprised him. Despite disapproving of him, she generally kept up a veneer of pleasant civility, laughing at his jokes and occasionally asking about the band. 'Where is she?' she said.

'She's with a client.' Dan emerged from the shed and closed the door behind him. He didn't want her nosing around, being critical of his work. 'She forgot her phone.'

'That's not like Kate.' It sounded as if she was accusing him of something.

'Is anything wrong?' he said, keeping his voice in neutral. No point winding her up.

She hesitated, her pale-blue eyes flitting around the garden, as if Kate might be hiding behind a shrub. 'Not really, I . . .' Confusion flickered over her face, which as usual was devoid of make-up. Her pink and white complexion was pinker than usual, her dark, grey-flecked hair tucked neatly behind her ears. In her white polo shirt, unstylish jeans and white tennis shoes, she reminded him of a gym teacher.

'What is it?' he prompted.

'I've got this nagging feeling,' she said with a hint of defiance, her colour deepening to red as she jiggled her car keys.

'A feeling?' Helen wasn't the type to say fanciful things. She wasn't intuitive, like Kate; she dealt in practicalities, or so he'd assumed. 'What sort of feeling?'

'A bad one.'

Caught unawares, they locked eyes, for possibly the first time ever. The look in hers stoked a feeling of worry in Dan. It wasn't unusual for Helen to fret – anxiety was her default setting – but this seemed more urgent.

'Would you like a cup of tea?' he said, feeling an impulse to put things on a more normal footing.

To his surprise, she nodded. 'That would be nice.'

He couldn't recall ever being in Helen's company alone and felt clumsy – as though his feet had grown – as he led the way through the house.

'Milk and sugar?' he asked, fumbling his way round the kitchen, glad he'd tidied up, but when he looked round, she'd gone.

He found her in the living room, staring through the window with the baffled air of a sleepwalker, somehow out of place in the crimson-walled room. He'd sometimes tried to imagine her going about her daily life – laughing, drinking, chatting, shopping – but found it almost impossible. Other than the hours she put in at the solicitor's office where she worked, he couldn't imagine how she filled her time.

'Milk and sugar?' he repeated, thinking he should know by now how his mother-in-law took her tea.

She looked at him unblinking, as if she'd forgotten he was there. 'Black, please.'

When he brought it through, she was perched on the edge of the sofa, clutching a pewter-framed photo of Kate and Saskia, holding champagne glasses and beaming at the camera. The picture had accompanied an article in the local newspaper with the headline INSPIRED INTERIORS BRINGS TOWN TO STANDSTILL, which reported how indie band Skinny Rivers had drawn a huge crowd at the opening of a new interiors showroom in Marlow, leading to a five-mile tailback on the M40.

In the picture, Helen was standing to one side, her body angled towards Kate, her face alight with pride. She looked younger and quite pretty in a fifties-style dress sprinkled with flowers that Kate had helped her choose.

'She's done so well for herself,' Helen said now, almost to herself. She jumped when Dan clattered the mug of tea onto the coffee table, slopping some over the side.

'Sorry,' he said, snatching a T-shirt off the back of the sofa and mopping at the spreading tea.

Helen didn't seem to have noticed, her shoulders bowed, eyes still fixed on the photo. 'How was she this morning?' she asked, finally lifting her gaze.

Dan found he couldn't meet her eyes. Playing for time, he balled up the damp T-shirt and lowered himself into the armchair, hands dangling between his knees. 'Fine,' he said, shifting uncomfortably. He had a feeling she knew he was lying, but before she could respond her phone trilled its old-fashioned ring tone.

He tensed as she pulled it from her bag and looked at the screen, her gaze unreadable.

'Everything OK?'

'It's Andrew,' she said, stuffing the phone back without answering it.

'Andrew?' Dan was intrigued to see colour suffuse her cheeks.

'Someone I used to know,' she said, casting her gaze to the floor, but Dan had a sense Andrew was more than that. Maybe she had a secret boyfriend after all. He and Kate had speculated about her mother's love life, but Kate maintained Helen was happy being single and not interested in having a relationship.

'Where does this client of Kate's live?' Helen asked, breaking into his thoughts with what seemed like deliberate force. 'Local?'

He frowned. 'Kate didn't say exactly. It's near Lexminster. Bluebell Cottage.'

'So, you don't know where she is?' Helen's voice had sharpened.

'It's not a big deal,' he said, trying to sound more light-hearted than he felt. 'I don't know where she is every minute of the day, but that doesn't mean—'

'She's nearly nine months pregnant, Dan,' Helen cut in.

'I know that.' He scraped his nails across the fuzz on his jaw, hating the disappointment in her eyes. 'Why are you asking about her client?'

Familiar lines cut across Helen's brow. She caught her lower lip between her teeth, giving the impression she was agonising about something.

'Helen?'

'It's going to sound odd,' she said, adjusting the hem of her top. 'There was this woman I knew, a long time ago. I saw her recently and a couple of days ago, I got this through my letterbox.'

She pulled a slip of paper from her bag and held it out. On it were written the words I KNOW WHAT YOU DID in black ink.

Dan frowned. 'What does it mean?'

'I think it's from the woman I saw, and I think she is the client that Kate's gone to meet. It's too much of a coincidence. From how I remember her, it's the kind of thing she might do, though I'm not sure of her motives. Maybe to get back at me.'

'But who is she?'

'Mary. I met her in a park when I lived in Leeds.' She was giving him a direct look.

'What happened?'

Her eyes darted away again. 'She was sitting on a bench, looking sad. We got chatting and she told me she'd lost a baby. I felt sorry for her.'

'And?' he coaxed, wondering where this was leading, and what it had to do with Kate.

'I suppose we . . . bonded.' Another pause, as though the memory of it bewildered her. 'She was a bit older than me, and we didn't have anything in common. I doubt our paths would ever have crossed under any other circumstances.'

He nodded for Helen to continue.

'I invited her round for coffee,' she said. 'I still lived in my parents' house then . . . sorry, that's got nothing to do with anything.' She looked at her hands in her lap. 'Mary was good with Kate, would sing to her . . .'

Dan waited. It was more than she'd said to him in one go in all the time he'd known her. He sensed she was relieved to get it off her chest.

'Once, she took Kate out in her pram for some fresh air and didn't come back for ages.' Her face worked briefly. 'I thought something had happened and was about to call the police when she turned up smiling, as if everything was normal.'

'Perhaps she'd forgotten the time,' Dan offered.

Helen shook her head. 'It happened again, a couple of times, so I started to make excuses for her not to come round, but she stopped me in the street one day and said she knew who I was. She said Kate was her baby, even calling her Lexi, and that I had to give her back.'

'God, that's weird.' A chill crept down Dan's spine.

'She said that she was better and wanted to prove to Patrick she could be a good mother.'

'Patrick?'

'The father of the baby she lost, I suppose.' Helen shrugged. 'She'd never mentioned him before, but she didn't talk that much about herself. She mostly focused on Kate.'

'Sounds intense.'

'She did tell me once that she'd had a breakdown in her teens. I wondered if losing her baby had triggered a relapse.'

'Hello?'

Helen's hand shot to her throat and her head whipped round.

Dan twisted to see Zoe posed in the doorway, her hair pinned up in a messy topknot. The sight of her in a midnight-blue maxi-dress, her eyes heavily outlined, was so surprising that, for a second, he thought he was dreaming.

'There was no answer at the door, so I let myself in,' she said, her gaze shifting from Dan to Helen and back, her face alive with curiosity. 'I thought you might need a lift to the gig tonight.'

Dan dared to glance at Helen, saw the way her face tightened, and inwardly groaned. If she didn't have a high opinion of him before, she definitely wouldn't now.

Chapter 11

Kate

I swim up through layers of sleep, a scent of lilac in my nostrils. My eyelids flicker until I am awake. I'm facing an open window. There's a full moon in the sky and the air is still, heavily fragranced by the garden.

Cocooned in a feather-light duvet, my pillow as soft as a cloud, I'm held between sleeping and waking, my breathing gentle. I can't remember the last time I felt this relaxed.

My eyelids droop and memories scroll past: my first kiss with Dan, the brush of his lips igniting something inside me. His wavy hair, trimmed and tamed on our wedding day, his lanky body confined in a tailored suit. He'd been touchingly keen to conform to all the traditions his family had denounced, and his eyes had glazed with tears when we exchanged our vows.

'I didn't think I'd cry,' he said at the reception, as we swayed drunkenly on the dance floor. 'It was the sight of you in that dress, and realising you'd chosen me to spend the rest of your life with.'

Mum's face when I told her I was pregnant: a mix of elation and something I couldn't decipher, quickly concealed. 'I'm so happy, Kate.' Her voice, thick with emotion – not exactly happiness, but something close.

Meeting Saskia four years ago in a busy coffee shop, when she sat opposite and chatted away, asking what I did for a living, before enquiring with a cheeky grin whether I'd like an assistant because she'd just been made redundant. Her joyful surprise – and mine – when I said yes.

This bedroom is so peaceful.

Drenched in sleepiness, I rub the swell of my belly, whispering soothing nonsense. The baby jabs my ribcage with an elbow or knee, and I smile. Will he be red-haired like me, or dark like Dan?

Thoughts slip in then drift away. I push my hand out and stroke the mattress beside me. *Where's Dan? Where am I?*

My eyes flick open once more and shift round the moonlit bedroom. I can just make out the shape of a dressing table by the window and a wardrobe jutting from the wall at the end of the bed. Beside it, a mirror reflects a frilly lightshade hanging from the ceiling.

I twist my head, and my heart seizes in my chest.

There's a shadowy figure in a chair near the door, head lolling forward, legs outstretched.

I scramble upright, stifling a gasp before it flies from my mouth. *Magda!*

She's sleeping, emitting tiny puffs of air, hands folded in her lap. Of course, I remember now. I'm in one of the bedrooms at the cottage, wearing some sort of nightdress. Not the nightshirt I brought with me. My hands grope at the soft material clinging to my body as events slice through the haze in my brain. I remember dropping some photographs on the kitchen floor before passing out.

I try to swallow, but my mouth has furred up. 'Magda,' I whisper, when my heart has stopped crashing around. She springs up, like a statue coming to life, moving quickly.

'You're awake,' she says, switching on a lamp by the bed.

I shrink back, blinking as the room bounces into focus. It's plain and shabby, the furniture dark and heavy, the candy-striped wallpaper peeling in the corners. The curtains framing the window are thin and old-fashioned, patterned with rosebuds. It's grown dark outside.

'It's OK,' Magda soothes, placing a hand on my forehead. Her touch is cool and gentle. 'I'm afraid you fainted, so I thought it best if you rested for a while.' She passes me a glass of water from the bedside table. 'I fell asleep too. I didn't realise the time.'

I take a long drink and offer her a weak smile.

'Thank you.' I replace the glass. 'I've never fainted before, but my blood pressure's low.' I'm trying to pinpoint the reason for passing out. 'The doctor's been keeping an eye on it,' I say, fingers plucking at the nightdress. 'Is this yours?'

Magda's expression is blurry with sleep. 'Your dress was damp where you spilled your lemonade earlier,' she said, though I couldn't remember it happening. 'It was all I could find that would fit you.'

'I did bring nightclothes with me.'

'I didn't want to rummage in your bag.'

I yawn, surprised and embarrassed that I was so out of it I didn't notice her undressing me. She must be stronger than she looks to have manoeuvred me upstairs and into bed.

Tiredness travels through me like a wave and I sink back on the pillows. 'Just as well I'd arranged to stay tonight.' I try for a smile.

'It's my fault.' The mattress dips as Magda perches on the side of the double bed and takes my hand in hers. 'It was far too hot in the kitchen for someone in your condition, and then I dropped a bombshell about . . . the past.' She lifts her eyes to look outside, and I notice they're shiny with tears. 'You were born on a night like this.' Her voice is rough with emotion.

'Listen . . .' I tug my hand from hers and struggle to sit up. 'All those things you said earlier, were they true?'

Her gaze snaps back to mine. 'All true, my darling.' She's

apologetic, but firm, as if now she's told me we can begin to move forward. 'I'm sorry if the shock was too much.'

My resistance seems to have drained away. 'So, my mum has been lying to me all these years.' My voice sounds croaky, and I reach for the glass and guzzle the rest of the water. 'Is that what you're telling me?' I prompt when I've finished.

'I'm afraid so.' Magda's gaze is unflinching. 'But for the best reasons, Kate. She obviously loved you very much and wanted to give you a good home, which I was incapable of doing at that time.'

I put the glass down and massage my forehead with my fingertips. It feels as if my brain has been replaced with sand. *I'm so tired*, is all I can think to say. I try to marshal my thoughts, to imagine getting out of bed and going downstairs, but it seems as impossible as climbing Everest in bare feet.

'Oh, my darling.' Magda shuffles up next to me on the bed and wraps her arms around me. 'You just rest, sweetheart. You probably need it.'

It feels good to sink against her squashy frame and prompts a flashback to climbing into Mum's bed one night when I was a child, during a violent storm. I was terrified of thunder and Mum confessed she didn't like it much either. She suggested we make up a story to take our minds off the crashing overhead. She started with a sentence, and I had to make up the next one and so on, and the story got sillier and sillier until we were both giggling, and I fell asleep pressed to her narrow body, her arm creating a protective barrier across me.

How can she not be my mother?

Tears spill over and I can't stop them falling. I glance through damp lashes at Magda. In the lamplight, she looks younger, cuddly in a thick cream cardigan she's slipped on, covering her dress. When she sees I'm crying, her arms tighten around me and she presses a gentle kiss on top of my head. 'Let it out; there's a good girl,' she urges. 'You'll feel better afterwards.'

I never do. Crying is meant to be cleansing, but I always feel soggy and limp afterwards. Besides, at home I mostly felt I had to put on a brave face, no matter what, for Mum's sake. Only now do I think that it should have been the other way around – that the night of the thunderstorm is the only time I can remember Mum putting on a brave face for me.

'Here.' Magda shifts and takes a tissue from her pocket.

'Thank you,' I say, when I've blown my nose. 'I can honestly say, I've never behaved like this in front of a client before.' It's a weak attempt at a joke, but Magda smiles and pats my hand.

'I'm not really a client,' she reminds me.

Unease pierces the blanket of cloud surrounding my thoughts before sleepiness descends once more. Her eyes are on mine. I can see my tiny reflection in her pupils, my hair flaring over the pillow. 'I need to know more.' I try to remember what she's already told me, but my thoughts are jumbled.

'It's a long story,' she says, after the briefest pause, and I sense her reluctance to elaborate. 'I wasn't in a very good place when you were born. I wasn't ready to have a child; I admit that.' She speaks with an air of an awkward confession, and I try to hold on to her words, not let them slip away. 'After you were born, I had terrible post-natal depression. I was in no state to look after a baby. I couldn't even look after myself.'

Unable to summon a suitable response, my eyes flicker around. Stupidly, I imagine how I would redesign the room: lilac walls, gingham bedcovers, plain white wooden furniture, and simple artwork on the walls ... My brain speeds up and slows down, like a car in a traffic jam.

'... when Patrick comes back, we could be a family.'

I seem to have missed something. 'What?' I shuffle into a more comfortable position, feeling at a disadvantage with her looking down at me, and I'm glad when she rises and walks round the bed. She sits on the window seat, fingers laced in her lap, her gaze off kilter as if she's seeing the past instead of me.

'I'm sure he would have stayed if he'd known I was struggling.

I knew if I got you back, he'd be mine again.' She flicks me a glance. 'I stopped drinking and took my pills.' *Pills?* 'But really, I knew the only thing that would keep me strong was having you both with me.' Her voice sounds disjointed, as if she's not sure what order to tell me things in. 'I didn't know where to find you, where to start.' I try to concentrate, ignoring a building pressure in my bladder. 'Jane has a lot to answer for, but I suppose it was no more than I deserved.' She rubs her elbow through her cardigan sleeve. 'I'd changed my mind about you, but by then it was too late.'

I prod around my feelings, but they're vague and unformed, forced back by a muffled fascination as Magda continues to talk.

'There was no one to ask where she'd gone. She had no family nearby after her great-aunt died, or close friends that I knew of. Her neighbour didn't know anything or said she didn't. I had no idea where to start looking.' I push the heel of one hand into my eye and rub it, willing myself awake. 'I told myself to focus on getting better instead and I did OK for a while, but I couldn't stop thinking about Patrick, or you, imagining how things would have been if you hadn't gone.' She makes it sound as if I got up and ran away on purpose, but I can't summon the energy to protest.

Outside, the moon dips behind the line of trees in the distance.

I force myself to sit further upright, fingers splayed on my stomach. The baby often moves at night, but now he's still.

I wonder vaguely what time it is.

'I thought Jane would stay in touch.' Magda lifts her hands and unties her hair, so it falls around her shoulders. 'I thought she'd bring you back one day, at least to visit. She should never have kept you.'

I can't think about Mum's part in this . . . whatever it is. *Not yet.*

Magda's words keep pushing in. 'She knew where I lived, yet she never sent so much as a letter or a photo to let me know you were OK.' She looks up at the ceiling, blinking fast as if she's about to sneeze, and I realise she's holding back tears. 'How could she do that?'

My blood feels like treacle, moving too slowly through my body. 'Why didn't you call the police?'

'It wasn't a police matter, Lexi.' She presses her hands to her temples, as if to contain her emotions. 'I deliberately let you go; do you understand? Eight months had passed by the time I was well enough to want you back. How was I supposed to explain that to the police?'

'They could have helped you find the baby.'

'Oh, Lexi, it wasn't that simple,' she says sadly, and I feel like collapsing under the weight of all the things I don't understand.

Magda swipes at her damp face with her forearm. 'We could do a DNA test,' she says suddenly, brightening. 'I've got a kit.' She nods. 'If you need proof.'

And that's when I know, with a shivering certainty, that she must be telling the truth.

Magda Trent is my mother.

Another thought drifts in: *This explains so many things*.

Why Mum was overprotective when I was growing up, always looking over her shoulder whenever we were out, as if we were being pursued. Not letting me out of her sight for long or making me promise to call her when she couldn't think of a convincing excuse to keep me at home. I was one of the first children at school to have a mobile phone, so she could keep track of me better.

She must have been constantly worried this day would come, that my natural mother would reappear and reclaim me. How could she have lived with that? I can't begin to imagine the thought processes that must have dominated her life.

'You're my mother,' I say, trying out the words, and a look of pleasure crosses Magda's face, swift and intense, transforming her into a stranger again, a woman I know nothing about, save that she gave birth to me thirty years ago.

My birth mother. It sounds unreal – the sort of statement that shouldn't apply to me yet makes even more sense if I can force myself to think about it properly. Mum and I aren't similar in any way; I've long accepted that. I'd simply assumed I must take after my unknown father. I'd never thought to question our differences, the way some of my friends used to do, fantasising they'd been swapped at birth and were secretly related to royalty.

Saskia once joked her mother must have had an affair because her sister looks so unlike anyone else in their family. 'I read somewhere there are all these men raising children who aren't theirs, and they have no idea,' she'd said, sounding scandalised. 'How can women be so deceitful?'

But what about mothers bringing up stolen children? It must be so rare and yet, according to Magda, it's happened. *I've been raised by a woman who's not related to me.*

'So, you met in the park.' I force the words through lips as dry as sandpaper. 'Then what?'

I can see Magda thinking, as if working out what to say. Or maybe trying to remember exactly how it happened. 'She asked if she could hold you,' she says quickly, as if to get it over with. 'You stopped crying right away and Jane seemed pleased, looked happy. She offered to babysit if I ever wanted a break. We lived quite close by . . .' She stops, her expression absent, as if she's lost the thread of what she's saying.

'So, you stayed in touch?' I prompted.

Another quick nod. 'She obviously felt sorry for me,' she says. 'Because I was struggling with you.' She flashes me a look. 'I said she could visit. To be honest, I was terrified of being left alone with you. I didn't think I could cope, and my father was no help; he was so busy all the time and had no interest in being a grandfather.'

My grandfather? Implications flood in. I could have grandparents, cousins I know nothing about. A whole family. I see us spreading like ivy, tendrils stretching and binding, dinners at Christmas around a long table laden with food, but feel strangely detached. 'Why was he no help?'

'Let's just say that my parents were devoutly religious. They didn't believe in unmarried mothers.'

The baby's pressing my diaphragm, making me breathless. I shift position and the room tilts like a galleon.

'My darling Lexi.' Magda's hands are cupping my face, thumbs stroking my cheeks. I instantly become drowsy, sensible thoughts fading to a pinprick. 'Please don't hate me.'

'I don't,' I mumble, wondering whether I should. She's lobbed a live hand grenade into my life, and nothing will ever be the same. 'I don't hate you,' I repeat, as she settles me back on the pillows and tucks the duvet around me.

I feel as if I've leaped backwards through time, am a child again. Is that Magda's intention? My eyes ache, as though I've had the flu. I need to ask her so many things, but my eyelids are drifting shut.

Didn't she mention something about my father?

I have to know.

'Shush,' Magda soothes, stroking my hair off my forehead. 'We've all the time in the world to catch up. We'll talk again tomorrow when we're both rested.'

My thoughts become fragmented. I catch Magda's breath on my face, brace myself for her kiss, but it doesn't come.

Chapter 12

Dan

The wedding reception venue was a vast, grey-stoned manor house just outside Oxford, and the dance hall was already packed by the time Skinny Rivers stepped on stage.

Dan was aware of a slight buzz of excitement, a faint echo of the way he'd felt the first time he performed in front of a crowd at a festival arranged by the music department at university.

He'd never really fed off an audience's attention the way Eric and Calum had, high on adrenalin for hours afterwards, leaping about and high-fiving, smoking and drinking, chatting up girls who lingered backstage – sleeping with them, in Calum's case.

Dan tended to lose himself in the music, his focus narrowing to his fingers on the strings of the guitar, and the melody inside his head, to Eric and Calum's amusement.

'You look so different when you're playing,' Kate had said, the first time she watched him perform, her expression pitched between admiration and shyness. 'It's as if nothing else exists.'

He knew she felt that same absorption when she was designing; she wasn't jealous of it, like previous girlfriends, and he'd felt a depth of love for her he hadn't known he was capable of feeling.

He still enjoyed being onstage, but tonight he was unusually jittery, his thoughts leaping like frogs.

As he and Eric adjusted their instruments, waiting for the newlyweds to take to the dance floor, he thought of Kate on his voicemail and wished he'd picked her call up. He could have told her he was unhappy about her spending the night away from home so close to giving birth. Or would that have only made her more determined to stay? Had things between them deteriorated so badly she'd rather stay with a client she'd only just met? He wondered who the client was and cursed himself for not asking. For all he knew, she could be spending the night with another man. He banished the thought as soon as it entered his head. Apart from being heavily pregnant, Kate wasn't the cheating kind; he just knew. She had strong views about it, despite, or maybe because of, her mother's affair all those years ago.

Zoe sauntered over, her piled-up hair as glossy as a raven's wing beneath the lighting rig. 'You all right?' she said, covering her microphone.

Playing for time, he tightened the shoulder strap on his guitar. He never used to need one, but these days his shoulder ached by the end of a set without it. 'I'm fine, thanks.' He kept his voice neutral, certain he could still feel the imprint of Zoe's hand, which had rested on his knee for most of the drive over.

'So that's the mother-in-law,' she'd said, once they were in her car. Her tone had been slightly mocking, but Dan knew she was miffed because he hadn't introduced her to Helen. Not that he'd had much chance. Seeing Zoe had galvanised his mother-in-law into action. She'd grabbed her bag, taken a gulp of cold tea and pushed past him out of the front door with a muttered goodbye. His mind flickered back to the story she'd been relaying before Zoe turned up, trying to make sense of it all. There was more to come; he was sure of that. But was Kate really with this woman? He thought of the note Helen had shown him. I KNOW WHAT

YOU DID. What did it mean? A shiver travelled down his spine.

'She didn't look impressed to see me,' Zoe had persisted, pursing her lips and drawing her brows together in a cruel imitation of Helen. 'What was she looking so worried about anyway?'

'Some problem she's been having with a neighbour,' he'd improvised. The truth had seemed too complicated to go into, especially as he wasn't sure what the truth was.

'I was worried about you when you rushed off this afternoon,' Zoe had continued, lifting her hand off the steering wheel and laying it on his knee. 'I'm here if you ever want to talk.' He felt her eyes flicking between him and the road, but refused to meet her gaze, turning the conversation to the gig.

Now, she was watching him again, eyes wide and luminous, the irises flecked with yellow. *Tiger's eyes.* 'You don't look OK,' she said, cocking her head like a therapist.

'I told you, I'm fine,' he repeated, sensing she'd love nothing more than to hear his marriage was in trouble. He didn't want to discuss it with Zoe.

'Let's get a drink afterwards,' she said, winding a loose tendril of hair around her finger, and he wondered if she'd overheard him telling Helen that Kate wasn't coming home. He had no idea how long Zoe had been in the house.

'Maybe,' he said in a non-committal way, hoping she would take the hint.

Zoe seemed to interpret this as a yes, breaking into a smile that lifted her face. 'Cool,' she said, sauntering off to take her position at the front of the stage. She turned to wink at him over her shoulder, which sparkled with some sort of glittery body cream, and Dan felt a pinch of irritation. Why couldn't she just focus on the music?

He missed his cue when the music began and came in late and pretended to ignore a 'what the fuck?' look from Calum – who was dressed appropriately for once, in a fresh white shirt and dark trousers. He grimaced an apology at Eric, but his friend was bent over his keyboard and didn't notice.

As Zoe launched into the first song – a Fleetwood Mac cover – he made an effort to focus, pleased when his guitar solo drew a spontaneous round of applause. By the time they'd played another seven songs, he'd managed to tuck his chaotic thoughts into a distant corner of his mind.

'We're on fire tonight,' Zoe declared as they stopped for a break, her face glistening with perspiration. Her eye make-up had smudged, and her hair was trailing around her shoulders, giving her a Gothic air.

She squeezed his hand as she passed, and when he jerked away, her smile slipped. She swayed over to Eric and stood on tiptoe to whisper something that made him laugh. As they left the stage with Calum, she flicked Dan a look he couldn't decipher. Was she trying to make him jealous?

He placed his guitar on its stand, the pleasure of the last hour or so draining away. Pressure began to build behind his eyes. He was tired and wanted to go home, but at the same time couldn't face the thought of an empty house.

'Kate couldn't make it tonight?' Eric asked, as they ordered soft drinks at the bar. He operated a 'no alcohol while performing' policy, after Calum got so drunk once, he threw up all over his drum kit.

'She's too pregnant for all this,' Dan replied, not wanting to mention that Kate wasn't coming home. 'And anyway, I don't turn up at her workplace every day, so why should she mine?'

'OK, I was only asking,' said Eric, the crease between his eyebrows deepening. 'This is hardly a normal workplace.' He indicated the high-ceilinged hall, where French doors opened onto a terrace strung with fairy lights, stone steps leading to grounds big enough to accommodate a housing estate. The floor was crammed with smartly dressed people swigging champagne, and the catering alone had probably cost more than Dan earned in a year. He couldn't imagine how much it had cost to hire the venue. It was a big step up from the cosy pub where he and Kate had held their wedding reception, but the upshot was they were being paid treble what they'd normally earn, thanks to Eric knowing someone who knew the groom, a hedge-fund manager with lots of money.

'Kate wouldn't have enjoyed it anyway,' he said, wishing he hadn't when Zoe picked up her glass and fixed him with her searchlight gaze.

'Oh? How come?'

'Too noisy, too hot. In her condition . . .' he began, making a dome shape over his stomach with his hands.

'Pregnancy's not an illness,' Zoe interrupted, raising her voice over a burst of chatter as a crowd of people elbowed their way to the bar. They began ordering drinks in an entitled way, clearly unaccustomed to being ignored.

'What do you know about pregnancy?' he asked Zoe, attempting a light-heartedness he didn't feel.

Her expression darkened. 'Let's just say it's a state I'm unlikely to find myself in.' Her eyes glittered with unreadable emotion. 'Some people aren't cut out to be mothers. I'm one of them.'

'How can you know until you've tried it?' Eric asked her, half-amused.

'It runs in my family,' Zoe shot back. 'I won't risk inflicting bad parenting skills on some poor unsuspecting kid.'

Dan exchanged a look with Eric. He wondered if she was going to elaborate, but suddenly she was all smiles again, slipping her arm through his. 'Don't look so scared, Danny-boy.' She lifted her glass of lemonade and darted him a mischievous look. 'I'm a good auntie,' she said with a grin. 'I'll be available for babysitting duties if required.'

Eric made a snorting noise, missing Zoe's hurt expression as he turned to greet the groom, who'd slapped him heartily on the back. He was bleary-eyed but beaming as he thanked them for playing and requested a couple of songs.

'I suppose I don't look the type who'd be good with kids,' Zoe said to Dan in a challenging way, as if daring him to dispute her. He wondered why, when it was Eric who'd looked disbelieving. If anything, Dan was reassured by her mentioning she was an auntie. It made her seem more real . . . more ordinary. Discomfited by the thought, he was relieved when his phone vibrated against his thigh and he had an excuse to turn away. 'Be back in minute,' he said, ignoring her outstretched hand as he downed his Coke and backed out onto the terrace. He noticed Calum in a shadowy corner, chatting up one of the bridesmaids, tracing a finger down her cheek. What a cliché he was.

'Dan?'

For a second, he didn't recognise the number, or the voice on the end of the phone.

'It's Saskia.'

'Oh, hi, Sass.' He got on well with Kate's friend and colleague, liked her a lot. He jabbed a finger in his ear to block out the swell of noise around him. 'Everything OK?'

'I think so, I just . . .' she faltered.

'Just what?' Despite the humidity a chill crept over Dan's arms.

'Oh, it's probably nothing, but I wanted to call Kate and let her know my consult went really well this afternoon.'

Relief coursed through Dan. 'She hasn't got her phone,' he said.

'No, I know, but I called the number she rang me from earlier. I thought it would be OK to have a word with her, but there was no response.'

'Maybe it was switched off.' Dan was struggling to understand why Saskia was bothered enough to call him. 'There's obviously not much signal there,' he said. 'She left me a voicemail I could hardly hear.'

'It wasn't that sort of no response, it was as if the number didn't exist,' said Saskia. 'I thought there might be a landline, so I looked in the diary to see if Kate had written it down.'

'And?'

'Nothing.'

Dan heard his name and turned to see Eric in the doorway, waving him over. 'Sass, I'm playing at a wedding tonight; I really have to go,' he said, brushing away a moth attracted to the fractured disco lights spilling out behind him.

'It's just that I went online and looked for the address, but that doesn't seem to exist either.' Saskia's words came at him in a rush.

'What do you mean?' He was only half-listening as he made his way back inside, giving Calum a poke in the ribs on the way. One of his hands had descended to the bridesmaid's silk-covered backside, and he looked annoyed at being disturbed. 'Maybe Kate wrote it down wrong.'

'You know that's not like her,' Saskia said. 'There's no Bluebell Cottage in Lexminster, or anywhere nearby. I ended up doing a pretty extensive search online.'

'Well, maybe the house name has changed and it hasn't been registered yet.' He was plucking words from thin air, keen to get off the phone, and to his relief, Saskia let out an embarrassed laugh.

'Oh God, I didn't even think of that,' she said. 'Actually, that happened when my folks moved. They still get post addressed to The Badger Den.'

'I can see why they changed it,' Dan said, amused. 'Did you try the postcode?'

'Yes, but it was linked to somewhere completely different, so I suppose Kate *must* have got it wrong.' Saskia sounded serious again. 'I've just got a funny feeling about it, because Kate always has the right contact details; it's just not like her.'

Dan thought of what Helen had told him and felt a pinch of unease.

'So, you're worried too?' said Saskia. 'It's odd for a person *and* an address not to be online these days.'

'Person?'

She hesitated. 'I could only find one Magda Trent on the whole of the internet, and she's a professor living in Michigan.'

'That doesn't necessarily mean anything.' Dan raised his voice as he shouldered his way to the stage, pushing his hair back off his forehead. It was warm outside, and even warmer inside from the press of bodies around him. 'Not everyone's on social media. If you searched for my parents, I doubt they'd come up.' He was still thirsty, but it was too late for another drink. He noticed that Zoe had slipped a silvery, sequined top over her dress, reflecting rainbow colours from the lighting. She blew him a kiss and he turned away. 'Listen, I've really got to go now, Sass.'

'OK, sorry for ringing, I—'

'No, it's fine. I'm glad you did,' he said truthfully. He wondered how much she knew about the state of his and Kate's relationship. 'You know she's staying there tonight?'

'Yes, she told me. I just wish I knew for sure where it was.'

'Me too,' he said, as Calum rushed past and jogged his elbow, sending his phone crashing to the ground.

'Fuck's sake,' Dan said. By the time he'd retrieved it from under a table, the line had gone dead and he didn't have time to call her back. He tried his best to focus on the rest of the set, but his mind kept zipping back to Saskia's call, and Helen's story, and by the time they'd finished he was unfairly annoyed with Kate for worrying everyone. When Zoe reminded him that he'd agreed to have a drink with the band before leaving, he didn't argue. Perhaps it would stop him worrying for a while.

'Go on then,' he said. 'As long as you don't mind driving me home again.'

Chapter 13

Kate

When I wake again the room is flooded apricot. Sunlight pours through the open window and there's a scent of roses in the air.

I yawn and stretch, feeling as if I've slept for hours.

Anticipation rolls through me, like the beginning of school holidays. When did I last have a holiday? Greece, two years ago with Dan, a tour of the islands, drunk on sangria, kissing under the stars.

I've worked non-stop since then and have forgotten how to relax.

I wriggle my toes and stare at an old-fashioned oil painting on the wall of a chestnut horse galloping through a field, mane flying.

Something niggles at the back of my mind.

There are sounds from downstairs. An aroma of fresh coffee and frying bacon drifts under the door and my mouth fills with saliva. I sit up, wincing as my back protests.

As I swing my legs out of bed, the baby kicks, and I stand for a moment, resting my hands on my belly, relieved by the tiny movements. I fainted, but there's no need to worry; I'm fine. *We're* fine – my baby and me. I love the way that sounds. *My baby and me. Me and my baby. Dan and me, and our baby.*

Except, Dan doesn't want a baby.

I shouldn't have sprung it on him like that, on his birthday. It wasn't fair.

My eyes travel the room. I like the sloping ceiling and uneven walls. The floorboards could be stripped back and varnished . . .

I'm starving. Eggs and bacon, swimming in fat with fried bread. Is it a craving? Did Magda have cravings when she was pregnant with me? Mum couldn't remember hers. Probably because she was never pregnant in the first place.

Oh God.

The events from yesterday flood back.

Magda Trent is my mother. I have a father called Patrick.

I have to ask her more . . . must write it down. Need a pen to make a list. I'm good with lists.

Thoughts slip past like eels, leaving only the vaguest impression. Probably natural after Magda's revelation. I've had a shock. A *big* shock. I try to feel it, but everything's removed. Instead, I feel oddly serene and it's nice.

'Mum is not my mum,' I say, trying the words out loud. They bounce off the walls and back, without much impact. I have an urge to laugh. I don't feel like myself anymore. Who am I if I'm not Mum's daughter?

'Breakfast won't be long, Lexi!' Magda's voice floats up the stairs, as bright and cheerful as the sun, and it seems entirely normal. Clearly, the past twenty-four hours haven't properly sunk in. I'll worry about it later.

Worry's bad for the baby.

There's a robe hanging on the back of the door. I pull it on over my nightdress, tying the belt inelegantly above my bump. I wonder what time it is, but don't have a watch. I can't see my phone or bag anywhere. Then I remember: I left my phone at home.

Some hazy notion that I might be able to tell the time from the sun's position propels me across to the window. Kneeling on the window seat, I rest my hands on the sill and peer out. The sky is a stretch of cloudless blue, in contrast to the garden, which dazzles and dances with colour. The hills and trees in the distance are washed with sunlight, and in a faraway field a tractor as small as a toy is turning crops.

'Lexi!' Magda calls again. There's an edge of anxiety in her voice.

'Coming!' I call back, vocal cords straining. Turning, I glimpse Magda's car on the drive, sun glinting off the roof. Something about the sight of it bothers me, but I can't work out why. Then I realise why. My car isn't there. Maybe Magda borrowed my keys and put it in the garage.

I pad to the bathroom for a wee, wondering vaguely where my sandals have gone. Something else missing, though it's nice having bare feet, no straps digging in, tiles cool beneath my toes.

As I rinse my hands and face, I notice a crack running across the sink and stare at it for a long time.

I lift my eyes to the mirror. My pupils have contracted to pinpricks and my hair's a tangled frenzy around my head. My skin's the colour of porridge. 'Alien,' I say, stretching the skin on my cheeks with my hands. 'Your mummy's an alien.' I pat my belly and giggle. 'I do apologise, sir.'

'Lexi!'

Her voice makes me jump. After roughly drying my hands, I drift downstairs, gripping the banister as if to anchor myself. Everything's swimming. I'm worried I might float away.

The bolts on the door have been pulled back. Magda must have been out. Perhaps she's an early riser, like me. Only, it isn't early. Entering the kitchen, I look at the clock on the wall and with a tiny jolt I see that it's ten thirty. I really have slept for hours.

'You looked so peaceful, I didn't want to disturb you,' Magda says, wiping her hands on her apron. Beneath it, she's wearing jeans and a lemon-coloured short-sleeved shirt. She looks younger, her hair draped over one shoulder in a simple plait.

'We both have red hair and freckles.' Finally seeing a likeness, I hold out my arm, pushing up the sleeve of the robe to show her. She grins with obvious delight, her face alive with . . . *joy*? No, not joy, not totally. There's a hint of sadness and longing there too.

'I'm sure it's not the only similarity,' she says, still smiling as she hands me a mug of instant coffee. It's milky and sweet, exactly how I like it. Only Dan ever gets it right. Mum hates coffee. She won't have it in the house. Says it makes her jittery.

A feeling of well-being floods through me as I sip the frothy liquid, returning Magda's gaze with more candour than I would have believed possible.

This could be the best thing that's ever happened to me.

What Magda has told me – it doesn't have to be a disaster. It's *not* a disaster. It's probably the most real thing, apart from meeting Dan and being pregnant, I've ever experienced. I'm not going to deny it.

Magda's my mother.

It could be a fresh start. Magda, me and the baby. I don't need Dan anymore. Don't need Mum, with her fussing, fussy, fretting . . . Maybe now I can distance myself and my baby from Mum, breathe freely without her looking over my shoulder, needing constant reassurances.

Thoughts tumble in and out like dandelion clocks.

Fuzzy, floating, flying—

'I thought we could eat in the dining room,' Magda says. I start, as if waking from a light doze. 'It's a bit dingy, I'm afraid, but it overlooks the garden. You said you liked the garden.'

Her face is expectant, one eyebrow arched.

I nod. 'It's beautiful,' I say. 'Let's do it.'

She releases a short laugh, the bones of her face relaxing. 'Let's do it,' she echoes. 'Go and sit down. I'll bring this through.' She waves a hand at the food she's been preparing. 'It's just bacon sandwiches, but everyone likes bacon sandwiches.'

'Unless they're vegetarian,' I quip. Bizarrely, Eric pops into my head. Dan's lovely friend, Eric, who can't bear the idea of killing animals for food. I haven't seen him for ages but can't remember why.

'You're not, are you?' Magda's smile fades. 'You ate ham yesterday.'

I smile, shake my head. 'No, I'm not. Sometimes I think I ought to be, but I'm not.'

'Me neither.' Her smile is back. 'Off you go then.' She makes a shooing motion. 'It's the first door on your left.'

I turn obediently and wander into the dining room. It's small and square, with yellowing walls and the same musty smell as the hallway. It's empty, apart from a polished oval table and two chairs in front of a pair of glass doors leading to the garden.

I try to open them, longing to breathe the sunlit air, but they're locked. I look around for a key but can't see one. Suddenly unsteady, I lean my forehead on the glass and close my eyes.

'Here we are.'

I turn to see Magda bustling in, a plate of bacon sandwiches in each hand. She sets them on the table and returns seconds later with a carafe of coffee, a jug of milk and a sugar bowl on a tray.

There's a slightly manic energy about her movements.

'Could we eat out there?' I indicate the paved area through the doors. 'We still haven't been out on the patio.'

Her expression flickers. 'Maybe later,' she says. She sits down. 'I can't find the key, I'm afraid.'

'OK.' I sit opposite, easing the dome of my belly behind the table. I'm hungrier than I'd realised, which might be why I feel so peculiar. I reach for a sandwich and eat quickly, crumbs spilling down my robe. The bread's rather stale and hasn't been buttered, but I don't say anything.

We don't speak while we eat, which is odd when there's so much to say, but it's a comfortable silence. The sort of silence I never enjoy with Mum, who seems compelled to talk all the time, though not about anything important.

'I must make a couple of phone calls,' I say at last, swallowing a mouthful of coffee. The sandwiches have left a strange aftertaste, as if the bread might be on the turn. 'People will be worried about me.'

People. A chink opens up in my mind. Mum will be frantic at me being uncontactable and Saskia must be wondering why I haven't checked in about her client meeting. 'Can I use your phone again?'

Magda holds up a finger, indicating I wait while she empties her mouth.

The cat – Arthur – appears in the doorway and meows. It's a plaintive sound that makes me think of a baby's cry.

'There you are, darling!' Magda throws me an apologetic smile as she rises and leaves the room with Arthur hot on her heels. 'Do you want some breakfast too?' I hear her moving around the kitchen.

'The phone battery's dead. It's so old, it doesn't hold a charge very long,' she says when she returns.

To my shame, I feel a twinge of relief. It means I can't call Dan, but the thought of talking to Mum gives me a dragging sensation in my stomach. There'll be so much talking to do – *so* much explaining. My mind hovers over her reaction to Magda's bombshell, then leaps away. I can't even picture it. Not yet. I need all the facts from Magda before I can face my mum.

Maybe Magda should come with me when I leave, and we can talk to her together. *No.* It wouldn't be fair to Mum.

But then, she hasn't played fair with me.

My mind spins in circles.

'I thought you might want to know a bit more about your father.'

As my thoughts zoom away from Mum and focus on Magda, a feeling of desolation sweeps over me. My whole parentage has been bogus. That story about Mum's affair wasn't even true. She couldn't have children of her own, so she took someone else's child. She kept me from meeting my father.

No wonder she's never met anyone since then or got married. She wouldn't have been comfortable keeping a secret so big from somebody else, no matter how she'd justified it to herself. Did her sister know? Cath has been in Australia for as long as I can remember, so probably not.

'Kate?'

I refocus on Magda with an effort. 'My father,' I say, the words clumsy on my lips. The picture I've built in my mind over the years is nothing more than a fairy tale, but my real father's still alive. With a feeling of unreality, I prop my elbow on the table and rest my chin on my hand. 'Tell me about him.'

'He was a doctor at the hospital where I was training.' Magda's voice is dreamy, as if it's a story she's repeated in her head many times but has longed to say out loud. 'Good looking, as you saw in the photo. He was the son of a colleague of my father's. Did I say my father was a doctor too? Anyway, Patrick came to the house one day – I can't remember why – but the moment I saw him I fell deeply in love. He was so different to anyone I'd ever met. I'd never had a proper relationship before.'

I listen to her voice as though hypnotised, while sunshine streams through the window. Arthur is sleeping in a pool of light on the floorboards, his body rising and falling with each breath. A peaceful feeling steals over me again, like being wrapped in a duvet.

'There was a steadiness about Patrick that appealed to me,' Magda continues, and I wonder why it did, but she's still talking. 'He was very well read too, had loads of books. He introduced me to the classics. I wasn't very academic, not in that way.'

What was Mum doing while Magda was busy falling in love with my father? I knew from old and difficult conversations that her teenage life had stalled for a long time after the death of her parents, that her aunt and her sister had done their best to take care of her, but I had no idea whether she'd longed for a career, or a family, to travel, what she was like before me.

'So, he was artistic too?' I say. Mum doesn't have a creative bone in her body, and I've often wondered where I got my eye for design. I'd wondered whether I took after my unknown father's side of the family.

'He certainly was.' Magda's eyes are still looking inward, as if picturing him clearly. 'He was gentle, tender and funny. The perfect man.' It's as if time and distance has rendered him a saint, yet he left her when she fell pregnant. 'I don't blame him for going,' she says quickly, as if guessing what's on my mind. 'He wasn't ready to be a father, and I was angry with myself for not being more careful.'

'So, I wasn't wanted?'

'Oh, Lexi, don't say that.' Magda reaches for my hand, and I let her take it. 'I would have felt differently if he'd been happy about me being pregnant, but when he left, I'm afraid I went to pieces.' She pauses, her face contorting, as if recalling that terrible time. 'But it never occurred to me once, not to have you, despite Patrick leaving and my father . . .' She stops.

'What?' But it's not too difficult to guess that he wanted her to have a termination.

'He thought I'd messed up my future. He wanted so much for me to be a doctor, like him.'

'It wasn't the fifties; women could still have children and go to work.'

'I wasn't very strong. Emotionally, I mean.' Magda's voice is stark with disapproval. Perhaps the memory of her old self disgusts her. 'I took after my mother in that sense.'

I feel afraid too, suddenly. It's all too much. The people she's talking about are related to me in some way. I have no idea now what kind of blood is running through my veins – my unborn baby's veins.

'He went abroad?' I say, the words thick in my mouth.

'Yes.' Her voice is a whisper. 'He didn't leave a forwarding address.'

Silence falls, heavy and somehow forbidding. Magda refills my coffee cup and I drink, desperate to slake the thirst I can't seem to shift.

'Kate?'

I blink and raise my head.

We're outside on a wooden bench on the patio, tall glasses of iced water on a mosaic-topped table in front of us, but I can't remember getting there.

'None of it really matters now,' I say through a yawn, unsure what I'm referring to. She was talking about my father. *Wasn't she?*

I glance down. I'm still in nightclothes and my feet are bare, the pearly-pink varnish on my toenails starting to chip. I never wander about in bare feet, even at home. I wear slippers, which Dan finds hilarious, teasing me about my granny-like tendencies.

Magda's hands wrestle in her lap. She's removed her apron and twisted her plait into a knot at the back of her head. Perspiration dampens her hairline. 'Post-natal depression's a terrible thing,' she says. 'It wasn't taken seriously back then.'

Post-natal depression. The words prick a hole in my consciousness. What if I get it? Would I recognise the symptoms? Would Dan? I've read awful stories about women suffering in silence, not knowing what's wrong with them, not wanting to admit to negative feelings in case their baby is taken away from them.

Like I was. By a woman Magda had thought was her friend.

'When Jane took you, I told myself you were better off, wherever you were,' Magda continues, as if she's a witch with the ability to see inside my head. She angles her body away from me as though ashamed. Or as if her memories are so painful she wants to escape them. 'I had to make myself forget you in order to move on, and to be honest it wasn't that difficult at first. I was relieved.' When her eyes flick to mine, they're oddly blank.

I can't think how to respond.

It's humid, the sun a hazy ball in a cotton-white sky. Even the drone of the distant tractor has stopped. A thrush drops lightly on the patio and cocks a beady eye at me before taking off, and I track its ascent into the branches of an oak tree beyond the perimeter wall.

'There's a storm coming.' I press my fingertips to my temples, glad of an explanation for the thumping in my head, startled when Magda lurches forward and deadheads a rose, its petals browning at the edges. Her movements are jerky, her cheeks darkened to scarlet. She looks upset and angry, but I can't work out why.

'You keep saying Mum took me, as if you knew nothing about it,' I say, marvelling that it feels almost normal to be saying such incredible words. Twenty-four hours ago, my life was trundling along familiar grooves. I was vaguely concerned about a room redesign that had gone over budget, and whether or not the nursery was going to be ready for the baby, about Mum's increasing need for pregnancy updates, and worried about Dan and me. It seems ludicrous now, as if those worries belong to someone else.

I look at Magda, waiting for a response. When none is forthcoming, I pick up my glass and take a sip, the icy liquid chasing away some of the dryness in my throat. 'Did you actually give Mum permission to . . . ?' I can't say 'take me'. It sounds too much like a true crime documentary. It conjures an image of a desperate woman, snatching a baby from a pram on impulse. I settle for 'raise me?' instead.

'She wasn't meant to keep you forever.' Magda swings round so violently her hair clip flies out and lands in a flowerbed bursting with small pink flowers. She doesn't bother picking it up and her plait uncoils like rope. 'If I'd known . . .' She pauses, chest heaving, hand clenched into a fist around the decaying rose petals, fighting some inner turmoil.

'You can't really blame her,' I say, swatting a fly from my face, some strong instinct to defend Mum rearing up. I'll have plenty of time to be angry with her later. 'Not if you'd made it clear you didn't want me.'

'I was ill!' Magda's voice is shrill, her face twisted, but just as suddenly she deflates, and the fight drains out of her. 'You're right,' she says, letting the rose petals flutter to the grass like confetti. 'She did the only thing she could.'

I try to picture it; Mum sneaking off with me in the dead of night, plotting to leave Leeds forever – the place where she'd grown up, the only place she'd ever known. It's so unlike the Mum I know, who does everything by the book, and blushes in the vicinity of a police officer. How did she even work out all the logistics? She must have made a deliberate choice to tread a careful path since then, to avoid attracting the attention of the law.

Oh God, Mum. What did you do?

'But why not make it formal?' I puzzle, shuffling to the end of the bench, where it's shaded by the roof of the cottage. Beads of moisture have gathered between my breasts, and I loosen the belt of my robe, clinging uncomfortably around my middle. 'Why not just adopt me, and tell me all about it when I was old enough to understand?'

'It wouldn't have been that simple.' Magda's face works briefly, as if she doesn't want to – or doesn't know how to – give me a satisfactory answer. She sits beside me again, too close. I feel stifled. The garden closes in and my breathing quickens. 'I think she thought you'd be better off never knowing,' Magda says at last, her gaze catching mine. 'Maybe she assumed I would never get better and be a fit mother for you.'

'But that wasn't her decision to make.'

Triumph flares in Magda's eyes, as though I've said the right thing, confirmed what she'd thought all along but hadn't liked to say. It's obvious now that she's been trying to portray Mum in a good light for my sake, but that her view of her is rather less forgiving. 'I was so glad to see how well you've done for yourself,' she says, abruptly changing the subject and laying her hand on my arm. 'I thought you might have gone into medicine, like Patrick, but I'm glad you didn't. It's a difficult job.' When she says his name, her voice softens, and she touches her hair in an unconscious gesture. A sense of hysteria presses down. There are so many thoughts competing for my attention, it's hard to stay focused, and my headache deepens with the effort.

I swallow more water, forcing it past the tightness in my throat. 'How did you feel when you saw me at the showroom?' I try to imagine meeting your child for the first time as a grown-up, but it's beyond me.

'I saw you in a newspaper originally,' she says, and I realise I didn't think to ask sooner how she found me in the first place. Her face stretches into a smile that's both secretive and proud. 'It was such a stroke of luck,' she adds, shaking her head as if she still can't believe it. 'I remember Jane mentioning having an aunt in this part of the world, you see. Every now and then, I'd try to find you. Occasionally I'd come and stay down here, hoping I'd bump into her.' It sounds highly unlikely, but I don't say so. 'And it's funny, because I don't normally read the papers, but someone had left one on the table in a café where I was having a coffee. I flipped through it and there you were.' She pauses and I hear my own heartbeat. 'With Jane.' As she lifts a hand to push back her hair, I notice a silvery scar threaded along the underside of her arm and wonder how she got it.

'I'd have recognised her anywhere.' Her tone becomes more clipped. 'She hasn't changed much at all, she's . . .' She appears to gather herself. 'I knew you were my Lexi straight away, with that lovely red hair.' She blinks a few times. 'I could hardly believe it after all that time. I hadn't decided if I was really going to go through with . . . with talking to you, but seeing that picture in the paper felt like destiny.'

Her gaze drops to my stomach, and I recall brushing against her in the doorway when I entered the cottage. *Was it only yesterday?* She twists around and places her hands on my belly, rubbing it lightly, smiling. 'My baby,' she murmurs, and I don't know which of us she's referring to.

He kicks, hard, and I gasp.

'Did you feel that?' Her eyes meet mine, awestruck.

'Of course I did.' Nausea rises in a rush. I push off the bench with difficulty and press my fists into my lower back. A piercing pain zigzags above my eyes, forcing them shut.

'Poor darling,' says Magda, standing up. When I lift one eyelid, she's watching me with laser-beam precision. She seems incredibly intense, but under the circumstances, I suppose she has every reason to be. 'Shall we go back inside?'

I draw warm air into my lungs and try to compose a sentence or two about getting dressed and calling Dan to let him know what's happening. I want to suggest arranging to meet Magda another time, once I've absorbed things properly, but a sudden squeal of hinges and the emergence of a man into the garden wipes everything from my mind. Magda tenses, her colour draining. Before I know what's happening, she cups my elbow and ushers me through the French doors into the dining room. Our plates are still on the table, a wasp dive-bombing the crumbs, and the sight of my coffee cup, half-filled with cold liquid, brings bitterness to my throat.

'Oh, it's the gardener,' Magda says before I can ask to borrow the phone, which hopefully is charged now, pulling the doors shut behind us. As she locks them, I wonder if I imagined her saying she couldn't find the key. 'He's Polish,' she elaborates, waving an acknowledgement.

I raise a hand to shield my aching eyes and observe the man, who is short and wiry with close-cropped dark hair, his naked chest as smooth and burnished as a piece of wood.

He glances in the direction of the house, but doesn't return Magda's wave, moving with confident strides in the direction of a shed tucked away in a corner. He reappears seconds later with a petrol mower and stoops to start the motor, muscles rippling.

It springs to life with an explosive roar that reverberates through my brain.

'He barely speaks a word of English,' Magda says with a smile. She tugs a muslin curtain across the doors, obscuring the view. 'Sadly, I don't have green fingers.'

I automatically look at her hands, as though verifying their colour, and she gives a stuttering laugh.

From nowhere, an image of Mum pops up, lovingly tending her window boxes at home. I see her look of concentration as she waters the cascading plants with her metal can, humming along to Radio 2 in the background. Radio 2 was the soundtrack to my childhood, with its genial hosts and middle-of-the-road music: gentle, soothing, and familiar. On Saturday evenings we'd sit on the sofa in front of some TV game show with home-made popcorn, laughing at—

'Lexi?' The name worms its way into my skull, jolting me back to the present. My head feels like a chainsaw has been let loose inside it. 'Are you OK?'

'Do you think I could have a shower?' I slur, picturing lukewarm water streaming over me, clearing my fuddled head. I can't read her expression, but her voice becomes sympathetic.

'Of course you can, sweet girl. It's not a proper shower, I'm afraid, just one of those hose attachments over the bath, but it works perfectly well.' She moves towards the door, her gait ungainly. 'I'll get you a fresh towel.'

My head feels like a cannon ball as I trudge upstairs behind her.

'I'd love a brand-new bathroom,' she says brightly. 'Perhaps you can help me with that.'

It's a shock to remember I arrived at the cottage with the intention of redesigning it – that I am an interior designer.

I wait on the landing while she rummages in a cupboard that houses an old boiler, finally pulling out a thick white towel and handing it to me. The sound of the lawnmower outside drills through my head.

'Be careful, won't you?' Magda's face clouds with doubt. She's probably imagining me slipping on the bathroom floor and bashing my head and having to look after me again. 'We don't want anything happening to you, or this little one.'

Her forefinger shoots out and prods my belly, and I find her attempt to be playful oddly touching. It's clearly not a role she's comfortable with and reminds me that, despite her bombshell, I don't actually *know* her.

'I'll be careful,' I promise, making my tone gentle, despite wanting desperately to be left alone.

Delight wreaths her face. 'I'll get you a drink,' she says, patting my shoulder as though my words have emboldened her. 'You must keep up your fluids in this weather, especially if your blood pressure's low.'

I've barely set foot in the bathroom when she reappears and places a glass filled with amber liquid on the sill above the bath. 'Iced tea,' she says. 'Very refreshing.'

'My clothes?' I'm vaguely aware that I haven't seen my overnight bag for a while.

'I'll put them on the bed.' She scratches the pink, crusty patch of skin above her elbow. 'I gave them a wash and popped them in the dryer; I hope you don't mind.'

'You didn't need to; I brought a change of clothes with me,' I say, but she's already backing out of the room, eyes discreetly lowered as I begin to disrobe. 'Call if you need me.'

The water trickling from the hose attachment is hardly generous. The pitiful flow causes the pipes around the cottage to clank and groan, but it's wonderfully cool on my overheated skin. I sit in the bath with my legs stretched out, and watch the droplets run off my distended stomach and pool around me, my mind drifting.

I eye the walls, imagine them tiled, white and blue, a stand-up shower in the corner with glass doors. A freestanding bath with clawed feet, chrome fittings, navy towels and underfloor heating.

I glance around for some shower gel – my toiletries are in my bag – but can only find a bar of lemon-scented soap on the side of the bath. I lather it over my face and under my armpits then rinse it off, soaking the ends of my hair.

Music rises from downstairs, operatic and dramatic, adding to the strangeness of the day. I close my eyes and lean against the cool enamel, stroking the mound of my tummy. I wonder what Magda's doing, and how she feels after everything she's told me. Is she worried I'll reject her? *Will I?* Two mothers. Having one is too much responsibility at times.

When the water runs cold and the pads of my fingers have shrivelled, I turn off the taps and awkwardly hoist myself out of the bath, noting that my headache has finally receded.

The air ripples my skin to gooseflesh. I pull the towel around me, but it's smaller than I thought and barely meets at the edges.

Retrieving the glass of iced tea off the windowsill, I knock on the door.

'Magda, I've finished,' I call wondering vaguely why she felt it necessary to lock the door from the outside rather than me locking it from the inside.

Seconds later, I hear her footsteps on the stairs and the key turns.

'Sorry about that,' she says. 'Just trying to keep you safe, stop you wandering about, especially near the stairs.'

'I'm fine,' I say, but can't deny the dizziness that overtakes me as I make my way to the bedroom. I scan the rumpled bed for my bag and clothes, but they're not there.

'I'll go and get your things.' Magda lets go of my arm – I hadn't realised she was holding it so tightly – and descends the stairs.

I wander to the bedroom window and look out. The lawn has been mowed into neat, vertical stripes, and the gardener is standing still, surveying his handiwork. He brushes his arm over his forehead then turns, as if sensing me watching and after a beat, raises his hand.

I shrink back, embarrassed to have been caught staring in nothing but a tiny towel, then immediately feel silly for not waving back.

The glass in my hand is slippery with condensation. I bring it to my lips, then pause. I've already had a cup of coffee today, and although I doubt there's much caffeine in iced tea, I don't want any more.

I place the glass on the bedside table and turn back to the window. The sky has sharpened to periwinkle blue, the distant treetops shimmering in the sun. It must be mid-afternoon.

The gardener whistles as he approaches the hedge with a pair of secateurs, and the sound cuts through the muddle in my head. The view pulls into focus, and I shove the window as wide as it will go and lean out, a pulse beating in my throat. Why would Magda move my car when it would have been perfectly fine on the driveway?

A smell of silage seeps in, tainting the scent of lilac, and a shiver moves through me.

I close the window, refasten my towel, and head for the door. Downstairs, Magda is singing – a light, happy sound that inexplicably brings me close to tears.

My mother. It doesn't feel real.

As I cross to the stairs, intending to get my bag – Magda must have got distracted – something catches my eye. One of the doors off the landing is ajar, a beam of sunlight slanting out across the bare floorboards. It must be Magda's room. I hurry over, clutching the stupidly small towel.

I push the door wide, wincing as the hinges protest, and pause on the threshold, immobilised by shock. Images leap out: a mural of dancing cartoon animals on the wall. A cream-painted chest and a changing mat on the floor. A mobile twirling from the ceiling with abstract shapes in primary colours casting odd shadows on the floorboards. Soft toys heaped on a shelf. A crib draped with delicate fabric. A wooden rocking chair by the

window.
What the hell?
My skin prickles.
This isn't Magda's bedroom. It's a nursery.

Chapter 14

Dan

Dan woke, but kept his eyes shut in an effort to ward off the hangover he could feel lurking. How much had he had to drink last night?

Memories thundered back: the wedding gig; Calum sneaking off with one of the bridesmaids; Eric shaking his head at Dan with a look of dismay; Zoe singing, eyes half-shut in ecstasy. Zoe often looked like she was having sex when she sang, according to Calum, who'd noticed it when she auditioned.

'Imagine what she's like in the sack,' he'd whispered, nudging Dan, who had to look away from the glint of lust in Calum's eyes, and the way his tongue flicked, lizard-like, over his lips. 'She's up for it; you can tell.'

But in spite of his disgusting comments, Calum had been too intimidated by Zoe to exert his so-called charms – or perhaps he sensed even then he'd be wasting his time.

Dan eased one eye open. The curtains were pulled back and sunlight rippled across the floral wallpaper. The sight of the gaudy colours made his head pound. He'd be glad when Kate got rid of it. *Kate.* He stretched one arm behind him and felt the empty mattress. He missed her.

Wincing, he reached for his phone on the floor beside the bed and squinted at the screen. No messages. The time leaped out: ten thirty. *Christ.* He couldn't remember the last time he'd slept this late.

Groaning, he swung his legs round and sat up, cradling his head until the spinning sensation settled. When he felt it was safe, he reached for the glass of water on the bedside table and drank it with a couple of painkillers he hadn't remembered putting there.

Standing, he lurched into the bathroom in his boxers, marvelling that he'd had the presence of mind to fold his clothes and place them on the chair by the window.

As he emptied his straining bladder, he tried to recall what had happened after Eric and Calum had left last night. He'd sat outside on the terrace steps with Zoe, looking at the stars, her head resting on his shoulder. He thought he might have pointed out Orion and the North Star and talked about growing up in Ireland.

He groaned again. Guilt crashed over him as he realised Zoe must have half-undressed him and put him to bed after driving him home. He supposed he ought to call and thank her and apologise for getting blind drunk. But first, he needed a shower.

Kate hadn't said when she'd be home, but it could be any minute. He imagined her reaction if she saw the state he was in. Then he reasoned that if she hadn't stormed out yesterday, he would have come home with Eric as usual. *Always take responsibility for your actions, son.* His grandfather's words rang in his ears, bringing a wash of shame. He still missed the old man. He'd have been horrified to see the hash Dan was making of his marriage.

He showered quickly and got dressed, feeling marginally better. He decided he'd put the washing machine on and run the vacuum cleaner round, ready for Kate's return. Maybe he'd find something in the freezer to cook for dinner. She could tell him about this new client, and they'd laugh at Helen and Saskia worrying that they hadn't been able get hold of her for five minutes, and Helen's story about a woman she used to know, who might have kidnapped Kate.

Maybe he would tell her how he'd been feeling lately . . . his mind reared away. *No.* He had to man up and be strong for her and the baby.

With a sigh, he headed downstairs, his arms full of dirty clothes.

As he made his way to the utility room, he became aware of sounds coming from the kitchen: cups clattering, a cupboard door opening and closing. A smell of frying bacon wafted past.

Shit. Kate must be home already. She knew he'd been drinking and must have put the glass of water and tablets by the bed and folded his clothes on the chair. At least she couldn't be angry, or she wouldn't be cooking breakfast.

Dan's spirits rose as he stuffed the washing in the machine and switched it on. In the hall, he checked his reflection. He couldn't do much about his bloodshot eyes, but at least his growing beard disguised the worst of his pallor.

He had a sudden flashback to Zoe's fingers trailing down his cheek, her eyes hooded and mysterious. 'I've never kissed a man with a beard.' Her voice, husky with longing.

Dan shook off the memory and rumpled his damp hair with his fingers. Nothing mattered now apart from Kate and the baby.

Entering the kitchen, he froze, trying to make sense of the scene in front of him. Zoe was standing at the oven in one of his shirts, her long legs bare, her hair a dark tangle down her back.

She looked over her shoulder and her eyes roved over him. 'There you are,' she said. She waved Kate's yellow silicon spatula at him. It was shaped like a hand. 'Sleep well?'

Shock rang through Dan, robbing him of speech.

'Bacon sandwich?' Not waiting for an answer, Zoe began buttering bread.

Dan watched, as though in a trance. 'What . . .?' His voice

was hoarse, and he cleared his throat. 'What are you doing here?'

Zoe swung round. 'How are you feeling?' she said, as though he hadn't spoken.

'What the hell happened last night?'

Her smile dimmed. She put down the spatula with exaggerated care and switched off the gas beneath the sizzling frying pan. She wasn't wearing make-up and he thought she looked younger, her skin clear and fresh, her cheekbones less defined. 'You really don't remember?'

'Stop playing games, Zoe.' It came out sharply, shock giving way to unease. 'If we'd had sex, I'm sure I'd have remembered.'

Her lips parted, then closed again. She raised her arms to thrust her hair back, and Dan noticed a ladder of faded scars on the insides of her forearms, thought about the long-sleeved clothes she always wore.

She's fragile. The realisation unsettled him further. He'd got used to thinking of Zoe as confident, arrogant even, used to getting her own way. Part of him had even admired her single-mindedness. The thought it might be an act was somehow frightening. It made him feel responsible.

'Of course we didn't have sex. You were drunk, you idiot.' She spoke in her usual drawl, a half-smile curling her mouth. 'I put you to bed with a glass of water and some painkillers.' Her long fingers plucked at the shirt, which parted a little to reveal a glimpse of her breast. 'I found this in your wardrobe; I hope you don't mind. I felt grimy so I had a wash, then sat in a chair by the window to keep an eye on you.'

The thought of her in their bathroom, using Kate's toiletries, watching him while he slept, made Dan feel weak. What had he been thinking, letting her in? 'What if Kate had been here?'

Her eyes widened. 'But she wasn't, Dan. You said she wouldn't be home.'

Had he told her that? What else had he told her?

He tried to think through the sick headache pushing at his

temples.

'Don't worry, you didn't spill the beans about your marriage,' Zoe said drily, as if guessing his thoughts and taking pity on him. 'I actually like that about you, Danny-boy. You're the most principled guy I've ever met.'

'So principled I get drunk with a woman who's not my pregnant wife and let her stay the night.'

She shrugged. 'But nothing much happened.' *Much?* 'You're blameless, Danny.'

'Are you testing me?'

'Maybe.' She cocked her head, the spark in her eyes confrontational.

'Zoe, I . . .' He wasn't sure what he was about to say, but the sound of a car engine caught his attention. Through the window he saw to his horror Helen's white Citroën pulling up outside. 'You have to go, right now,' he said.

Zoe's eyes grew big. 'But I've made breakfast.' She indicated the buttered bread and the bacon congealing in the pan. 'You need to eat.'

'My mother-in-law's here.'

'Ah.' Zoe turned to where he was looking, her expression darkening. 'So she is.'

A thick, dark panic gathered in the pit of Dan's stomach. 'It looks bad you being here, Zoe. You must see that.' He started chivvying her out of the kitchen, like a character in a bad sitcom. 'You have to leave, or hide, or . . . something.'

'Oh, Danny.' She was laughing at his discomfort now, her hands on his shoulders, but there was a glint of sympathy in her eyes. 'You don't know which way is up, do you?'

'Please, Zoe.'

Letting go, she kissed her fingers at him and slipped upstairs, just as a series of knocks hit the front door. 'I'll get dressed and see myself out,' she called from the landing, clearly enjoying the drama. 'Just keep her down there.'

'Zoe—'

'You'd better let her in before she breaks the door down,' she said and disappeared from view.

With a creeping sense of dread, Dan wrenched open the door to find Helen on the doorstep, eyes puffy as though she hadn't slept.

'What's all this about?' His too-hearty voice sounded jarring, even to his own ears.

Helen didn't seem to notice. She craned her neck, peering past him into the hallway. 'Is Kate back?'

He suppressed a surge of irritation. Couldn't she see Kate's car wasn't on the drive? 'Not yet,' he said, hoping she couldn't smell the alcohol oozing from his pores.

'Do you mind if I come in and wait for her?' Not waiting for an answer, she brushed past him and into the front room.

Biting back swear words, he followed, trying not to glance upstairs. It struck him that he hadn't spotted Zoe's clothes anywhere, and he wondered with plunging despair if they'd been on the chair and he'd bundled them into the washing machine with his own.

His hands were clammy, and his stomach churned with acid. 'I've no idea what time she's coming back,' he said to Helen. He sounded curt, but she was clearly preoccupied, pushing open the window to let in some air, and tweaking the curtain into place.

'It sounds silly, but I can't settle,' she said, a hint of apology in her eyes as she turned to face him.

'Me neither,' he said, hoping it might explain his twitchiness.

'Something smells nice.' She sniffed the air like a terrier, and he realised she was making an effort to act normally, even though she'd never called round on a Sunday morning before. 'Breakfast?'

'I was going to have a bacon sandwich,' he lied. 'Would you like one?'

She shook her head. 'I've already eaten, thanks.' He didn't believe her but didn't push it. The thought of eating made him want to gag.

Helen finally came to rest on the arm of the sofa, and he wondered how he was supposed to entertain her until Kate turned up. What if she didn't come home for hours?

What was Zoe doing?

Crossing the room, he switched on the television and turned the volume up. 'Thought I'd catch the news,' he said, not caring that he sounded odd as long as Helen didn't guess there was a woman in his bedroom. She'd risen again and started pacing, as if staying still was impossible. 'Listen, that woman I told you about yesterday,' she said, completely out of the blue. 'I keep thinking about her.'

'What?' Dan, facing the open door behind her, noticed Zoe sneaking down the stairs like a pantomime baddie, holding her high-heeled sandals aloft. She was wearing the midnight-blue dress again and had fastened her hair up in an untidy heap. Pausing, she dramatically pressed a finger to her lips, the whites of her eyes gleaming. Seconds later, Dan watched her slip through the front gate, and hurry across the road to where she'd presumably parked her car.

Grateful, he shoved all thoughts of her aside and turned his attention to Helen, standing with her knuckles pressed to her mouth, seemingly deep in thought.

'Go on,' he said, trying to recall what she'd been saying. Something about the woman, Mary, she'd mentioned before.

He dropped in the armchair. 'What is it?'

'Oh, it's probably nothing.' Helen waved a dismissive hand, at odds with the intensity of her tone. 'It sounds so silly, only . . .' she paused.

'Go on.' He was intrigued now, his headache retreating a little. She looked so serious, standing there in her pale-pink T-shirt and ironed jeans, one hand on her chest. He felt almost fond of her. 'Spit it out, Helen.'

'I think she's dangerous.'

Dan's heart knocked against his ribcage. 'Why?'

'I don't want to believe it.' Helen sounded wretched. 'She came round to the house and apologised for what she'd said about Kate being her baby and cried for ages. I felt like I couldn't abandon her. Her mum died when she was twenty, and I knew how that could affect someone. And her father wasn't very supportive. Religious, apparently.' Helen hesitated. 'But she got into the house one day, while I was out. She'd had a key cut and was waiting in the kitchen in the dark. She had a knife, Dan.'

Fuck.

'I don't think she intended to use it,' Helen said quickly, as if reassuring herself more than him. 'She put it down as soon as she saw Kate in my arms, but it was the last straw.'

'Did you call the police?'

Her mouth twisted. 'No.' She must have seen something in Dan's face and sounded almost pleased when she said, 'She was vulnerable, Dan. I tried to get her to see a doctor and she promised me she would.' Her gaze fell to her feet in their white trainers.

'And did she?' Dan's fingers kneaded at his forehead; he already knew the answer.

'No.' Helen's voice dipped. 'She began following us around, saying she wanted her baby back. That I was ruining her life.'

'Jesus.'

'Anyway, that's when I decided to move away and start afresh.' Helen closed her eyes, as if reliving the past. 'I had an aunt down here, my father's sister. She looked after us after our parents died, until Cath, my sister, turned eighteen.' He'd never heard Helen so much as mention her parents' deaths before. 'Anyway, I stayed with my aunt in Abingdon, until I got a job and found somewhere of my own to live.'

'Sounds a bit extreme.'

'I'd been in a rut anyway,' she said with a little shrug. 'It was a relief to get away, actually. I thought Mary would get better without us around, reminding her she'd lost her baby.'

'What a mess,' Dan murmured.

'Kate and I were fine.' A flush spread across Helen's cheeks, as if he'd criticised her. 'The important thing was to keep her safe, and I told myself I could do that somewhere new.' Her chin lifted. 'I made sure she had a happy childhood.'

Dan could see she desperately wanted to believe that and felt a flash of pity that she hadn't realised how hard she'd made it for Kate to relax around her. 'But what has this got to do with anything?' His stomach gave a loud growl. The thought of a bacon sandwich was suddenly appealing, but he was riveted by Helen's story.

'Lately, I've had this feeling of being watched,' she said, her voice troubled. 'Then I saw Mary once, when I was out shopping, and it all came flooding back, especially with that note through my door.'

Dan felt a prickle at the back of his neck. 'You're sure it was from her?'

'I don't know for sure. The note was anonymous, but I can't think who else it could have been from. No one else would write that, would they? She must have found us and still thinks I took her baby all those years ago.' Helen's frown deepened, cutting a groove between her eyebrows. 'I haven't seen her for over thirty years,' she said. 'But I'm certain it was her. I wonder whether something had prompted her to look for us.'

He leaned forward. 'Does Kate know any of this?' Even as he asked, he knew she couldn't, that she would have mentioned it.

Helen's lips trembled. 'Of course not,' she said. 'It all happened a long time ago. I didn't want to worry her.'

'But?'

'Oh, Dan.' The words burst out, uncharacteristically emotional. 'What if the client Kate's gone to see really is Mary?'

Chapter 15

Kate

'What are you doing?'

With a yelp of surprise, I turn to see Magda standing on the landing.

'It was supposed to be a surprise,' she says, with an air of puzzled disappointment.

'I don't understand.' Heart thumping, my gaze flicks back to the nursery. 'Did you do this?'

'Don't you like it?' She joins me in the doorway, surveying the interior with a critical frown. 'I thought it best to keep the colours neutral,' she says. 'We can always change them if you don't like it. We have time.'

'You did all this by yourself?'

'Of course!' Her brow softens as she turns to face me. 'I thought I should sort out at least one room before you came.' She offers a tentative smile. 'The most important room.'

When I don't respond her shoulders visibly sag. 'Obviously I'm no expert,' she says. 'I should have waited for your input.'

'No, it's fine,' I say automatically, trying to make sense of it.

'It's . . . it's perfect.' *It is.* It's as lovely as anything I could have designed, and yet . . . there's something horribly presumptuous about Magda's actions, as if she's taken for granted we'll instantly bond and become a family, before I've had time to absorb the magnitude of it all.

'You will stay here, won't you?' she pleads, gripping my wrist. 'Please say you'll stay.'

Does she mean come and visit, or not go home?

I'm still draped in the flimsy towel, which reveals more than it covers. I snatch the edges together, dislodging her fingers. A breeze quivers the curtain at the window and as I catch a glimpse of blue sky, a disturbing thought takes hold: *I'm going to be trapped in this doorway with Magda forever.*

'I really can't stay,' I say feebly. 'It's such a lot to take in; you must see that. I need to talk to Dan, and Mum.'

Magda imperceptibly stiffens. 'Get dressed and have some lunch first.' She turns me away from the nursery with gentle but firm precision and closes the door behind us. When she leads me back to the room where I spent the night, I don't object and fret vaguely about my fluctuating energy levels. Maybe I'm still in shock or delaying the moment I have to return to the real world.

'There we are.' My clothes are laid out on the bed, neatly pressed, next to my overnight bag. 'Come down when you're ready.'

'I'm not really hungry,' I protest, my mind flitting back to the crib, and the wooden rocking chair by the window. I'd planned to buy one, imagining myself breastfeeding in it. Dan had teased me, saying it was something mothers in films did, and what was wrong with breastfeeding in a pub garden, or the local swimming baths?

Dan. A wave of loneliness grips me. Sometimes, we go to Mum's for a Sunday roast, but I hadn't arranged anything this weekend because I was planning to finish decorating the nursery.

How can all this have happened without me talking to him? It's been so long since we had a proper conversation about anything meaningful. I try to imagine his input – *Take it slowly, Kate. Think of the repercussions . . .*

No. That would be Mum's advice. *Take it slowly*. It's her default response, as if being spontaneous or following your instincts must always end in heartbreak and disaster.

But hadn't she acted on impulse when she took me and raised me alone? Surely that was a decision based on instinct. Had any part of her regretted it? But if she'd wanted to give me back at any point, surely she could have? Maybe she'd been afraid of the repercussions.

My head swirls.

'A slice of sponge cake?' Magda pipes in a fake bright voice from the bottom of the stairs, and her obvious attempts to keep me with her suddenly strike me as sad. I suppose it wouldn't hurt to stay for a quick cup of tea and a slice of cake. I want to leave on good terms and not upset her.

I fling off the inadequate towel and drag my clothes on, flushing a little at the sight of my neatly folded knickers, uncomfortable at the thought of Magda ironing them. Had I really been in the garden earlier without any underwear on? I hunt in my bag for my hairbrush and pull it through my tangled curls and my mind becomes less foggy, as though I've loosened my thoughts. The shock of seeing the nursery hits me afresh.

How am I going to explain this to everyone?

Magda's paying the gardener as I enter the kitchen, thrusting a note into his outstretched hand. He flicks me a glance over her shoulder, his gaze dark and direct, and I detect a question in them. I give a half-smile, wondering whether he assumes I'm Magda's daughter. I give her a sideways look, seeking similarities once more. Do we have the same bone structure? We're both curvy, that's without question, and our hair's a similar shade. How would it feel to introduce her as my mother? Weird. Not right. A mother's more than biology; a cliché, but true. There's no getting away from the fact that Magda didn't raise me. She hasn't earned the title of mother. On the other hand, it seems Mum has lied to me my entire life.

Something tips inside me and I lean against the worktop. An ache rips through my lower back, unlike anything I've ever experienced. I close my eyes and try to breathe through it, and when I open them the gardener's expression has changed to mild alarm.

Alerted to my presence, Magda waves him out and shuts the door. She steers me gently to the table, murmuring that I should put my feet up. 'You mustn't overdo things this late in pregnancy,' she coos. 'You know if there'd been any other way, I wouldn't have told you the truth like this.' Her eyes are large and watchful. She doesn't seem sorry. She looks excited. Maybe she's hoping I'll go into labour.

Panic constricts my breathing. I can't let that happen. Dan *has* to be there when our baby is born. If he's not, our marriage might never recover.

I blow out little puffs of air, the way I've seen women in labour do on television, then stop myself. *You're not in labour.*

The squeal of the garden gate cuts through the open window. The gardener's leaving. A feeling of hysteria bubbles up. I want to call him back, tell him to go and get Dan, but it's too late. And anyway, he doesn't speak English.

My thoughts are growing muddled again.

'What is it, sweetheart?' Magda's rubbing soothing circles between my shoulder blades, her probing gaze seeking mine, but pain is circling my insides again and I can do nothing but emit an animal-like noise that seems to come from outside of me.

'Just a bit of backache,' I manage as it fades. I shift from Magda's touch, twisting my face into a smile. I must look demonic because she blinks and backs away. 'I think I stayed in the bath too long.' I'm trying to convince myself as much as Magda, but she looks unsure, her fingers fluttering like moths.

'You're sweating,' she says with a touch of alarm.

'It's so hot.' I pass a hand over my forehead, and it comes away damp. I stare at my palm, close to tears.

Magda tears off and passes me a sheet of kitchen roll and I dab at my clammy skin. My hand is shaking, and she pats my shoulder, as if to reassure me. 'OK?'

I nod, unconvincingly. 'Some tea and cake?' I say, dipping to pet Arthur, weaving through my ankles, his sides vibrating. 'I'm hungry now.' It's not true, but food might settle the gnawing sensation inside me.

The sponge cake looks perfect: golden and airy, perfectly grouted with jam and buttercream. Magda makes a performance of cutting me a generous portion and sliding it onto a blue and white china plate.

'There you are,' she says, placing it in front of me. She returns to the worktop and leans against it, looking as though something's troubling her. 'Eat up,' she murmurs, nibbling at her thumbnail – something I do too, when I'm thinking.

Unsettled, I toy with my spoon, studying my distorted reflection in the back: bug-eyed and wild-haired. It doesn't look like me, which is fitting. I've never felt less like myself.

The odd feeling starts up in my stomach again. I begin to eat quickly, hoping to stave off another pain, but as soon as my plate is cleared, I want to be sick.

'So, how long have you been married?' Magda asks, as if she knows how I'm feeling and wants to distract me.

'Six years,' I manage, appreciating her effort to make me feel better. 'Dan was my first serious relationship.'

'First love is a powerful thing. I don't think it ever leaves you.' Her voice is knowing. 'I knew when I met Patrick that I'd never want another man.'

I wonder if Mum had loved my father. Then I remember – he wasn't my father. Patrick is. Patrick, who left, but might have come back if he'd known about me. *If Mum hadn't taken me away.*

'You could have had more children.'

Magda shakes her head. 'I never met anyone else that I wanted to have children with,' she says matter-of-factly.

'I'm sorry.' Arthur leaps onto the table and stalks up and down, tail switching from side to side, and when the silence stretches, I say, 'What do you hope will come of . . .' I flutter my hand between us, 'our meeting?'

She pulls Arthur towards her, and he nestles against her chest. 'What do you mean?'

'I mean, what do you see happening when all of this comes out?'

'Comes out?' she echoes. Frown lines appear. 'When the baby comes out?'

A shockwave passes through me. What doesn't she understand? 'When people find out you're . . . that you're my birth mother.' It sounds all wrong, but I guess I'm going to have to get used to saying it.

'Do they have to know?'

'What?' My scalp prickles. 'Of course they do, Magda. I can hardly keep it a secret.'

'Maybe I don't want to share you, Lexi.' She focuses her attention on Arthur, but the tips of her ears have reddened. 'She's had you to herself all this time. Isn't it my turn?'

'It's not a competition, Magda.' My heart is thumping unevenly. 'I can't keep it from Mum.' I hate the way I stumble over the word *mum*. 'There's room in my life for both of you, and guess what?' My voice becomes too bright in an effort to banish whatever that look in her eyes is. 'My baby will have two grandmothers instead of one. That's two more than I ever had.'

'Oh, darling,' she says at once, pausing in the act of fondling Arthur's ears. 'Patrick's parents are still alive, as far as I know. I've already written to him, telling him all about you coming home. I'm sure he can't wait to meet you, to introduce you to the rest of his family.' Her voice is rushed, breathless, as if she can't believe she hasn't already told me.

I'm quiet for a moment, digesting it. 'Does he . . . does he have other children?' What I mean is, do I have brothers and sisters? I'd longed for one or the other, even though Mum had made sure I didn't go short of company when I was growing up, always careful to invite Josie on our yearly trip to the seaside, or camping, during the summer holidays.

'I don't know.' Her lips cut a thin line across her face. 'But you're our only child. We can go and visit him.' Magda rises with alacrity and reaches into the folder she took the photos from the day before. 'He lives in Vermont. He's had a very successful career over there.'

My head whips up. 'You've been in touch all this time?'

'I've followed his career,' she says, evasively. 'You're going to get on so well together; I know you are.' She hands me a newspaper cutting. 'He's hardly changed at all.'

'Do you think I should talk to him first? Email him, or something?'

'Maybe.' She sounds distracted. 'Or we could just fly out there. I've got tickets.'

'Tickets?'

'Open-ended, we can go any time.' Her gaze slides off me like oil. How had she known I would agree to go? It's far too soon, but I don't say so. She's obviously concocted a fantasy reunion in her head. I can't bear to disappoint her.

Instead, I look at the picture of a middle-aged man with swept-back hair and a small greying beard, and read the words *Vermont cardiologist, Patrick Gilmore, has won recognition for his work at a local teaching hospital . . .*

Another ache grips my insides, like a pair of firm hands.

I bite my lip so hard I taste blood. *Please make it stop.*

My breathing comes fast and shallow. It hits me that my baby hasn't moved for a while. Doesn't that happen just before labour? I read it somewhere, or maybe my midwife told me.

I suddenly long to see her, feel her cool hand on mine, hear her voice reassuring me that everything's going to be fine. We'd discussed me having the baby at home – Mum wasn't keen on the idea, so I had agreed on the hospital – but I don't want to have him here.

'He's so handsome and talented.' Smiling proudly, Magda retrieves the cutting and I arrange my face into what I hope is a relaxed expression. Underneath the table, I clutch my belly, breathing a little easier as the pain ebbs away. 'I always knew he'd be important.'

I try to speak, but my tongue feels thick. The horrible feeling is happening again, as if everything is sliding away and it's hard to focus my eyes. Magda's still studying the cutting, her face intent.

'Let me show you another one,' she says, snapping the folder shut. 'I won't be a moment.' Flicking me a look that suggests her mind is elsewhere, she smiles slightly. 'Back in a minute.'

Before I can process what's happening, she's left the kitchen and I track her ascent by the groan and creak of the stairs.

My eyes feel sore as they wander around the kitchen. I don't know what I'm looking for until I spot my tote bag, wedged in a gap next to the fridge. I rise quickly and almost fall. My legs are as weak as cotton, and my brain feels foamy. What's happening to me? If it's labour, it's not like anything I've read about or been told. Should I call the hospital?

It's suddenly imperative that I get to my bag. Shuffling awkwardly – *where are my sandals?* – I grip the edge of the table, then the worktop, for support. I make it to the fridge, my ears attuned to movements upstairs. Magda sounds like she's rooting through drawers in her bedroom.

Retrieving my heavy leather bag takes a superhuman effort. Sweat trickles down my sides as I heave it out. Returning to the table is too much effort, so I sink to the floor and dig around inside my bag, not knowing what I'm looking for until I realise they're missing. My keys. I take out my laptop and rummage some more, then go through the pockets on either side, throwing out tissues, a tin of lip salve, a well-thumbed book of baby names.

They've gone.

Pain spirals. I shift onto all fours, panting like a spaniel. I feel so sick. Maybe it's something I've eaten. Probably the bloody sponge cake I hadn't wanted.

I thrust my hair out of my eyes, but it immediately flops back, and as the pain rumbles past, I roll back into a sitting position and lean against the fridge. 'For God's *sake.*' I register panic, thick and hot before it drifts away. My emotions feel muffled, as if they're hidden behind a pane of glass.

Has Magda hidden my keys to keep me here?

My eyelids flicker shut, and I drag them open.

I want Mum.

A sob tears at my throat.

Upstairs, a door closes, and Magda's footsteps cross the landing. My breathing falters.

'Lexi!' She drops whatever she is holding and hurries over, taking in the sight of me on the floor. 'What on earth are you doing?'

'Can't find my keys,' I mumble. Sleep is stealing over me, soft and warm like a blanket.

'Oh, my darling, I borrowed them to get your samples out of the car,' she says, helping me up, hands firm beneath my armpits. I feel as fragile as an old lady. 'I thought we could look through them together, like you said.' She gives a light laugh. 'A bit of mother–daughter bonding after all the revelations. What do you think?'

I don't know what I think. As I tilt against her, I spot my keys lying next to the kettle, my book of swatches beside them. Now I feel stupid. 'Sorry,' I mumble. 'Going mad.'

'Don't worry.' Her face looms over me, eyes stretched. They're shiny and pleased, her hand at my elbow surprisingly strong. 'Let's go and sit down and you can tell me what I need to do to turn this place into a palace. Not a guesthouse, but a home for us all.'

Chapter 16

Dan

Dan stared at Helen, absorbing her words. 'But what would this Mary want with Kate?'

Helen moved over with a lurch and took his hands in hers – a gesture so unexpected, he felt almost afraid. 'Don't you see?' Her pale-blue eyes searched his. 'It's the baby she wants.'

Dan yanked his hands from hers. Helen was talking as though it was actually happening. 'Why the hell would she want our baby?'

'It's payback, Dan.' Her eyes beseeched him. 'She believes I took hers, so now she wants mine.'

'But it isn't yours.'

'Oh, Dan! You know what I mean.' Her voice was clipped. 'The baby's as good as mine in Mary's warped little mind.'

'Christ.' He ran his hands over his face. 'That's why she put the note through your door.'

Helen nodded. 'The more I think about it, the more it feels like it's true.'

He watched a shudder run through her. 'Helen—'

'Where's her phone?' she said, stepping away from him.

'In the bedroom, why?'

'Maybe there's something on there.'

Before he could respond, she was out of the room and halfway up the stairs.

'Wait.' He followed her, his heart pumping so hard he could feel it in his head. What if Zoe had left some trace of herself in the bedroom? To his relief, he couldn't see anything out of the ordinary – just an indent in the pillow he'd slept on, the duvet still rumpled where he'd thrown it back, and the shirt she'd worn, bundled up on the floor.

He doubted Helen would have noticed anything out of the ordinary anyway. 'This is crazy,' he said, as she snatched Kate's phone up. It wasn't password protected and he longed to grab it off her – maintain Kate's privacy, though he knew she had nothing to hide. 'She'll probably be back any minute.'

Ignoring him, Helen swiped at the screen. 'Didn't you say the client phoned her?'

'Yes, but—'

'There's no caller ID.' She drew in a shaky breath. 'We need to ring the police.'

'And tell them what?' Dan felt out of his depth. He'd never seen his mother-in-law like this and wondered what Kate would do. 'Everything you've told me is speculation, Helen. Don't you think you might be overreacting?'

She hesitated, and he read her reluctance to repeat what she'd told him to the police. Maybe she was doubting her own story.

'Oh God, you're right,' she said at last. 'I'm being ridiculous.' She clattered the phone down, blotches of colour standing out on her neck. 'It's just . . . she's heavily pregnant' – *Not that again*, thought Dan – 'and it's not the right time to stay somewhere overnight.'

'Look at it like a business trip.' Dan held his palms out. 'It's not the first time she's stayed over at a client's and everything was fine then. She'll come home fired up with ideas, you'll see.' His words seemed to swell in his throat and he had to stop for a moment. 'You know she always wants to do the best job she can,' he finished.

'That's true.' Helen's eyes shone with tears and Dan realised he hadn't properly understood how deep-rooted her anxiety about Kate was. Then again, if what she'd told him about this Mary was true – and he only had her interpretation of it – he supposed her worry was natural, to an extent. 'Even so,' Helen continued, and he felt a sag inside. 'It's out of character for her to rush off without her phone and to not call me—'

'We had an argument, OK?'

Helen's eyes snapped to his. 'What?'

Dan tried not to squirm. 'I've been an idiot lately.' He pushed his toes through the pile on the rug by the bed. 'Worried about how the baby is going to change things.'

'Of course it's going to change things,' Helen snapped. 'It's how you deal with those changes that counts.'

'I . . . I know. I haven't been dealing with it very well.' He felt a rush of relief at saying it out loud.

'And you think she's glad to have a night away from you?'

He nodded. 'Partly,' he said, rubbing the back of his neck. 'She's pretty fed up with me at the moment and is probably glad of an excuse to have some space.'

'Well, you can hardly blame her.' He had Helen's full attention now. 'Who was that woman?'

'What?' He looked at her, puzzled by the switch of focus. 'What woman?'

'The one who turned up here yesterday.'

His heart gave a great thud. 'She sings with the band,' he said, feeling his face heat up. 'Her name's Zoe.'

'Why was she here?'

He forced himself to hold Helen's viper-like stare. 'She was giving me a lift to the gig.' He wished he didn't sound so shifty.

'Is that all?'

He pressed the back of his neck again, trying to free the knots there. 'Helen, I—'

'Are you having an affair, Dan?' Although her voice had changed tempo, as if hoping to invite a confession, her eyes were glacial.

'No, of course not,' he said firmly. 'She does like me, though,' he confessed, not realising he was going to say it. 'Kate doesn't know.'

Helen studied him for a moment, and whatever she saw in his clammy face must have satisfied her. She nodded curtly, her gaze defrosting slightly. 'She doesn't need to if it's not serious.'

Another swoop of relief. Thank Christ she hadn't seen Zoe creeping out earlier. 'Thanks, Helen, for not judging me. I've made it clear to her plenty of times that I'm not interested.'

'You really need to grow up, Dan,' she said, and he realised he was far from off the hook. 'Kate needs a husband who's going to support her, not one who's out chasing women.'

'I'm not.' He felt a bolt of outrage. 'What do you take me for?'

'Do you wish Kate wasn't pregnant?'

'Of *course* not.' He put as much conviction into his voice as possible. 'I was freaking out a bit, that's all.'

'You've had plenty of time to get used to the idea.'

'I know, I . . .' He struggled to find the right words, wanting her to understand. 'I'm a bit worried I might not be up to the job. Of being a father,' he said.

'Very few men are.' She spoke so quietly, he had to strain to hear her. Silence fell and her gaze flickered downwards. Dan had no idea what she was thinking. Her mask was back in place.

He walked around the bed and put Kate's phone back on charge, catching his reflection in the wardrobe mirror. It was almost a surprise to see that he looked the same. He felt as if the last twenty-four hours should have marked him in some way.

Behind him, Helen seemed frozen to the spot. She looked out of place among the embroidered pillowcases and floral hat boxes – a recreation of Kate's great-aunt's bedroom that Kate had said made her feel safe.

He turned to face his mother-in-law. She'd lost her shape

against the light coming through the window and seemed like a stranger again. 'What is it?'

'I don't really know.' Her voice was strained. 'I still have a feeling that something's not right, and I'm so worried about Kate and the baby.'

The thumping in his head increased, but he knew he had only himself to blame. All the stuff with Kate, and whatever was going on with Zoe . . . His insides felt scraped out.

'I'll go and put the kettle on,' he said, willing Kate to come home now, so they could put an end to this nonsense.

Helen moved towards him. He had a feeling she wanted to cry or slap him. He even braced himself but, instead, she shook her head and made a strangled noise, then shoved past him, and ran downstairs.

He found her in the kitchen, staring at the wall, her back rigid. 'Helen, I'm sorry,' he said, feeling helpless.

'Just call me when she's back.'

Before he could respond, she'd picked up her bag and left, closing the back door quietly behind her.

Chapter 17

Kate

Fragments of a dream float to my consciousness. I've been stung by a giant wasp that keeps growing bigger, hovering about me, its black wings blocking out the sun.

I wake with a cry, hands pushing at the heavy air.

I'm in bed. Outside, dusk has fallen.

What happened?

I remember sinking onto the mole-coloured sofa downstairs. The pains had stopped, and I was feeling better. I'd been talking to Magda about colour schemes, and she'd seemed interested, asking intelligent questions. At one point, she got up to make a pot of tea.

When she came back, she asked about Dan's family, whether they were supportive; did I get on with them? I found myself telling her how much I'd liked Cass and Rory the few times we'd met, but that Dan and his siblings and parents weren't a typical family, and apart from his sister Rosie, we rarely saw them.

It had been oddly cosy, sitting there with the sun dappling the floorboards, just talking – something I rarely did at home. There always seemed to be something pressing to do.

'What about you?' I'd asked Magda, aware of a reluctance to stand up and leave and deal with whatever would follow – half-scared that if I moved the pains would start again. 'What was your childhood like?'

She'd taken her time before replying, smoothing her hand across the cushion between us. 'My mother – your grandmother – died when I was twenty,' she said at last. It was clear from the way her eyes sought refuge in the floor that it was still a painful subject. 'My father was . . . he was a difficult man; let's put it that way,' she continued. 'He was a doctor with very high standards and high expectations of me and my brother.'

'You have a brother?' I'd wanted to laugh. Out of nowhere, I suddenly had relatives popping up all over the place. A giddy anticipation had taken hold and I'd bombarded Magda with questions – where did he live, what was he like, did he have children?

Laughing, she'd held her hands up, said firmly that it was a story for another time.

Eventually, as the sun began to sink, I said I ought to go. I didn't like driving in the dark and would prefer to find my way home before daylight faded.

Magda rose, tucking a strand of hair behind her ear. She said I should stay for dinner, but I refused.

What then? Had I stood up too swiftly and fainted again?

I can't even remember getting up off the sofa.

Remnants of anxiety from my dream course through me. The duvet's too heavy and I try to shove it away, but my arms feel weighty, as if the blood's stopped circulating.

My hands shoot to my belly. I think of my little boy tucked inside, safe and warm, with feathery eyelashes and tiny hands curled into fists.

'He'd be so upset if he knew you didn't want him,' I'd rehearsed saying to Dan on my way home from the hospital scan, but Dan had seemed so genuinely sorry to have missed the appointment, I didn't have the heart in the end. Instead, I pinned the scan-photo to the fridge door with a heart-shaped magnet and caught him staring at it later with a complicated expression.

Mum had a copy too, which she'd brandished at strangers outside the hospital, as if she was the only woman in the world ever to become a grandmother. *Mum, who's not my mum.*

A sound escapes me, not quite a sob. *What's wrong with me?* I'm like a shadow, or someone pretending to be me. I feel as if I don't exist anymore, as though I'm slowly slipping away.

I skim the room and catch the fluorescent beam of eyes from the top of the wardrobe. I let out a smothered squeal.

Arthur!

'You scared the life out of me,' I scold, heart juddering.

But the cat's presence is comforting, and when he dive-bombs the bed and pushes against me, I hold onto him, caressing his silky ears. 'I shouldn't be here,' I whisper into his fur. 'I have to go home and face the music.' *Music.* I hear it downstairs now, soft and dreamy. I think of Dan, strumming his guitar, and my heart twists with longing.

Arthur leaps off the bed and onto the window seat, where he settles down. Thirst crowds in. Fumbling towards the lamp, I find the switch and click it on. My lower belly aches, as though I've been doing sit-ups, and a formless worry niggling at the edge of my mind begins to take shape.

At least I'm dressed this time. My dress is rumpled and twisted beneath me, but I haven't the energy to free it. The pull of sleep is powerful and I try to fight it.

I have to call Dan. Maybe he can come and get me. He'll be able to find the cottage. *But he doesn't have the car.*

Eric will drive him. Eric's a good friend. Dan needs good friends because his family are hopeless, as much as I like them. They moved their family from commune to campsite to squat, and Dan's little sister nearly drowned in a lake. His upbringing was the opposite of mine, I'd told Magda. I used to think that was why we were drawn to each other – he wanted stability, and I was attracted to his romantic, bohemian background. Only it wasn't romantic. It was shambolic, and frightening at times, at least for Dan. And although his parents were pleased about the baby, they'd already warned us not to expect them to be hands-on.

'Because of them, I think Dan's scared to be a parent.' Magda had listened, not speaking, her silence drawing more words out. 'I haven't talked to him about it; I don't know why. We used to be a team.'

'We'll be a team now; you'll see.'

Must stay awake.

A cramping feeling spreads from my back across my belly, tightening and squeezing like a belt. I swing my legs round and sit for a moment, aware of a whimpering noise coming from deep inside me. I lower my chin to my chest, praying the pain won't strengthen.

A sound from the room below brings my head up.

'Magda?' I don't feel right. I drop back down and lift my legs onto the mattress. Trying not to groan, I tug the duvet over my bulk as Magda comes upstairs, the sound of each stair cracking like a gunshot.

A draught brushes my cheek as the door opens.

'Lexi?' Her voice is hesitant. 'I've brought you some fresh water,' she says, approaching the bed when she sees that I'm awake. 'How are you feeling?'

'Not good,' I manage. She must be fed up of having to look after me. 'Listen, I need to get home.' I try to sit up again. The room spins. 'If you could just give me a hand, I'll be on my way.'

'Oh, my sweet, you're in no fit state to go anywhere.' She puts down the glass and, leaning over, strokes my hair from my forehead. 'You fainted again; don't you remember?'

'No, I don't.' I struggle onto my elbows, perilously close to tears. 'Something's happening to me; I feel drunk,' I slur. Not that I've been drunk for ages.

'Don't you worry now.' She eases me down, her hands insistent on my shoulders. She smells of something faintly medicinal that makes my throat clench. 'I've called the hospital to ask their advice,' she adds.

'You have?'

'I was worried you might be going into labour.'

'I thought that too,' I say in a rush, grateful to put my fears into words. 'I didn't want to say, but I was having pains earlier.'

'Well, they suggested waiting until we're sure you're having contractions.' She takes my hand and holds it tightly. 'Until then, the best thing to do is lie still. You can't risk driving home.'

Anxiety scratches my overheated skin. 'I have to call Dan,' I say, trying to free my fingers. I can see two of Magda, zooming in and out of focus. 'He has to be with me if the baby's coming.'

She pauses, then says, 'I've already called him and told him you fainted and that I was looking after you.'

'What?'

'His number was in my phone from when you called him yesterday. I hope you don't mind.'

Another memory floats back: the sound of her voice downstairs, low and reassuring. 'What did he say?'

'He's very worried, of course.' Her tone is rather flat, and I wonder whether she got the opposite impression.

'He should be with me,' I fret, tears flooding my eyes.

'I'm sure he'll come; don't worry.' She gives my hand a reassuring pat before letting go. 'I told him where to find us, just in case.'

I feel a pinch of fear, imagining him leaping on his motorbike, riding haphazardly along unfamiliar roads. Another image materialises: Dan flopping in front of the television with a beer, not wanting to get involved.

Out of nowhere, I think of the singer who joined the band at the end of last year – Zoe something, tall and pretty with silky black hair.

I'd gone to Eric's apartment to drop off some paint samples, while they were rehearsing. She didn't see me, but I noticed the way she looked at Dan – as though she was starving, and he was a delicacy she longed to sink her teeth into – and the way her long fingers seemed drawn to touch him. I hadn't mentioned it; it hadn't occurred to me he might be attracted to her, but now I wonder whether they're having an affair and that's why he's been lukewarm about the baby.

A muffled sob escapes, and at once, Magda's arms enfold me. 'What is it, sweetheart?'

'I think Dan's seeing someone else,' I blurt into her shoulder. 'That's why he doesn't want this baby.'

'Oh, Lexi.' She rocks me back and forth, whispering against my hair. 'I'm going to take care of you, just like I should have been doing all along.' She presses kisses onto my hair, and when my tears are spent, stands up. 'Now, you stay there,' she says tenderly, eyes gleaming like marbles. 'I'll bring us a sandwich, then I'm going to sit here and keep an eye on you.'

She leaves before I can raise a protest.

Drying my eyes with my hand, I reach for the glass. I bring it to my lips and pause, aware of a metallic tang coming from the water. I raise the glass to the light and swish it around. Tiny particles rise from the bottom, clouding the liquid. I sniff the water again. Nothing. Probably lime-scale.

Nauseous, I put the glass down and shuffle out of bed, standing unsteadily on the rug. Despite everything Magda has said, I can't stay.

Maybe I could call Mum, ask her to come and get me. But it would be too awkward, take too much explaining. And I'd have to leave my car behind.

I'll just have to risk driving home and pray my head stays clear and the contractions, if that's what they are, hold off.

Stumbling around the bed, I recoil from the sight of my puffy face in the mirror, glistening with sweat, eyes slitty from crying.

I open the bedroom door and hear Johnny Cash singing 'Walk the Line'. The landing is dimly lit by a glow from downstairs, but it's enough to see my way. I force myself to the bathroom on legs that feel like foam. After using the toilet, I splash my face with cold water, trying to ignore the aching prowl in my belly.

Back on the landing, my eyes glance off the door of the one room I haven't been in. With a feeling of déjà vu, I cross the strip of crimson carpet and press down the wrought-iron latch. The door opens with a haunted-house squeal that makes me freeze. My heart flips, but the music downstairs is loud enough to cover any sounds.

Not stopping to ponder my motives, I ease inside, fingers groping the wall for a switch. I press it and a naked bulb illuminates the room, which is small with a sloping ceiling underneath the eaves.

There's a metal-framed bed pushed up against the wall, covered in an embroidered blanket, and a couple of flat pillows tossed in the middle. Propped at the end is a black suitcase, unzipped.

Magda's room?

There's no furniture, apart from a walnut desk beneath the window, with a narrow drawer underneath.

I lumber to the uncurtained window, bashing the corner of the bed with my knee on the way, but there's only a darkening sky outside, and my own reflection staring back like a ghost.

I've lost all sense of time, and the energy that's carried me this far starts to seep away. I cast my eyes to the floor as I rub my lower back to ease the gnawing ache. The boards are old and pitted, probably riddled with woodworm, and I notice a phone poking out from under the desk. It's broken, the screen a spider's web of cracks. It's the one I used yesterday.

Crouching with difficulty, I pick it up. It's definitely the same phone. Perhaps it stopped working after Magda called Dan and she destroyed it, threw it in here in a fit of frustration.

If only I could call him now. I would tell him not to come,

that I'll find my own way home.

Grunting, I thump down onto my bottom, spreading my legs to accommodate my belly. I pick the phone up and switch it on. Despite the cracks, the screen lights up and shows a bar of signal. Enough to make a call?

I'm about to dial Dan's number when an urge to ring Mum overwhelms me. But what would I say? I bang my forehead with the phone. *THINK!*

Saskia. She'll take me to hers. She won't judge me, never has. I can pick my car up another day. After the baby's born. Mum can come with me, and we'll talk to Magda together.

Aware my thoughts aren't making much sense, I try to prise Saskia's number from the depths of my mind but draw a blank. Tears of frustration burn my eyes. I think of my phone, with all my numbers stored inside, in my bedroom at home.

There's a clatter from downstairs and I drop the phone. The suitcase has fallen open, spilling clothes into its lid.

Downstairs, the music stops, and with an icy clarity I realise I'm snooping in Magda's room, and she might not be happy.

Grasping the edge of the desk, I haul myself to my feet, swaying as the room rotates. *What's that?* The drawer is slightly open, something glinting inside. I tug it out, the action provoking a loud rattle of the contents, and a couple of brown pill bottles roll into view, their labels torn and faded. My heart picks up speed as I think of how peculiar I've been feeling since yesterday, am still feeling now. Is it possible she's been drugging me? But she mentioned taking her pills, so maybe they're hers.

A noise makes me jump. *She's coming upstairs.*

Sliding the drawer shut, I turn to leave, eyes grazing the open suitcase on the floor. On top of a couple of scarves and a navy jacket is a tiny white knitted matinee coat with pearly buttons – the kind of garment I'd jokingly asked Mum if she was going to knit for the baby.

Why does Magda have baby clothes in her suitcase?

I remind myself she knew I was pregnant before I came, so it shouldn't be that surprising. All the same, the sight of the tiny coat makes me uneasy, just like the nursery did. It's as if she expects to be a grandmother before I've had a chance to accept she's my mother. It's almost as if being a grandmother is more important.

I shove the thought away. It's natural she's excited about the baby. It must be like a second chance for her.

These thoughts are flooding my head as I wrestle the suitcase shut, and I reach the door just as it opens.

'Kate!' Magda looks comically surprised, as if she hadn't really expected to see me there. 'What are you doing?'

'I . . .' I lick my lips, decide to be honest. 'I was curious,' I say, a shot of adrenalin bolting through me. 'I wanted to look around.'

'Oh, OK.' She moves to let me pass, seeming bemused.

'It's the designer in me,' I continue. 'I can't resist a strange room.' *Not so honest after all.*

'I thought . . .' she pauses, a hand at her throat. 'How are you feeling?'

'Much better,' I lie. My stomach's tightening again, but I'm not going to react. I don't want to be back in bed at her mercy, however well meaning she is. I want to talk to Saskia. I want to leave. 'Can I use your phone again?'

Her brow furrows. 'I told you, I already called your husband. And the hospital. They said—'

'I know,' I cut in, blood roaring in my ears. 'But I want to talk to my friend.'

A strange expression crosses Magda's face. 'I'm afraid I dropped the phone in the kitchen and it's broken.'

I can't tell her I've found it, or she'll know I've lied about what I was doing in this room.

'That's a shame.' I look away from her scrutiny, try not to glance at the drawer containing medication. *Now what?*

I try to give an impression of authority, despite the shakiness in my limbs, and head out of the room. 'I know I should probably rest, but I really want to go home,' I say again, holding onto the banister to steady myself as I go downstairs. I don't know where I'd rather be at the moment but it's suddenly, startlingly, obvious that I shouldn't be here.

I enter the kitchen as swiftly as my bulk will allow, blinking in the brightness of the striplight overhead, eyes scouring the worktop for my keys.

'You can't go.' Magda follows and places a restraining hand on my arm. 'Please, Lexi.'

'Kate,' I say, automatically. 'I need some space to think about everything that's happened.' *Where are my keys?*

'You have to stay.' She shifts her hand and moves in front of me, and there's something unyielding about her presence: like a brick wall or barbed wire fence. 'We've got to go and see Patrick. In my letter, I told him to expect us.'

'What?' My eyes snap from the kitchen table — perhaps my keys are in the fruit bowl — to her face. In the harsh light she seems to have aged. Her eyes are ringed with shadows and lines and her hair looks faded, with glints of grey showing through the reddish dye. 'I can't meet him yet, Magda. Please try to understand.'

'Don't call me that.' Her eyes burn like coals. 'I'm your mother.'

'It's not that simple,' I say, feeling helpless. I should never have suggested an overnight stay. If only I could turn back time and not know the things she's told me. 'Mum is the one who raised me and I'm going to need time to—'

Her hand flies out and slaps me hard across the face. 'How dare you?'

I clutch my cheek, the shock of it ringing through me. Lifting my eyes, I stare at her in horror.

Her expression mirrors mine, her face the colour of parchment. She presses her knuckles to her mouth. 'I'm so sorry.' It comes out as a muffled whisper. 'I shouldn't have done that, Kate, forgive me.'

As if the blow has dislodged a veil, I can suddenly see clearly what should have been glaringly obvious all along.

Magda is seriously unstable.

I think of the pills, and the broken phone on the floor. Maybe she's mentally ill – prepared to do whatever it takes to keep me now that she's found me.

In the tortured silence that follows, I finally spot my keys on one of the chairs, and like an engine roaring into life I make a lunge for them.

Magda still seems frozen, her expression blank.

I haven't got my bag, my feet are bare, and my cheek is burning as though branded, but I can't risk staying in this house a second longer.

The cat flap opens and Arthur slides into the kitchen. Magda doesn't move.

Not looking at her, I edge past, and when I reach the back door, I wrench it open and flee into the night.

Chapter 18

Dan

Dan couldn't settle after Helen had left. The look on her face, the things she'd told him, his confession about Zoe liking him. *Christ*. If he was hoping to keep his mother-in-law on-side, he was doing a terrible job. He felt destabilised, his world shifting around him. His headache was like a power drill in his skull, his throat like sandpaper. He stuck his head under the tap and swallowed ice-cold water, then made some toast and forced it down.

Afterwards, he cleared away the debris from Zoe's aborted attempt at breakfast, cleaning the pan thoroughly and shoving it to the back of a cupboard.

If only it was as easy to wipe away the memory of her standing in the kitchen, in one of his shirts. What had she been thinking?

What had he? The fact he'd let a woman stay in his and Kate's house overnight made him want to cry.

He had an urge to call his mother but knew it wouldn't help. His parents had always had a relaxed approach to marriage, believing love ebbed and flowed, and could only be sustained by allowing each other a certain amount of freedom. Which, as far as Dan could tell, meant his father had affairs, and his mother forgave him.

He hadn't been back to Ireland since marrying Kate but was suddenly overwhelmed by a longing for the majestic mountains and lakes of Killarney, where he'd lived on and off with his grandfather before coming to England.

He knew Kate was curious about the places where he'd grown up. Maybe they could visit after the baby was born. He could show them Castle Ross, Torc Waterfall and Carrauntoohil – the mountain his grandfather had once climbed.

He realised with a jolt it was the first time he'd imagined going somewhere as a family – not just him and Kate – and though he still couldn't picture an actual child, the thought was cheering.

Slightly restored, he wondered whether to go to his studio and finish the baby's cradle or make a start on the nursery. Kate had already prepared the walls and bought some tins of paint. Surely, he could get a coat on before she returned.

Relaxing his shoulders on a sigh, he was about to leave the kitchen when his phone rang. Hoping it might be Kate, he was pierced with disappointment when he recognised the number.

'Hi, Eric,' he said, knowing there was no point ignoring the call as his friend would simply come round. 'Good gig last night.'

'I hope you didn't spoil it by doing something stupid.' Eric's voice was tight.

'Like what?'

'You know I'm talking about Zoe.'

Dan's spirits plunged. 'I had too much to drink and she drove me home; that's all.'

'Really?' Something in Eric's tone made Dan's chest tighten. 'That's not what she told me.'

'You've spoken to her?'

'I've just been round to her flat.'

'What for?' Dan realised he didn't even know where Zoe lived – that most of their interactions involved him ducking her barbs and flirtatious innuendoes while trying to think of suitable comebacks. He couldn't recall a single adult conversation with her about ordinary, everyday things.

'I tried your phone first thing, and you didn't reply. I wanted to check you were OK.'

'I was hungover,' Dan muttered. 'What did she say?'

A pause. 'That she stayed at yours.'

All Dan's muscles clenched. 'What?'

'Is it true?' Eric sounded combative.

'No! At least, not in the way you think,' Dan said. 'I didn't know she was here until I got up; I really didn't. She was in the kitchen, making bacon sandwiches.'

'For fuck's sake, Dan.' He couldn't work out if Eric was disappointed or disgusted, but it hardly mattered. Either way it was bad. 'She didn't say as much, but she implied it was more than that.'

'Well, it wasn't.' A nerve twitched under Dan's eye. 'Maybe she wanted it to be, but it wasn't.'

'And you?'

'Me, what?'

'Did you want it to be?'

'Christ's sake, Eric.' Dan swallowed – felt sick. 'I thought we were on each other's side, no matter what.'

Eric made a snorting sound. 'I wouldn't be much of a friend if I encouraged you to fuck up your marriage.'

Dan closed his eyes. 'I know, and I appreciate it, Eric. But I promise nothing happened, and nothing's going to happen.'

'So, where's Kate?' Eric's voice mellowed a fraction. 'Obviously she wasn't there to greet your visitor.'

'She stayed with a client overnight.'

'Weird.'

'Not really,' he said. *Was it?* 'It's a guesthouse that's being done up and she wanted to get a feel for it.'

'Female client?'

'Obviously.' He batted away an impulse to tell Eric what Helen had told him, and her feeling that something was wrong. His friend's sympathies were clearly stretched to breaking point as it was. 'She'll be back later today.'

'Good,' Eric said. 'I told Zoe to either back off or leave the band.'

'What?' Dan slapped a palm to his forehead. 'You shouldn't have done that,' he said. 'She's a good singer. I thought you said she needed the job.'

'We can always get another singer,' said Eric. 'And she doesn't *need* a job, not for the money anyway. You should see her flat. No, scrap that,' he added quickly. 'You shouldn't go anywhere near her flat. But what I'm saying is, it's not some dive above a shop. She's either loaded, or someone's paying for her to live there.'

Dan absorbed Eric's words, unsure how he felt.

'I should have checked her out properly, mate.' Eric exhaled, and Dan pictured him raking a hand through his curly hair. 'She could be seeing loads of married men for all I know.'

Dan thought it unlikely. He knew on some level that Zoe was in love with him, and suspected Eric knew it too. But he didn't argue. 'What did she say?'

'Told me to eff off and mind my own business.' Eric laughed abruptly, and Dan was struck once again with the thought that – in spite of himself – Eric liked Zoe. Maybe more than liked her. 'She said you're both grown-ups and you can make up your own mind.'

'Well, you've nothing to worry about. It's all in hand. I promise.' Dan hoped it was true.

'It'll be a good job when that baby arrives,' Eric shot back. 'If that doesn't sort out your priorities, nothing will.'

When he rang off, Dan pushed his confusing thoughts aside and went up to the spare room, where he prised the lid off a tin of paint with a screwdriver. SUNSET YELLOW, according to the label. It certainly matched the sunshine streaming through the window, which overlooked the garden at the back of the house. Beyond, was a view of hills, dotted with sheep and cows. It was an airy and peaceful room – perfect for a baby.

Dan picked up the smallest paintbrush. He knew he should get changed, but it was already afternoon. It was suddenly imperative that he painted at least one wall before Kate came home.

He opened the window, then shook the dust sheet over the floor, climbed the stepladder and began pushing paint around the edges of the room. The motion was soothing, and when he'd finished, he found a paint roller and covered the rest of the walls.

He stood back to admire the effect, which gave the impression of sunshine, even though the sun had now moved round the front of the house. He wondered if he had time to hang the duck-patterned blind that Kate had bought and was on his way outside to fetch his drill when his mobile rang again.

Unknown number.

'Kate?'

Silence. 'Hello?' His heart was racing.

'Is this Dan?' The voice was female, soft and well-spoken.

'Who is this?'

'I'm Magda, Kate's client.'

Now his heart was drumming. 'What's happened?' Helen's story rushed into his head. 'Is she OK?'

'She's fine.' A little laugh, presumably meant to reassure him. 'She wanted me to let you know she's going to stay here again tonight.'

'What?' His palms were sweating. 'Why?'

A soft sigh. 'There's a lot to see here,' she said. 'Kate's putting together a quote for me.'

'But . . .' How to say what he wanted to say without shouting or sounding controlling. 'I thought she was coming home today.'

'She changed her mind.' He couldn't work out her tone but sensed an underlying disapproval.

'She's heavily pregnant.'

'I do know that.' An incredulous laugh that made Dan feel embarrassed.

'I'm sorry, I just . . .' Why hadn't Kate phoned him herself? 'I'd like to speak to her, please.'

The pause that followed went on so long, Dan wondered if she'd already left to fetch Kate. He saw himself in the kitchen window, paint smudged on his forehead, a yellow streak on his T-shirt. He was a mess. 'Hello?'

'I'm afraid she doesn't want to speak to you.'

'Sorry?' Dan felt a coldness in the pit of his stomach. 'What do you mean?'

Another soft sigh, as though weighing up what to say. 'She's been telling me about your problems.'

'Problems?' He sounded like an echo.

The woman tutted, as though becoming impatient. 'She tried to call you a couple of times and when she got your voicemail, she became upset. When I asked her what was wrong, it all came out. About how you don't want this baby.'

Dan felt the ground was falling away from him. Kate had told a complete stranger that he didn't want their baby? It was so unlike her, he couldn't believe it . . . yet it made a weird kind of sense. She wouldn't tell her mother, and probably even Saskia didn't know the full extent of how she felt. Wouldn't it be easier to talk to someone who didn't know them?

Christ. So much for Magda being some crazy woman, out to ruin Kate's life. He was the one in danger of doing that.

'Can I just talk to her, please?' he said, wiping his free hand on his jeans. This was awful – worse than anything he'd imagined. 'I'm sure we can sort this out.'

'I'm sorry but, as I said, she doesn't want to speak to you right now. I'm just letting you know she's fine, and that she'll be home when she's ready.'

Her disapproval sparked a flash of anger.

'I appreciate your concern, but our marriage isn't really any of your business—'

She'd hung up.

Dan stared at his phone, his mind racing. *What the hell?*

He pressed redial, but the call wouldn't connect. No caller ID either. *Shit.* He wheeled around, clutching his hair.

Kate had poured her heart out to a stranger and didn't want to speak to him. He didn't even know where she was.

Overcome with dizziness, he rested his hands on the worktop and dropped his head between his arms. *Kate.*

Fear grabbed his heart like a fist.

Was she planning to leave him? He groaned. Why hadn't he picked up her calls? Now she'd talked to this Magda woman and realised she didn't want him anymore.

Straightening, Dan scrubbed his face with his hands.

You don't want this baby.

It wasn't true. He *did* want this baby. He wanted Kate. He wanted to tell her he was sorry, to beg her to give him another chance.

He felt as if someone had shaken him awake.

His phone pinged and he looked at the screen: a text attachment. He opened it and stared.

It was a photo, softly lit. Zoe had snapped herself, smiling sleepily into the camera. She was naked, from what he could see, one tanned arm draped across a man . . . his mind did a shift. He recognised the duvet cover.

'It's me,' he muttered. He was sleeping, head to one side, but easily recognisable. *Jesus Christ.* What was she playing at? The photo suggested they'd had sex, but he knew they hadn't. Was it a warning? Did she intend to send the photo to Kate?

There was a message underneath. You look so cute when you're sleeping 😊 xx

Dan felt his brain short-circuit. Breathing hard he replied, This ends now, Zoe. I love my wife. He pressed send then deleted the photo.

He let out a frustrated howl that bounced off the walls of the kitchen. Their kitchen. The place where he and Kate had cooked, eaten, laughed, talked and even made love. He remembered how she sometimes mimicked Nigella while cooking, making innuendoes until his eyes were damp from laughter.

He had to talk to her.

He sat heavily at the table and stared unseeing at the whorls and scratches in the wood. With no way of contacting his wife, a conversation was impossible. He had no choice but to wait for her to come home. But what if she was so upset with him, she decided to stay where she was?

He shook his head. Kate never took time off work. Tomorrow was Monday. She'd be back at the showroom, no matter what. She would swing by Saskia's first to freshen up if she didn't want to come home.

He would have to speak to her there.

If only I knew where she was.

He sat until the light outside changed.

Zoe didn't reply to his text.

Kate didn't come home.

He went over Magda's words again and shivered. The impact of her call was somehow more shocking than the photo Zoe had sent. He remembered her accent had altered towards the end of the call, as she became more impassioned. It had sounded familiar.

A punch of adrenalin brought Dan to his feet. Helen's northern inflection had faded over the years, but a trace of it still lingered. Magda had the same accent. Or was he imagining it, Helen's story still fresh in his mind? *No.* He was certain. He should ring Saskia, and ask if she had the woman's address. As he sank his head to his fists, another thought bounced in.

CCTV.

Kate had it installed at the showroom earlier in the year, after a couple of teenagers smashed the front window and made off with an expensive chandelier. Maybe this woman – Magda – had been caught on camera.

Heart thumping, Dan called a startled Saskia and asked her

to meet him at the showroom.

Then he rang Helen.

'Is Kate back?' Her anxious voice ripped through him.

'No,' he said. There was a loaded silence. 'I want you to look at something.' Still no response, just the sound of her ragged breathing. 'I'm coming to get you.'

Chapter 19

Dan parked the motorbike on the tree-lined street outside Helen's terraced house.

The sun hadn't yet set, but a light glowed from a downstairs window. He remembered the first time Kate brought him home, and how awkward he'd felt in Helen's small, neat living room. Far from the welcome he'd imagined, after hearing about Kate's childhood, he'd found the house rather sterile – despite Kate's efforts with bird-patterned wallpaper and clever lighting – and Helen vaguely hostile.

He'd wanted to show her he was serious about Kate but realised, too late, he'd brought mud into the house on his boots and trailed it across her cream carpet, and in spite of Helen's assurance that it didn't matter, he knew she'd written him off.

As he'd prattled nervously about his family – parents of no fixed abode, siblings scattered round the globe – her face had stiffened further. When he told her about the band, and that despite his degree he didn't have a 'proper' job yet, her disapproval had swelled.

Her assessment of him was sealed when Kate revealed it was Dan who had persuaded her to drop finance and switch to interior design. Helen reacted as though he'd talked Kate into opening a brothel and hadn't really relaxed until her showroom was up and running and Kate had proved she could manage perfectly well without either of them.

Now, he watched Helen step onto the porch, zipping up a thin jacket.

'I've got a spare helmet,' he called, indicating the seat behind him.

Her gaze shot to her car, parked in front of him, and he thought for a moment she was going to refuse. Then, she pulled the door shut and hurried towards him.

'Where are we going?' Her eyes gripped his, reflecting the sinking ball of fiery sun behind him.

'Inspired Interiors,' he said.

She frowned. 'Is Kate working?'

He shook his head. 'I'll explain when we get there.'

She cast a doubtful look at the motorbike. 'I've never been on one of these,' she said. 'Am I dressed properly?'

He looked at her and nodded. 'Hold on to me and try not to move around too much,' he said. 'You'll soon get a feel for it.'

Without further comment, she pulled on the helmet and allowed him to fasten it for her, then swung her leg over the leather seat. When he revved the engine and pulled away, she gripped the sides of his leather jacket. He was reminded how scared Kate had been the first time, before she relaxed against him, looking over his shoulder and whooping with joy.

He doubted the ride would elicit the same response from Helen, judging by her rigid position.

Despite his impatience, he rode more slowly than usual, easing the bike carefully into tight bends and turns. No point frightening his mother-in-law any more than she already was.

When they arrived, the normally bustling pavement outside Inspired Interiors was deserted. Sandwiched between a charity shop and a dry-cleaner's, Dan had thought it a poor location at first, but Kate had assured him it was perfect. She wanted to appeal to everyone, not just wealthy clients, and a beechwood sign above the door proclaimed there was 'a design to suit every budget'.

Although the cream-and-grey-painted exterior was tasteful, it wasn't intimidating, and the window display of a stripy sofa and curtain, material and wallpaper samples was homely and inviting.

He parked the bike and helped Helen dismount. She climbed off as though her muscles had been injected with cement, but although her hands shook a little as she removed her helmet and her hair was pasted to her head, he noticed her eyes held the same spark Kate's had after that first ride.

Helen ruffled her hair with her hand and peered past him into the showroom, where some lights were on. 'Looks like Saskia's here.'

'I asked her to meet us,' he said.

He moved to the door and rapped the glass with his knuckles. Was he doing the right thing? Kate could have changed her mind about coming home, might be arriving at that very moment, surprised to find the house empty.

Saskia hurried over to unlock the door. 'What's going on?' she said, flicking panic-stricken brown eyes to his when she recognised Helen behind him. In the past, Helen had been almost as disapproving of Saskia as she was of Dan, convinced Kate gave her too much leeway and that one day she'd either set up her own business, or run off with the profits.

'She just wants to protect me,' Kate had said, when Dan pointed out it was unhealthy the way Helen didn't trust anyone's motives where her daughter was concerned. 'It's what mothers do.'

His mother didn't. Neither were very good role models.

The showroom smelled of vanilla and leather – a comforting scent that made him think of his grandfather.

'I don't suppose you've heard from Kate again?' he asked Saskia, after pressing a kiss on her cheek. He jiggled his keys, affecting a casual air that wouldn't have fooled anyone.

'Not since the phone call yesterday,' she said. 'Is she not home yet?' Normally on the verge of smiling, her heart-shaped face was sombre, and her usually sleek blonde hair was mussed up, as if she'd dashed out without checking her reflection.

Dan's heart gave a little lurch. 'No,' he admitted quietly.

Helen had been standing as if rooted to the polished floorboards, gazing at a display dresser lined with jewel-bright vases, but now he felt her hawk-like gaze on him, demanding answers.

He knew he should mention the phone call from Magda, but the words lodged in his throat. He would wait until they'd looked at the CCTV footage, before saying anything. It was unlikely Kate's client was the woman Helen had told him about, but if it was . . . He punched down the thought. He was ruling it out, that was all.

'Does that work?' he said, pointing to the camera discreetly positioned high in the corner to cover the front of the building.

Saskia caught the direction of his gaze and nodded. 'Why?'

'Could we have a look?' Glancing at Helen, he saw that she understood what he was getting at.

'Look at what?' Saskia hooked her hair behind her ears, eyes flicking from him to Helen and back again. 'What's going on, Dan?'

'Probably nothing,' he said, but she clearly didn't believe him. Helen had never turned up on a motorbike with her son-in-law. 'It's just this client that Kate's with . . .' His voice trailed off. He ran a hand over his hair, unsure how to continue. He waited for Helen to speak, but she stayed silent.

'What about her?' Saskia studied him as she zipped up the grey hooded fleece she was wearing with pyjama bottoms. The heat of the day hadn't penetrated the interior, and it was chilly inside. 'Do you think she's genuine?'

He looked at Helen, who shook her head imperceptibly. 'Maybe not.' Saying it out loud made his stomach plunge.

'Oh.' Saskia's mouth wobbled briefly. She looked younger, just as Zoe had earlier, somehow vulnerable. 'Come on, I'll show you,' she said, moving behind the counter Dan had made from recycled wood what felt like light years ago. 'It's linked to the computer,' she said, switching it on.

Helen joined them, walking as though on marbles, and the three of them watched in silence as the system booted up. Dan could hear Saskia breathing and smell Helen's coconut-scented shampoo. Or was it the other way round? His senses felt heightened and he drummed his fingers on the counter to release a flow of energy.

'Here we are,' said Saskia at last, logging in and pressing an icon on the desktop labelled NET SURVEILLANCE. 'State-of-the-art stuff,' she added, her hair falling forward as they studied a list of instructions on the screen. 'We've barely looked at it since it was installed, so you'll have to bear with me.'

Dan resisted the urge to grab the mouse and do it himself. He wouldn't know where to start, any more than Helen did. He could sense her impatience too. Glancing over, he saw her teeth grinding her bottom lip.

'I take it you want to see what this client looks like?' Saskia raised enquiring eyes to his. 'Magda Trent?'

He nodded. 'Just curious,' he said, knowing it sounded ridiculous – that it was obviously more than that – but she didn't comment. She flicked through the diary beside the keyboard, then tapped a date into the computer and pressed playback.

Immediately, the area by the door flickered into focus, people visible on the sunlit stretch of pavement outside. Helen pushed her head close to the screen, her arm brushing his. Her scrutiny was intense, and he suddenly felt afraid.

'Roughly what time did she come in?' he asked Saskia. It was a waste, watching a whole day's footage.

Saskia cast her eyes upwards in thought. 'It must have been around two thirty,' she said. 'We'd had a fabric delivery, and I was out the back.' She sped the recording forward so that people scuttled by cartoon-style.

Dan's ghost of a laugh died abruptly. 'Wait,' he said. 'What about her?'

Saskia rewound and hit pause, freeze-framing a woman pushing through the door. She was curvy, with curly brown hair in a ponytail, sunglasses covering half her face.

'I didn't actually see her.' Saskia squinted at the screen. 'But I don't think that's her, from how Kate described her. She was older.'

'It's not her,' said Helen firmly, eyes still glued to the image. 'I mean, if she's who I think she is, that's definitely not her.'

'Who do you think she is?' Saskia's dark eyes were troubled, her mouth turned down at the corners.

'It's a long story,' Dan said, apologetically. He was embarrassed all of a sudden, couldn't think now what had possessed him to come. His hangover headache from earlier pounded back and he longed to be home – preferably cuddled up on the sofa with his wife.

'Wait a minute.' Helen's eyes narrowed and he looked at the computer. Time was ticking over in the corner while figures moved past the store like characters in a silent film. 'There!' She jabbed the screen with her finger. 'Freeze it,' she ordered in a strangled voice.

A wide-eyed Saskia did as she was told. 'What are we looking for?' She sounded bewildered, but Dan tracked Helen's gaze to a woman paused on the threshold, one hand holding the door open. She looked ordinary: plump, indeterminate age, plain clothes, flat shoes.

'Can you zoom in?' said Helen. 'Please, it's important.'

Dan's pulse started to race.

'I don't think we have the software for that,' Saskia said, sounding panicked. She pressed a few keys, but nothing happened. 'I'm sorry, I can't.' She sounded close to tears, but before Dan or Helen could speak the image unfroze. The woman lifted her head, giving a clear view of her unremarkable features.

'Oh my God, I knew it.' Helen emitted a high-pitched noise that raised the hairs on Dan's arms. 'It's her,' she said. 'It's Mary.'

Her words cut through his frozen brain. 'Are you sure?'

'Who's Mary?' demanded Saskia.

'I'm sure.' Helen squeezed her eyes shut. 'She's older, obviously, and she does look different, but I'd know her anywhere.'

Fear grabbed Dan's heart like a fist. 'She called me earlier,' he confessed, and heard Helen's sharp intake of breath. 'She said Kate was staying with her again tonight, that she'd told her we were having problems, and she didn't want to come home yet.'

'Kate wouldn't talk like that to someone she hardly knows.' Saskia sounded outraged.

'Why not?' said Dan, not daring to look at Helen. 'Maybe it's easier than telling the truth to any of us.' His throat constricted. 'I've been a crap husband lately . . .'

'None of that matters,' Helen interrupted, her face bloodless. 'The point is, she has Kate where she wants her.'

He hated how dramatic that sounded. 'What do we do?'

'Kate could be in danger, Dan.' Helen's eyes reddened with tears. 'I think we should call the police.'

'What do we tell them?' He tuned in to Saskia's plea to explain what was going on. 'My wife is staying with a client who called me earlier to say Kate was fine and is staying overnight again, but my mother-in-law thinks she's a baby snatcher out for revenge.'

'What?' Saskia's face was a mask of disbelief. 'Is this a joke?'

'Does it look like we're joking?' Helen rounded on Saskia, her lips a line of fury. 'I would hardly make something like this up.'

'Do you believe her?' Saskia turned to Dan, her eyes glossy with tears of shock.

'I don't know what to think,' he said truthfully, shaking his head. 'But something feels off. Kate wouldn't just refuse to speak to me or have a stranger call me to say that.'

'I know I'm right.' Helen turned to him. 'Trust me on this, Dan, please.'

He stared, trying to untangle his thoughts and work out what to do. A car hooted outside, and Saskia's hand flew to her mouth.

'We don't even know where she is,' he said, clutching his throbbing temples, remembering how Saskia hadn't been able to find the address.

A terrible silence fell, and Dan felt the full force of Helen's fear and worry. Was this all his fault?

'Hang on,' said Saskia, distracting the flow of his thoughts. Two bright spots of colour stood out on her cheeks. 'I could look her up on Google again, but I could only find one Magda—'

'Try Mary Trent,' Helen said, voice tight.

They gathered around the computer screen as Saskia typed the name in.

'Oh my God – look at this.' She clicked on a link to an old news article, referencing a Mary Trent dismissed from a hospital in Leeds, twenty-five years ago, for stealing a newborn baby.

'What?' Dan stared, words jumping out at him, while Helen murmured that she wasn't surprised.

'She didn't go to jail as she returned the baby safely but got a two-year suspended sentence.' She looked at them. 'I doubt she ever worked in a hospital again.'

'And she didn't give up looking for the baby she believed was hers,' Helen said.

They fell silent again for a moment, taking it in, until Saskia said, 'When I spoke to her yesterday, Kate said the cottage was in the middle of nowhere, and mentioned a farm nearby.'

'Go on,' Helen instructed. Dan sensed a force field of energy building around her and felt it pass through him.

'She said it was called Cherry Field Farm, and I said it couldn't be, because cherries don't grow in fields.'

It was unlike Kate to get things wrong, and Dan knew from Helen's expression she was thinking the same. 'Maybe it's called Cherry *Tree* Farm,' he said, his heart beginning to race. 'That would make more sense as cherries grow on trees.'

Saskia nodded. 'That could be what she meant.'

'Look it up.'

But she'd already turned back to the computer and was typing into Google again.

'There is a Cherry Tree Farm,' she said, voice tight with excitement. 'It's on the other side of Lexminster, closer to Oxford.'

'We'll go in my car,' Helen said to Dan. 'I can use the satnav.'

Dan snatched a flyer from the desk and scribbled the postcode on the back.

'It'll be dark by the time we arrive,' Helen said curtly. 'We need to get going.'

Dan looked through the window and saw she was right. Dusk was gathering, the sky a bruise of purple and grey. 'Maybe we could call the farm first.'

'There's a number here.' Snatching up the phone, Saskia dialled, biting her lip like a frightened child, and Dan felt a stab of guilt for dragging her into whatever was going on. 'No answer,' she said, when the tension of waiting became unbearable. 'Should we call the police, just in case?'

'It might still be nothing,' he said, praying he was right. Even if it was, he wanted to meet this Magda, the woman who knew so much about his marriage. 'I'll ring you as soon as we've found Kate.'

He looked for Helen, but she was already outside, pulling her helmet on like a seasoned motorcyclist.

A circling fear swooped down, prompting Dan to turn back to Saskia. 'If you haven't heard from me in an hour, call them anyway.'

Chapter 20

Kate

The gravel on the drive digs into my soles, but I can only think of escape, Magda's slap replaying in my head. I've never been hit before. Mum rarely even raised her voice to me when I was growing up, never mind her hand.

Why did Magda lash out like that? Even if she's ill, or distraught at the thought of me leaving, it's no excuse.

Catching my breath on a sob, I wheel around, certain she's right behind me, but the doorway to the kitchen is empty. Inside, Arthur is curled on the flagstone floor, oblivious.

Turning, I try to get my bearings. Moonlight trails across the garden, muting the colours to a washed-out grey, but there's enough light spilling from the cottage to make out Magda's Vauxhall in front of the garage. She must have taken my keys and put my car inside after removing my samples from the boot, but why?

To make it harder for me to leave.

An owl hoots mournfully, jolting me into action. I stumble towards the garage, one arm outstretched in case I fall. Despite the slap – or perhaps because of it – I suddenly feel more alert, as though my reflexes have snapped back into balance. As I manoeuvre clumsily around her car, images fight for space inside my head: the photo of Magda and Mum (who had taken it?); the tenderness in Magda's eyes when she revealed who she was; the nursery she'd lovingly painted; her face when she talked about Patrick; the bedroom with the drawer of medication and the suitcase with baby clothes . . . My mind reaches for something just out of my grasp, and I let it go. I need to keep calm for my baby's sake. Something is happening, despite my due date being nearly three weeks away.

You were two weeks late. Mum's voice in my head. *It was a cold start to May. I think you were hanging on for the sunshine.*

The truth slams into me again. Mum's been lying to me. She was never even pregnant.

Swallowing another sob, I fumble for the garage doors. They're solid timber and even though I know they're going to be locked, I rattle them anyway. They don't budge. I stand on tiptoe to peer through a glass panel set into the wood, but it's too dark to see inside and my bump gets in the way.

I let out a cry of frustration. I don't want to go back inside to ask Magda for the key, but what are my options? I'm barefoot, in the middle of nowhere, with no bag or phone, or any means of getting home.

I sag against the garage doors, my breathing ragged. I feel a movement deep inside, as if the baby's sighing, and grip the place I imagine his head to be. 'I'm so sorry,' I whisper. 'Please hang on in there, baby.'

Something scuttles down the side of the garage and I jump. I try to see the gap in the hedge that I drove through when I arrived, but there's only darkness in front of me. I remember the gate the gardener used to enter the garden, and the farm sign I passed in the lane. *The farm.* It can't be far away. Perhaps I can make my way there and ask to use their phone.

Immediately, I realise it's a bad idea. I could fall, or lose my way in the dark, or it might be further away than I think. What if I find it and there's no one there, and I can't find my way back?

A hysterical image rises, of me squatting in a rutted field in the middle of the night, giving birth. No one would know where I was.

My resolve starts slipping away. I should go back inside and talk to Magda. She's probably mortified now she's had a chance to calm down. Maybe I'm overreacting to the slap. It's not like she's chased me with a kitchen knife and the whole point is that she wants me to stay. She *wants* me.

She wants the baby more.

Ignoring the persistent voice, I push forward, resting a hand on the bonnet of Magda's car. I puff air up into my fringe and try to think, but a contraction is building, and panic takes over once more.

I slump forward, concentrating on the feel of cool metal against my burning forehead. Where the hell is Magda?

When I raise my head, the moon has gone, the garden vanished under a shroud of darkness. I drag myself in the direction of the cottage, flinching with every painful step.

'Lexi? Where are you, darling?' I freeze. 'Lexi?' She sounds puzzled, as if she can't understand why I fled. 'Are you out there?' Her voice draws closer, then her outline fills the doorway, blocking the light. 'Lexi?'

She must know I'm out here. Has she forgotten what she did? My mind flashes back to the pill bottles. Maybe she takes something that affects her mood. It would explain her soothing me one minute, angry the next. 'Do you have the key for the garage?' I call on impulse. 'I need to get my car out.'

'Your car?' Her outline stiffens. 'You don't have a car, silly.' *Oh God.* 'Come inside now; you'll catch your death of cold.' It's not cold; it's mild. No breeze, just the waft of warm, sweet, honey-suckle-scented air. 'Lexi.' Her tone sharpens. 'Come back now.'

Some instinct propels me towards the garden. I duck into the darkness, hoping she won't spot me.

Her footsteps crunch across the gravel. 'This is silly, Lexi.' Her laugh sounds unconvincing. 'Think of the baby.'

As if I can think about anything else. The grass is cool and damp between my toes, and I try and tether my mind in the here and now. I need to find the gate. Shoving my hair off my sweat-slicked face, I search the shapes in front of me. When I reach the end of the garden, I scrabble through thick shrubbery, and almost cry out with relief when my hands meet the rough brick of the wall. Fronds brush against my shins, releasing a scent of lavender. I'm certain the gate is close by.

'Lexi, I'm really not in the mood for hide and seek.'

Her voice is still some distance away. I wonder if she thinks I'm wedged beneath her car. Suppressing a feverish sob, I drag my hands across the wall until they find a gap. Dipping my fingers, I feel the cool metal of the wrought-iron gate and fumble for the latch, but I've forgotten about the rusty hinge. As I push the gate open, an ear-piercing squeal slices the air like a siren, and the moon chooses that moment to reappear, as effective as a spotlight.

'There you are, Lexi.' She's closer than I thought. I imagine her moving stealthily towards me, like a panther – or one of those predatory stone angels I'd seen in a sci-fi drama, who move closer when no one's looking. 'You really shouldn't be out here in your condition.'

Ignoring the ache in my back and belly, I burst through the gate and emerge into a weed-choked lane, strips of moonlight filtering through a canopy of branches above. I start to run, but it's an odd, lumbering movement, like wading through thick mud. I clutch at my belly, each step threatening to pull me to my knees, the keys I'm still clasping, digging into my palm.

'Where are you going, Lexi?' Magda's right behind me, breathing in heavy puffs. 'You're going to give birth very soon.' Her voice is soft, oozing concern. I think of a hawk watching a sparrow. 'You're putting the baby at risk.'

I muffle a panicked sob. Where's the farm? Maybe it's in the other direction. The earth is pitted with tractor marks, but it's impossible to tell which way they're going. I keep stumbling forward, panting like a dog. My lungs feel like they're about to burst into flames. *I want Dan.* I want him. We can get past our problems; I know we can. *Please God, let our baby be safe.*

'Why are you doing this, Lexi?' Magda sounds perplexed. 'Please, come back with me.'

I stop and double over, hands pressing the sides of my stomach. My swollen ankles feel like they're about to burst, and something has stung my foot. 'You hit me,' I rasp, trying to catch my breath.

'Oh, Lexi.' When I raise my head and look round, I see her forehead is wrinkled with bemusement. In the sliver of moonlight her eyes glitter with tears. 'I shouldn't have done that and I'm truly sorry, but you don't have to run away.'

As the tightening in my belly increases, all the fight goes out of me. It suddenly seems ridiculous that I'm out here, trying to run from a middle-aged woman who bakes cakes and makes her own lemonade. It feels wrong to be out here in the dark with the baby coming. Maybe I should surrender and go inside. Maybe it's safer there.

'Please come back, Kate.'

I prefer it when she calls me Kate. It's less creepy. I think of being back in that bed with Magda keeping watch and a bolt of dread shoots through me. 'I don't know,' I say, eyes raking the shadows around me for signs of life. If I saw the farmer, would he help me?

'Kate?' Her hand circles my wrist. Her fingers are icy cold.

She's your mother. 'I need to talk to someone.' My teeth have started to chatter. 'They'll have a phone.'

'Who will?' Her clasp tightens.

'The farmer.'

'What farmer?' Her eyes are penetrating, like shards of glass, and there's a shrillness to her tone. 'Nobody lives around here apart from me.'

I move my free hand to my chest, feeling my rapid heartbeat. Why is she lying? My brain sparks with questions that fizzle and die like damp fireworks. Only one thing seems certain. She's not going to let me go until I've had my baby. 'Dan's not coming, is he?'

'No.' Her voice softens again, ripe with sympathy. 'He doesn't deserve you, sweetheart.'

'Did you even call the hospital?'

She shakes her head, a downward tilt to her lips. 'We don't need them, Lexi.'

As the words leave her mouth a spasm of agony rips through my belly. I cry out, my hand reaching for support, meeting spiky foliage, and the reality of my surroundings sinks in. I have to go back with her. Everything else can wait.

As Magda's arm closes around my shoulders, I hear the sound of an engine. Half turning, I see the beam of headlights bouncing over the bumpy track towards us.

'Come away.' Magda pulls me with her, and we fall against the hedge.

'What are you doing?' I try to free myself. The headlights swing away, then the engine dies and a couple of car doors slam. There's a rise and fall of voices, followed by a shout of laughter. 'Let me go, Magda.' I try again to pull away, but her fingernails dig into the flesh of my arm, trapping me against her.

'Ow!' I strain against her. 'What are you *doing?*'

'I'm trying to stop you from making a terrible mistake.'

She makes it sound obvious, like something we've discussed, and out of nowhere it hits me again with the force of a punch – how sleepy I've been, how relaxed . . . how disjointed everything seems. The tablets in the bedroom drawer. 'You've given me something.'

'Only to take the edge off the shock, my darling.'

I've been drugged. I try to speak, but shock at her admission has robbed me of speech.

'Don't worry, sweetheart, I know what I'm doing.' She's placating again. 'We can't have you leaving, now I've finally found you.'

'But I'm having a baby,' I whimper, my mind ranging chaotically for things I've read about medicating during pregnancy. I wouldn't even take an aspirin for a headache, and besides, I'm super sensitive to tablets – even paracetamol. 'What about the baby?'

'Come on, Lexi.' Her soothing voice continues. 'You need to come back to the cottage and lie down. I'll run you a nice hot bath to help with the contractions, if you like.' She chuckles and the sound of it chills me. 'I stayed in the bath for almost the whole of my labour,' she says. 'You were practically a water baby.'

'It's not due yet.' I finally wrench away from her and start moving down the lane, legs buckling. Where did the headlights go? Can't be far now.

'You're going the wrong way, silly.' Her arms encircle me from behind. I push against them, but she's strong. I long to take my baby bump off and hide it somewhere safe so I can run.

'Please let go of me,' I plead, struggling in the cage of her arms.

'I really don't want to, but I'm going to give you something to help you calm down.'

'No, no. Please don't, Magda.'

Her grip loosens. She fumbles for something in her pocket, and I catch a gleam of something sharp. A needle and a syringe. I wriggle frantically, and her arm tightens across my chest.

'Just a little scratch, you'll hardly feel a thing.'

She pushes up my sleeve and jabs the needle into my upper arm while I try to squirm away.

'Sorry, my darling.' She squeezes me tightly. 'Don't fight it.'

Almost immediately, the certainties I'd felt lose shape and I soften against her. Her breath shushes through my hair, warm on my scalp. 'It'll help you relax, my love.'

My eyelids droop and my limbs grow heavy.

'Come on now; can you make it back?' Her arms shift me about. I feel like a puppet, draped around her. My anxiety drifts away like smoke. I'm weightless, and Magda's eyes are large with kindness and understanding. Her voice is the soft rustle of leaves through the overhanging branches. 'Here we go, one step at a time.'

I try to trace the outline of the moon with my eyes, but it's too much effort to look up. I glance down and the ground looms at me, ridged and unyielding. My knees ache. Everything aches. 'Sorry,' I murmur, grasping at Magda with cotton wool fingers.

'Nothing to be sorry for, darling girl.'

Her arms are like steel bars, preventing me from falling, but I cling to her anyway. We seem to be moving for ages before the cottage weaves into view, its lights like a beacon in the darkness. I'm certain I can hear faint music in the distance and think of Dan, strumming his guitar and singing softly, his voice plucking at my heart. I can't be without him, we're inseparable, our roots tangled together. 'Dan,' I say in my head. 'Our baby's coming.'

Other feelings rise up. I'm eight years old and have toothache, but it's spreading all over my body. It's in my back, my spine, my belly, and it's getting worse. *I want my mummy.*

I groan and retch, and the feeling subsides a little.

Steps. Going upstairs.

Magda's struggling. I'm a deadweight. 'It'll soon be over, darling.' Her voice is a tickle in my brain. 'Here we are.' I'm sinking down and down through clouds, eyes closing.

'Everything's going to be OK.'

Chapter 21

Dan

Helen gripped the steering wheel, her knuckles white, and Dan wished she'd go faster. He'd never been in a car with her before but wasn't surprised that she drove like an elderly person with poor eyesight.

'There's no point speeding,' she said tightly, as if reading his thoughts. 'It wouldn't help Kate if I crashed, and we ended up in hospital.'

But he wasn't ashamed of wanting to race through the night to get to his wife. He needed to know she was OK. He wanted to meet this Magda, or Mary, or whoever the hell she was, and see for himself what had compelled Kate to confide in her things he was certain she hadn't told anyone else. He drummed his fingers on his knees, willing the car on.

He'd tried phoning Kate when they'd got back to Helen's, hoping she was home, curled on the sofa, checking her messages, but it went to voicemail. It was almost 10 p.m. Normally at this time on a Sunday, she'd be soaking in the bath with a book and a chamomile tea. She'd given caffeine up since becoming pregnant, had gone off coffee altogether.

He felt perspiration on his upper lip and opened the window a fraction, glancing at Helen. In the intermittent light from passing cars her face had a ghostly pallor, the skin stretched tightly over her cheekbones. She was listening intently to the robotic instructions issuing from her satnav, even though they were still on the road outside Marlow.

'I can't believe it's really her,' she said out of the blue. It was the first time she'd referred to the woman they'd seen on camera since they'd left the showroom. 'You know how you imagine a scenario over and over in your head, but you try to convince yourself you're being ridiculous, and that everything's going to be fine?' She threw him a look and he nodded, recalling all the ways he'd managed to convince himself he was going to be a terrible father, based on his childhood experiences. Had his dad really been that bad?

He remembered Rosie visiting once, just after he and Kate were married. Kate had been out working when Rosie called round after a gap year in India and started reminiscing at the kitchen table about their 'idyllic' childhood. As she'd recounted memories of stories around the campfire, of Dan singing her to sleep at night, of how much she'd learned about nature thanks to their mother, who'd trained as a teacher, and how enriched their life had been compared to friends', he'd wondered why she hadn't mentioned almost drowning in the lake. She'd been surprised when he mentioned it, and he realised how different their perceptions of growing up had been. Where he'd seen instability and danger, Rosie had seen adventure, fun and excitement. He hadn't pushed it, content to let her tease him for 'selling out' by settling down with a wife, knowing she adored Kate.

Recalling that conversation now, in the confines of Helen's car, he suddenly remembered his mum teaching him to play the guitar during the long evenings in the squat, clapping with delight that he only needed to hear a tune once to be able to recreate it. How had he forgotten that? That, and that the woodworking his dad had taught him had been his entire career so far.

'I told myself Mary was bound to have moved on by now.' Helen's voice delivered him back to the moment. 'I thought that she'd have married, had more children. Stepchildren, even.' She shook her head. 'But looking back, I think I always knew deep down she was ill.' Another sideways glance at Dan. 'I mean mentally ill,' she clarified. 'The breakdown in her teens was obviously part of it. Maybe she never properly recovered.'

Dan's blood chilled. 'But Kate obviously likes her,' he pointed out. 'She'd never have decided to stay there otherwise.'

'She drew me in once, remember?' He heard Helen swallow. 'The truth is, we don't know what she's capable of.' She paused and he knew there was more. 'I tried to talk to her, you know, before I left Leeds.' She changed gear and turned off the main road. 'I wanted to say goodbye, and check she was OK, I suppose.' Her eyes flicked to the satnav, checking the route. 'She always used to visit me, not the other way round, said the house where she lived was a dump, but when I went to the address she'd given me, I suddenly remembered that I'd briefly met her before.'

'What?' Dan's head jerked round.

'I went to that road once before when I was heavily pregnant with Kate. My boss's secretary had been off work ill and he wanted someone to check on her. I lived nearby, so I offered, but there was no answer when I knocked, so I tried the house next door, hoping someone might know how she was.'

'And?'

Helen's eyes narrowed as she stared ahead, as though reliving the scene. 'The door opened, and this person peered out. A youngish woman, maybe a bit older than me. I couldn't see her properly, but she was in a bad way, looked like she'd been crying a lot, her hair all over the place. Anyway, she didn't know what I was talking about, looked totally confused, and when I asked if she was OK, she slammed the door in my face. It wasn't until

I went back to the street that day that I realised it was *her*. I'd thought there was something familiar about her when I met her in the park but couldn't pin it down. She looked so different.'

'God,' said Dan. 'It's hard to take in, to be honest.'

'Anyway, she wasn't there when I called to say goodbye. A neighbour said he hadn't seen her for a long time.' Helen's voice sounded hoarse. 'That's when I wondered if anything she'd told me was true,' she said. 'She mentioned her father was a doctor and lived in a big house, and that he'd disowned her when she fell pregnant, but I don't know if that was true either.'

'And you never saw her again?'

A quick shake of the head. 'I didn't like it.' The whites of her eyes shone in reflected light from the winding road. 'It felt like unfinished business. As if she wasn't done with me.'

Christ. He couldn't vocalise the effect her words were having, feelings gathering in his chest. 'Is that why you . . .' he hesitated. But surely it didn't matter what he said now, given their situation. 'Is that why you've always been so overprotective of Kate?'

'Have I?' She blinked, tears glistening on her eyelashes. She took the next corner too quickly and Dan jolted forward, his hands shooting out to the dashboard. 'Shit! Sorry.' He'd never heard Helen curse and his feeling of unreality deepened. 'I suppose the experience with Mary made me more cautious,' she went on, as though nothing had happened. 'But that wasn't the only reason.'

'Oh?' Dan rubbed his shoulder, which had jarred when his arm shot out, wondering what was coming next.

'Kate's father,' she began, then stopped.

This was uncharted territory. Helen never talked about Kate's dad to her, never mind to Dan. The air between them hummed with tension. Outside, trees and houses passed in a shadowy blur, the rising moon casting a silvery glow across the countryside. According to the satnav, they were ten minutes from their destination.

'He was the main reason I decided to move away,' Helen

continued, just when Dan thought she wasn't going to speak again, and he carefully closed the window to hear her better. 'Mary was the catalyst, but I couldn't stand being in the same town as him, knowing he didn't want us.' Dan held his breath, not wanting to snap the fragile thread of her confession. 'I'm sure Kate's told you he was married. The oldest story in the book.' She gave a half-laugh. 'They were childhood sweethearts, expected to marry,' she went on in a rush, and must have pressed her foot down because the car suddenly gained speed. 'Her father owned a chain of restaurants and put him in charge of the business, said if he ever hurt his daughter, he'd ruin him, make sure he never worked again.'

'Surely he could have stood up to him?'

'It was . . . complicated. His father was a powerful man. He could have ruined his life.'

Dan didn't comment.

'I loved him,' Helen said simply. 'When I fell pregnant . . .' she swallowed, 'he told me it had to be over and that it was best if I didn't contact him again.'

'Shit,' Dan said softly. 'That's harsh.'

'I took full responsibility,' Helen said, in the more matter-of-fact style he was used to. 'I knew he was married when we met, so it was my fault too.' He wanted to ask how they'd met, feeling he was close to finally unravelling the mystery of his mother-in-law, but she was still talking. 'I suppose at first, I hoped having the baby would change his mind, but I was wrong.' She slowed the car and took a right turn. 'It certainly wasn't how I'd planned to be a parent,' she said, shaking her head. 'I wanted to give my daughter the sort of childhood I'd had, before my parents died.' It was as if she couldn't stop talking now she'd started. 'I never wanted to be a single parent.'

'Why choose a married man?'

'You can't choose who you fall in love with, Dan.'

It was the most un-Helen-like thing she'd ever said, and for a moment he almost forgot why they were in the car, and where they were going. 'Why haven't you told Kate any of this?'

She shot him a look of genuine surprise. 'I didn't want her to know her father didn't want us,' she said, as if it wasn't blindingly obvious. 'Plus, I was angry with him, so I decided to move away and start afresh. Pretend he didn't exist. I didn't want any complications after that. It was just me and Kate, a perfect little unit. We didn't need anyone else.'

Dan thought Kate might have begged to differ, but in a way, he understood Helen's reasoning.

'At first, I wondered whether he would try and find us, but I think he was probably glad that we'd left.' She didn't sound bitter, which was either a testament to how much she loved him, or she'd genuinely forgiven him. 'Plus, there was the small matter of me changing my name.' Dan's head shot round again. 'I started using my middle name instead of Jane, and took my aunt's surname,' she said.

So, Helen wasn't Helen at all. She was Jane. Dan wondered what other surprises she had up her sleeve. 'It can't have been easy, moving so far away with a baby.'

'I had my aunt,' she said, lifting her chin. 'We were happy, actually, in spite of everything that had happened.'

'What about your sister?' For a moment, he wondered if he'd gone too far and she wouldn't answer, but maybe it was the intimacy of being in the car, enclosed by the darkness outside, but she answered right away.

'Cath never approved of me seeing Andrew.' *Andrew.* The name rang a bell. 'She'd been friends with his wife at school. We had a big falling out about it.' She said it rather defiantly, as if the memory still stung. 'Cath was older than me,' she said. 'She was like a mother to me after our parents died and couldn't cope with me growing up and apart from her. I'm sure she only went to live in Australia with her boyfriend to punish me for not listening to her.' He wondered if that was true, or just Helen's perception. He remembered how Kate had wanted her aunt to come to their wedding, to swell the numbers on her side, and to meet the cousins she'd never seen, but her mother had been adamant Cath wouldn't want to come and Kate had dropped it.

'So, your sister never knew about this woman. Mary?'

'Of course not.' Helen's voice was sharp. 'She was in Australia by the time all that happened.'

'Did you tell your aunt?'

'Why would I tell anyone?' In profile, Helen's brows were heavy, her expression strained. 'I'd got myself into another situation I had to get out of. It was embarrassing, actually. Bad character judgement on my part. Why would I tell anyone that?'

A memory triggered in Dan's brain. When Kate had found out she was pregnant she insisted they didn't tell a soul until after her first scan, because she was worried she might miscarry. 'It happened to Mum before she had me and there were problems after I was born. That's why she couldn't have any more children,' she'd explained. 'Telling people I'm pregnant too early would be tempting fate.'

In a daze, he'd gone along with it, hoping by the time they did announce it, he'd be as enthusiastic about having a baby as Kate was.

Helen had miscarried.

A thought crept in, so terrible Dan felt immobilised with shock. What if she was lying? What if she *had* taken that woman's baby, and that was the real reason she'd moved away?

What if she wasn't Kate's mother?

He tried to think. Perhaps she'd been out of her mind with grief after miscarrying, still desperate about the break-up with the baby's father. People did crazy things in the heat of the moment. Maybe Helen was the one who was unhinged.

What if she'd been lying all along?

He must have made a sound because Helen swung her head towards him.

'Don't worry; we're almost there,' she said briskly, and it struck him how much stronger she was, emotionally, than he'd realised. He wondered whether her constant veneer of anxiety hadn't been about keeping Kate safe, but to do with protecting herself. He remembered how calm she'd been when she asked him if he was having an affair with Zoe, compared to her seemingly unfounded panic over Kate's whereabouts. Her own affair with a married man had probably made her less judgemental. Or maybe she'd been worried all along that she'd be found out one day.

Had this woman – Mary – tracked Kate down in order to tell her the truth? And if she had, what would that do to Kate?

And Helen?

His mind veered wildly as Helen swung the car down a weed-choked path just wide enough for one vehicle.

'Look, there's the sign,' she said, pitching towards the windscreen in order to see better, slamming her foot on the brake.

In the car's headlights Dan made out the words 'Cherry Tree Farm' painted roughly in blue on a chunk of wood fixed to the trunk of a tree. His heart thrashed in his chest. Kate had driven down here less than two days ago, innocently thinking she was meeting a client, and he tried to imagine what she'd been feeling. Excited, probably, at the thought of a new project. Tired, too, after a bad night's sleep. He knew she struggled to get comfortable now she was so big and suffered with heartburn. He wished he'd offered to rub her back, or read to her, like he used to do when they first got together and she couldn't unwind at night, because she was so busy planning her days. She'd been angry with him too, for behaving like a moody teenager that morning.

And how would she be feeling now? What had this woman told her exactly?

'Try not to worry; we're almost there now.' Helen's determined voice scattered his chaotic thoughts and he realised he was staring at nothing. She dimmed the headlights and his reflection in the windscreen unnerved him; he was wild-haired and wide-eyed like a fugitive. 'We could ask at the farm or drive on a bit further and see if we can find the cottage.'

'Let's ask at the farm to be sure.' His voice was stiff, as if he hadn't used it for ages. He felt Helen's querying gaze but couldn't quite look at her. If he was right and she was lying, was Kate safer with the stranger than with her? Did he really know what Helen was capable of?

'OK.' Helen obediently switched off the engine and clambered out of the car, moving swiftly into the shadows. He followed, stumbling on the hard, uneven ground. His legs felt weighted down, like they did in dreams when he was running from an unknown assailant.

'Quick,' Helen urged, picking her way past a pick-up truck and a dusty Jeep parked in front of a sprawling two-storey farmhouse. Smoke curled from its chimney, despite the mildness of the evening, infusing the air with a rich scent of pinewood. One of the outbuildings was ablaze with lights, and classical music drifted from an open window.

Inside the farmhouse, a dog started barking disjointedly.

'Dan?' Helen was at the door, her slender figure cast into shadow by the overhanging porch. 'What are you waiting for?'

She sounded anxious, more like the Helen he knew, and emboldened by the knowledge that she was waiting for him to take charge, he strode to the door and pounded it with his fist.

Chapter 22

The barking in the farmhouse grew louder and the porch light sprang to life. The door opened to reveal a tall man with a thatch of thick fair hair and a beard speckled with grey.

'Get back, Skip,' he ordered the black-and-white collie frantically trying to push between his legs. 'What's the emergency?' he enquired, studying Dan and Helen through wire-rimmed glasses that magnified his eyes. He was in socked feet, a knitted waistcoat straining across his belly. 'Sounded like the hounds of hell were after you.' He was more amused than concerned.

'Sorry about that, sir.' Dan exchanged a glance with Helen. They hadn't planned further than getting here and he wasn't sure how to start. 'We're looking for a property we believe is in this location.' He sounded like a police officer. 'Bluebell Cottage?'

Helen shifted impatiently and he willed her not to blurt anything out. His mind was still slippery with uncertainty, and he wished he'd had the nerve to ask her to wait in the car. Not that he thought she'd have listened.

The dog barked again, making them jump, and the farmer bent to calm it. 'Sorry,' he said, not looking remotely sorry. 'He's just being a good guard dog.'

'That's OK.' Dan attempted to stroke the dog's nose, but it gave a low growl and he straightened, feeling rebuffed.

Helen was frowning, her face flushed. He sensed she'd like to grab the farmer by his collar and demand he tell them where her daughter was.

'Bluebell Cottage.' The man pushed his glasses up the bridge of his nose with a meaty finger, his eyebrows pulling together. 'There's nowhere round here with that name, and I should know. I've lived here long enough.' He turned his head and bellowed, 'Ruth!' Pulling the door wider, he stepped back, throwing out his arm. 'Come on in. My wife might be able to help.'

Helen peered back over her shoulder, as if the last thing she wanted was to step inside, while Dan crossed the threshold with the sense of stepping into another life.

The dog ran off, claws clattering the tiled floor, into the depths of the house where a smell of roast dinners lingered.

Helen joined Dan with obvious reluctance as a short woman, with a cap of white hair and a lively face, emerged from one of the rooms, drying her hands on a tea towel.

'Don't shout like that, Bernard,' she chided her husband, flicking the tea towel at him and rolling her eyes at Dan and Helen, as though it was normal for visitors to turn up unannounced. 'Can I get you both a drink?'

'No, thank you,' he said. Helen remained immobile. 'We're looking for a cottage and wondered if you could point us in the right direction.'

'Bluebell Cottage,' Bernard elaborated, wagging his head back and forth, hands dug deep into the pockets of his baggy trousers. One of his toes was poking through a hole in his sock. 'Ring a bell, Ruth?'

His wife shook her head and looked thoughtful. 'The only other house down here is the Andersons' place, but that's called Little Acorn.'

Dan felt a kick of disappointment. Glancing at Helen, he saw her mouth pinch at the edges.

'Mary could have made the name Bluebell Cottage up to throw us off the scent,' she muttered. In the buttery overhead light, her eyes looked bruised, and her fingers toyed with her bag.

'Bit far-fetched,' he said, aware two sets of eyes were watching their exchange with open curiosity. 'Little Acorn must belong to someone else.'

'It used to,' said Ruth, and they turned to look at her. 'The Andersons put it on the market earlier this year, after he got a job abroad. Not that I knew them that well,' she went on, leaning against a narrow table laden with papers, books, keys and pens. Dan noticed various sizes of wellington boots lining the skirting board, and children's coats hanging among the adult ones. It had the feel of a happy family home. 'They used it mostly as a holiday cottage,' Ruth continued, her bird-like eyes darting between them, as if picking up some tension. 'It's a bit out of the way, so there wasn't much interest and as far as I know it's still empty.'

'It was to let, the last I heard,' said Bernard, scratching the side of his beard. 'But I don't think anyone's living there.'

'Are you sure?' Dan's heart had started thumping. 'My wife . . .' He cleared his throat. 'My wife went to see a client yesterday, and we think it was at that house.'

'You think?' A frown creased Ruth's face.

'She said it was close to a Cherry Tree Farm, and she'd been driving this way from Marlow for about forty minutes.' He seemed to have slipped back into detective mode. 'We're fairly certain it's somewhere around here.'

'How come you don't know for sure?' Ruth folded her freckled arms and cocked her head, eyes suddenly wary.

'It's a long story,' Dan said, rubbing his jaw, not daring to look at Helen. A confused silence fell. 'Anyway, we thought the place was called Bluebell Cottage, but when we looked it up, we couldn't find it,' he pressed on. He was sweating beneath his leather jacket.

'So, what does your wife do?' Ruth seemed to be looking for something in his face.

'She's an interior designer.'

Her eyebrows shot up. 'That place does need some work,' she conceded. 'The Andersons put in a new kitchen, but that was about it. I'm sure potential buyers were put off. They wouldn't want the bother of doing it up.'

'Lovely garden, though,' mused Bernard.

Out of the corner of his eye, Dan saw Helen edging back towards the door. Was she planning to slip away without him?

'Maybe it's a different Cherry Tree Farm and a different house,' suggested Ruth, tracking his face more closely. Maybe she thought he was an abusive husband, stalking his escaped wife.

'I'd know if there was another Cherry Tree Farm,' said Bernard with a bark of laughter, apparently oblivious to any undercurrents. 'And I can tell you there isn't. Not in or around Lexminster, at any rate.'

Dan glanced at Helen. She was still poised for flight, ignoring the dog who'd returned to frisk around her ankles.

'You sound worried about your wife.' His eyes snapped back to Ruth. Hers were narrowed, but with concern or suspicion he couldn't tell. 'Is there a problem?'

'We just need to check this place out and make sure she's OK if she's there,' he said.

'Why wouldn't she be?'

Helen made an unintelligible noise and Ruth's eyes swivelled towards her. 'This is my mother-in-law, Helen,' he said quickly, hoping she wasn't about to break down and start shouting. He wouldn't put anything past her anymore. 'We're a bit worried because my wife is due to give birth in a few weeks and we can't get hold of her.' He paused then added, 'She was meant to come home today, but hasn't.'

The couple's attention sharpened. 'Shouldn't you call the police?' said Ruth, at the same time as Bernard said, 'And you're certain she was visiting a cottage down this lane?' He removed his glasses and put them back on again.

'As certain as we can be,' Dan said. 'We're not sure it's a police matter yet,' he added to Ruth, praying it was true. 'We just need to know she's OK.'

'Dan, we should go.' Helen's voice came at him through gritted teeth. 'We're wasting time. We can find it on our own.'

As he opened his mouth to reply, one of the doors off the hallway opened and a woman came out, a small, curly-haired girl clinging to her like a koala. 'What's going on, Mum?'

Ruth kept her eyes on Helen as if trying to commit her to memory. 'This man's looking for his wife,' she said, and Dan thought how unlikely it sounded, like something from a film. 'He thinks she's staying at Little Acorn.'

'I thought it was empty,' said the woman.

'So did we, but I suppose it might have been let,' acknowledged Bernard. 'It's not like it's right next door. If the tenant wants privacy, they're not likely to introduce themselves.' Swinging into action, he bent to retrieve a pair of well-worn boots from a mat at the foot of the stairs. 'I can lead the way there if you like.'

The woman, a younger replica of her mother, held the child closer, as if worried they might try to abduct her. American voices floated from the room behind her, followed by whooping applause, and Dan recognised *The Big Bang Theory* – one of his and Kate's favourite shows.

'Why don't you ask Tomasz?' the woman said. 'He'll know if someone's moved in.'

'Of course,' said Ruth, her eyes leaving Helen as she turned to look at her daughter. 'Why didn't I think of that?'

As the woman returned to the room and closed the door, Bernard looked up from tying his boot laces. 'I don't know if he's here.'

'Who's Tomasz?' Dan felt light-headed, wished they could hurry up and stop wasting time.

'He's one of our farm labourers, a Polish chap,' said Bernard, gesturing for Ruth to pass him his keys. She picked them from the detritus on the table with practised ease and threw them to him. 'He used to garden for the Andersons to earn some extra cash.'

Dan struggled to see the connection and could tell from Helen's closed expression she was close to breaking point.

'I saw him heading that way yesterday morning.' Bernard undid his waistcoat buttons and tucked his shirt into his trousers. He sounded apologetic. 'I meant to ask where he was going, but his English isn't very good, and I had to get the wheat from the top field in.'

'Does he live here?'

'In one of the outbuildings,' said Ruth. 'We did it up last year. We don't charge rent and we pay him a decent wage,' she continued, as though Dan might think they were taking advantage of immigrants. 'He's supporting his parents and four sisters back in Poland.'

'Is he here, though?' Bernard said. 'He spent last Sunday at his girlfriend's.'

Dan remembered the pick-up outside. 'We heard music when we arrived,' he said.

'Oh yes, he loves a bit of classical.' Ruth's brow lightened. 'He's quite a cultured young man.'

Helen was already through the door, crossing the yard, her bag bouncing off her hip.

Dan followed, Bernard close behind.

'Let me talk to him,' he said to Helen, who was slamming her palm on the door of the wood-and-brick building. Though worried her wild-eyed face would scare the man, Dan was starting to catch her desperation. It seemed as though no one was going to respond. A piano concerto was building to a crescendo, filling the air around them with frenzied notes. Dan doubted whoever was inside would hear someone knocking at the door.

He moved to the nearest window and rapped on the glass. Blood pumped through his veins, intensifying the jagged pain in his shoulder from when Helen had braked sharply. 'Come on,' he muttered.

'This is ridiculous,' said Helen. 'Let's just go.'

Bernard grabbed the door handle and gave it a vigorous rattle. 'Tomasz,' he called in a booming baritone and, finally, the music stopped.

Within seconds the door was wrenched open, and a dark-haired man appeared. He looked to be in his late twenties and was naked from the waist up, faint light from the farmhouse picking out a tattoo on his tightly muscled chest. He seemed astonished to see them, his dark eyes flitting from face to face.

'You OK, Mr Walker?' His accent was strong, the emphasis on 'OK'.

'Sorry to disturb you, Tomasz,' Bernard said, politely. 'We would like to ask you something.'

Tomasz adjusted the waistband of his jeans. 'Sure,' he said, folding his arms, emphasising the bulge of his biceps.

In the room behind him, a blonde-haired woman was curled on a leather sofa, her naked shoulders rising from a blanket, and Dan's mind flashed to Zoe. It felt like weeks since he'd found her frying bacon in his kitchen. How he wished he could wipe the last few days out and start again.

'Who lives down the lane?' Helen burst out, as if she couldn't contain herself, and part of a nursery rhyme popped into Dan's head: *One for the little boy who lives down the lane.*

He thought of Kate, certain she was waiting for him to rescue her. He remembered how he'd let Rosie down, all those years ago, because he'd been playing football instead of looking out for her. She'd almost drowned because of him. He wouldn't let Kate down.

'The house down the lane,' he said loudly when Tomasz didn't reply. 'Who lives there?'

Tomasz screwed his face up and looked at Bernard for clarification. Bernard pointed somewhere over the rooftop, then mimed a digging motion. 'Mrs Anderson,' he said, shaking his head.

Tomasz's face cleared. 'No, no Mrs Anderson,' he agreed. 'New lady.'

Dan's heart jumped so hard it hurt. He looked at Helen, who was staring at Tomasz with the force of a laser beam.

'What is her name?' she said slowly, her head jutting forward.

Tomasz's eyes grew wide. 'Mrs Trent,' he said, with an exaggerated shrug. 'Wait.' He held a finger up. 'Other lady.'

'Other lady?' Dan spoke at the same time as Helen said, 'I knew it.' her voice trembling with barely suppressed emotion.

Tomasz shaped an arc over his stomach and made an agonised face. 'I think baby come.'

'No!' Helen's shout startled them all.

'He might just mean pregnant,' Dan pointed out, but even as he said it, horror rolled over him. 'Shit,' he said, scrabbling for his phone. 'We need to call an ambulance. Or the police.'

'*Policja*?' Tomasz scanned their faces. 'Is problem?'

Helen's hand gripped Dan's sleeve. 'We can't wait.' Her face was moon white. 'We have to go there now.'

'I'll take you both.' Bernard laid a hand briefly on Dan's shoulder. 'We'll be there in less than five minutes.'

He could only nod gratefully and follow the farmer to his Jeep. He jumped in next to Helen, who was already strapping herself into the front seat, seeming barely aware of his presence.

'Can I do anything?' Ruth shouted. She ran across the yard as Bernard revved the engine and reversed, spraying gravel everywhere, her jaw slackening with shock as they roared past her into the lane.

In the wing mirror, Dan saw her run to Tomasz, no doubt to ask what was going on, and hoped she'd have the sense to call for help.

Chapter 23

Kate

Pain squeezes my insides, forcing my eyelids open. I'm back in bed. No duvet this time, just a thin white sheet that I bunch between my fingers as my contraction gathers strength.

I can't pretend it's not happening. I'm in labour.

Sweat beads my forehead as I puff out air. Swallowing a cry of agony, I push a fist to my mouth and bite my knuckles. It feels like my insides are being crushed in a vice. The pain's stronger than earlier and my mind peels back to the injection she gave me in the lane outside.

What has she done?

A whimper escapes. I want Dan. I want to go to hospital. I don't want to be here.

I writhe and grind my teeth. I throw off the sheet then yank it back over my belly. The effort of being quiet makes me nauseous. I wish I could go back to sleep but know I mustn't.

Grasping the edge of the mattress, I heave onto my side, keeping my breathing shallow until the contraction eases.

My hair hangs damply over my eyes. I shove it back and try

to think. My head feels like a sponge. Thoughts become blurred, no beginning, no end.

I stare at the window that's become familiar. Outside, the sky is vast and black. The silence is dense. I've never felt so lonely.

A sob fills my throat. This wasn't how I'd envisaged giving birth.

'Having a baby is a force of nature; it can't be stopped.'

Who had said that? I can't remember but pray it's not true. I can't have my baby here; I can't. I bury my face in the pillow and let out a groan.

Think.

Breathe.

Footsteps on the stairs. My heart trips. No use pretending to be asleep. She'll know.

A strip of light from the doorway lands on my face. Magda comes over and snaps on the lamp by the bed, looking at me as though I'm an animal she's run over. She lays towels on the bed, disappears, and returns seconds later with a bowl of steaming water.

As though hypnotised, I watch her wring out a pale-pink flannel. She smooths it over my sweat-glazed face, making clicking noises with her tongue. My mind clutches blindly for something to say, but I start to cry instead, tears sliding into my ears.

'There, there,' she soothes. Her palm is cool on my cheek, but when I raise my eyes, her gaze slides off me.

She drops the flannel in the bowl, twitches aside the sheet and rolls her sleeves up.

'What are you doing?' My voice is too small, and she doesn't reply. Her face has a boiled look, pink and shiny. She's humming a lullaby: 'Rock-a-bye Baby'.

Pain circles and spreads, stealing my breath. I turn my head and grit my teeth. I won't give her the satisfaction of seeing how much it hurts.

'Won't be long now,' she says, in a sing-song voice that ripples my flesh into goosebumps. 'I'm going to help you through it, sweetheart. Just try to relax.'

I stare at the landing through the bedroom door and imagine charging downstairs into the night and running all the way home.

The pain recedes. I try to push upright, but my arms are feeble, and the weight of my belly keeps me pinned to the bed. 'I need to go to hospital.'

'Of course you don't.' Her eyes warm up. She looks at me with affection as she slips her hands into a pair of latex gloves. 'It's a perfectly natural process,' she says. 'You'll be fine.'

'What if something goes wrong?'

'Hush now, lovely. Nothing will go wrong.'

She moves her hands to my knees and eases them apart. There's a blast of cool air and my mind empties until only one question remains: *How can this woman possibly be my mother?*

Mum would know I needed Dan to be with me when the baby comes. She wouldn't behave like this in a million years. I know she's longed to control me at times, but in the end, she's only ever wanted what's best for me. She didn't even ask if she could be at the birth, though I know she was dying to – she waited for me to invite her.

'What the hell are you doing?' I snap my legs together so that Magda's hands fall away.

'Just checking to see if your waters have broken.' Her tone is that of a midwife now, calm and reassuring.

'They haven't.' Hope surges. The birth could still be hours away and my contractions aren't coming any quicker.

'It doesn't always happen when labour's induced.' After removing a glove and feeling around the bed beneath me, Magda flicks the sheet back over my belly. 'I was going to break them for you, but we can wait a little longer for nature to take its course.'

For a moment I wonder if the sedatives she's plied me with are still playing havoc with my mind. 'Induced?'

'Something I've been slipping into your drinks and food,' she says, as if it's something we'd discussed. 'It's herbal, so it's perfectly safe; don't worry.'

I feel like she's slapped me again. 'You can't possibly know that.' My voice is a panicked squeak. 'My baby's due soon; it doesn't need inducing.' Fear clogs my lungs, shortening my breath. 'For God's sake, Magda.' I press my palms against my leaking eyes. 'How could you do this?'

She tugs my hands away and brings her face so close to mine I see flecks of black in her irises. 'Don't you think I've waited long enough?' Her smile is tinged with sadness. 'Please try to understand,' she says, stroking my burning cheek. 'And try to keep calm, sweetheart. I don't want to have to put you to sleep again.'

Sedatives *and* herbal medication? I start to cry, wheezy, frightened sobs. What has she done to me? To *us*?

'We need you to be alert to push her out.'

Her? I screw my head away from her touch, seeking a means of escape, but even if there was one, my body won't cooperate. I'm completely at Magda's mercy. 'Was this your plan all along?' I manage, feeling faint with shock. 'To put me in labour?'

'I wanted to maximise our chances of being a proper family,' she says, the bed creaking as she rises. 'If you go to hospital and speak to Jane' – it takes me a second to realise she's talking about Mum – 'it won't happen, you mark my words. She'll talk you out of seeing me again.'

'She won't, I promise.' My voice is climbing towards hysteria. 'I'll explain everything; she'll understand. We can talk it through and—'

'She's good at talking,' Magda cuts in, wringing the flannel out in the bowl of water, her expression setting like cement. 'I won't take that risk again.'

'You know this isn't right.' I grab her arm, digging my fingers in. I want to hurt her. 'You don't have the right to induce or deliver my baby.' Saying it aloud makes it real and brings a wave of sickness. 'When my family finds out, they won't want you in our lives.' She shakes my fingers off and wrings the flannel out again, water beading on the bedside table. 'It's not too late, Magda,' I continue, desperate to get through to her. 'If you call for help now, I'll say I went into labour unexpectedly. I won't tell them what you've done.'

With a plunge of despair, I realise she's tuned me out. She's humming a low continuous note like someone mediating, staring at a patch of wall with a blank expression.

Panic swirls through me. What if she won't let me go? Maybe she intends to keep me and the baby locked up here with her. I think of the nursery she's prepared, and imagine the cupboards and freezer stocked with food. We could be here for months, without anyone knowing where to find us.

Another thought blows in like an icy breeze. *What if the baby's the only thing she wants and I'm dispensable?*

Before I can process this, another contraction sweeps through me. An involuntary howl of pain escapes and Magda snaps back to attention.

'Breathe through it,' she says, taking my hand, blowing sharp breaths out, head bobbing, and for a crazy second, I wonder if I've hallucinated that she'd slapped me, sedated me, and brought about my labour. She's exuding such matronly warmth it seems impossible. Then I remember the look on her face when she hit me, and I know it's true. She's so scared of losing me, her reasoning's skewed. She's doing whatever she thinks she has to.

Because she wants the baby. This time the voice won't leave. It grows in volume as my contraction eases, until the words pulse in my ears. *She wants the baby, not you.*

Something she said earlier filters back, and as soon as I feel able, I take a couple of deep breaths before speaking. 'Magda, could I please have a bath?'

She'd been looking at me with something like pride as we rode my contraction together and it takes her a moment to refocus.

'I'm sorry?'

'It hurts so much,' I say, truthfully. I'd planned on not using any pain relief in hospital and realise how naive I've been. It hurts like hell.

'I'm afraid being induced can extend labour and make the pain more intense.' Magda gives me an apologetic grimace that makes me want to scream, *You did this to me!* But I realise I'm afraid of her reaction. Her hair's fallen loose around her face, and in the lamplight the whites of her eyes look bloodshot. It's as if she's starting to unravel, and it's easier to believe she might not have my best interests at heart after all. 'Your contractions are further apart than I'd like,' she says, glancing at her wristwatch, a frown crossing her forehead. 'Maybe a hot bath would help.'

I think of the key in the bathroom door and a blast of optimism clears the debris in my brain. I probably have less than ten minutes before my next contraction. Enough time to follow Magda to the bathroom and lock her in.

'I'm not sure there'll be any hot water left,' she says, edging slowly towards the door. 'I'll have to go and check.'

As she leaves, I hoist myself into a sitting position and swing my legs over the side of the bed. Nausea rises as the room tilts and sways, but I bite my lip and force myself to stay upright until it settles.

'The tank's still warm,' Magda says seconds later, eyes widening when she sees I'm sitting up. She holds a hand out as if to restrain me. 'You stay there while I run the bath.'

Calmer now that I have a plan, I muster a feeble smile. 'You're being so kind,' I say. 'I appreciate you looking after me like this.'

Her smile falters as confusion flickers over her face. For a second, I think she's going to ask me who I am and what I'm doing here, then whatever she's thinking fades from her eyes, and she turns into Magda again.

'Why wouldn't I look after you, you silly goose?' Her eyes crinkle into a smile. 'Now, lie back down and I'll come and get you when your bath is ready.'

'It feels better sitting up,' I tell her, feeling a spark of pain deep in my belly. *Stay put, baby*, I plead. *You can't come out just yet.*

Magda hesitates, so I clumsily drop back on my elbows, resisting the urge to tug my dress down over the orb of my belly. *Go*, I urge her. *Just go*. 'I think there's another on its way,' I say weakly, praying there isn't.

'Just breathe, like we did before.' Magda pats the air in front of her and blows a breath out to demonstrate. 'I'll be right back.'

I track the soft pad of her footsteps across the landing and wait for the clank and groan of the pipes when she turns the bath taps on. 'I'll bring the radio upstairs,' she calls out, sounding almost happy. 'There's a Mozart concert on I think you'll like. He's Patrick's favourite composer.'

Patrick. I suddenly wish I'd insisted Magda call him. I want to talk to him. I've so many things I'd like to ask Patrick about her, about everything. Would he really have stayed with her if Mum hadn't taken me away? Maybe he could talk her out of her crazy plan to deliver my baby and care for it as though it was hers.

Feeling myself start to drift off, I bolt upright in a panic. Magda has to stay in the bathroom. 'No music. I'd . . . I'd rather just talk to you,' I improvise, and jump when her head pokes round the door.

'Lie down,' she says, wagging a finger. 'I'll help you through in a moment.'

I've no choice but to do as she says. However, as soon as she withdraws, I roll awkwardly out of bed, onto all fours, feeling a jolt in my spine. *Sorry, baby.*

I'm becoming familiar with the pattern of contractions and sense another one coming. I hesitate, breathing fast, stifling a frantic sob. Blowing air out in little gasps, I cross the floor on my hands and knees, entering the landing. Focusing what little energy I have, I shuffle over to the bathroom, where steam is billowing underneath the door. There's a swish and splash, as though Magda's running her hand through the bath water. I recognise the scent of lily of the valley, which used to be my great-aunt's favourite. Magda's clearly pushing the boat out, creating some kind of fantasy birthing area and, for a second, I imagine the pleasure of sinking into a bubble bath and giving myself over to my labour – of letting nature take its course. Magda won't let anything happen. She's obviously desperate for me to have this baby.

I think of Dan and Mum, their horror when they find out I've given birth without their knowledge, and tears leap to my eyes. Dan wouldn't want this for me, and neither do I.

I grab the struts of the banister and pull myself up, pausing a second to swallow a sobbing groan that's threatening to erupt. It's been less than ten minutes since my last contraction. They're coming closer together.

Magda's singing pauses and the taps go off with a clunk of pipework.

Shooting a hand out to the wall to steady myself, I push my way to the half-open door, feeling on the verge of collapse. The pain is cresting, burning like the hottest fire, but I keep my eyes fixed on the little brass key sticking out of the lock.

As I reach the door, it starts to open and my hand flies to the latch. With the element of surprise on my side, Magda lets go and the door slams shut in her face.

'Lexi?' The latch wiggles as Magda tries to open it. 'What are you doing?'

The weight of my belly is dragging me down, the pain relentless. I drop into an ungainly crouch, panting wildly now. My arms strain at the sockets, but I don't let go of the doorknob.

'Kate?' Magda's voice sharpens into anger. 'Let me out of here now.'

She pulls the door hard, and it opens an inch, but desperation gives me strength. I yank it back, pain jarring through me. My fingers fumble with the key and I manage to turn it. For a second, it meets resistance and, sobbing, I give the door a final tug and the lock slides into place. *Thank you, God.*

I let go and fall back, gasping air into my lungs. My face is damp with sweat and tears and my palms are slippery. My elbow throbs where I bashed it on the floor.

'Please unlock the door, Kate,' Magda pleads, her voice low and desperate. 'You really don't want to do this.'

Oh, but I do.

The frame trembles as she pulls at the door, then bashes it with her fists. 'I'm trying to help you, you silly girl,' she cries. 'Think of the baby.'

I am. I need to find the phone and call for help.

My contraction has faded, but I know the next one won't be long. Teeth chattering, I half-crawl to Magda's room as the banging and shouting from the bathroom grows louder. Another cracking noise splits the air, more splintering wood, but I daren't look round. The cottage is old and I've no idea if the lock on the bathroom door will hold.

I reach Magda's bedroom and scramble crab-like across the floor to where I left the mobile, but as soon as I get there, I know she's beaten me to it.

The phone has gone.

Chapter 24

Dan

The Jeep jolted over potholes as the road narrowed to a dirt track, its headlights picking out darting insects. Above, a tunnel of branches blocked out most of the sky.

Dan searched the darkness either side for a break in the foliage, as if he knew better than Bernard where they were going. Beside him, Helen's eyes roamed the blackness.

'Where is it?' she demanded when they'd been driving for about two minutes.

'Not far,' Bernard said calmly, his gaze intent on the road. 'Can I ask what's going on?'

'My daughter needs help.' Helen's voice was taut. 'That's all you need to know.'

Dan felt compelled to elaborate, to break the unbearable tension more than anything. 'We think this woman had an ulterior motive for contacting my wife,' he said, emotion squeezing his throat. *Please let them be OK.* The thought of anyone wanting to harm Kate or the baby – *his* baby – was unbearable. Why hadn't he checked Kate had her phone with her? He should have run after her instead of watching her drive away. 'If my wife's about to give birth, she should be in hospital, not stuck out here.'

The Jeep hit a bump and he bashed his head on the roof.

'Sorry,' said Bernard, grinding the gears and slowing down. 'We haven't had any rain for so long the ground's rock hard.'

Dan was relieved when he didn't ask them anything else and tried to quash thoughts of Kate, crumpled at the bottom of a staircase, or being held hostage, tied up with a knife to her throat.

Was Helen right? Did Mary want the baby as some sort of payback?

He recalled her voice on the phone, calm and reassuring, telling him Kate was fine, but there'd been that undercurrent of disapproval – a sense of feelings being restrained. He'd thought they were directed at him, based on what Kate had said about their marriage. He couldn't – didn't want to – believe this woman meant to hurt Kate, whatever Helen had told him.

A twitchy silence prevailed, until Bernard brought the car to a juddering halt. 'This is it,' he said, though Dan could see no signs of life. Bernard switched the engine off and leaned over to retrieve a torch from the glove compartment. 'Come on then.'

Dan and Helen got out and stood uncertainly, like visitors to another planet. The air was thick with the smell of leaves and lavender. An owl hooted somewhere, and wildlife rustled in the undergrowth. It was hard to imagine anyone living out here.

It was exactly the sort of place someone might choose to hide.

Helen darted around the car, silhouetted briefly in the headlights. Dan followed on legs that felt hollow, blood pulsing thickly in his throat.

'See?' Bernard was parting a thatch of tangled ivy to reveal a wooden plaque fastened to a gate post. The pencil beam of his torchlight picked out the words 'Little Acorn' in black letters. 'Tomasz needs to cut this back,' he said, pulling the leaves away. 'Nobody would guess it was here.'

Beside the fence post was an opening where a gate had once

been and Dan walked through it onto a gravelled area. There was the cottage, etched against the sky, several of its windows lit up. He scoured the drive for Kate's Nissan, but there was only one car parked there and it wasn't hers.

He heard Helen's intake of breath and guessed she'd noticed too. She rounded on Bernard like a snake, hissing though gritted teeth. 'What if it's the wrong place?'

'There's nowhere else,' said Bernard mildly, swinging the torch around. 'It's either here, or you've got the wrong address.'

'Maybe Kate's already left,' Dan said, but his palms prickled with sweat. Something wasn't right.

'Or' – Bernard swung the beam in the direction of the cottage – 'her car's in the garage.'

'Why would it be in there?' Unexpectedly, Helen began crying. 'What do we do now?' she said through gulping sobs, tears racing down her face.

Dan met Bernard's gaze and shrugged his helplessness. 'Let's go and knock,' he said. He moved to the door, feeling as if the darkness was chasing him, biting at his heels. Raising the brass knocker, he rapped the door several times, Helen beside him in the porch, her arms hugging her waist.

'Try opening it,' she said, even as Dan was twisting the handle and pushing his shoulder to the door.

'It's locked,' he said, though he'd known it would be. Pressing his ear against the wood, he thought he caught a trace of music from inside.

'Someone's definitely there.' Heart beating faster, he knocked loudly, then stepped back and cupped his hands round his mouth. 'Is there anybody there?' he shouted. 'Hello?'

Dan caught a glitter of intent in Helen's eyes as she opened her mouth.

'No,' he said sharply. 'If she knows it's you, she might—' he stopped abruptly. He didn't want to think about what might happen. 'Magda!' he yelled instead. 'I just want to talk to you.'

Nothing.

'I'll go back and call for an ambulance from the landline,' said Bernard. 'We don't get much mobile signal out here.' Dan turned to see him retracing his steps to the lane.

'Thanks,' Dan called, wondering if Bernard was starting to suspect something was amiss. Maybe he'd call the police too. Dan hoped so. He wondered whether Saskia had. He'd lost all sense of time but was sure they'd been gone longer than an hour.

As Bernard was swallowed by the darkness, Helen darted over to one of the windows and peered through it. 'There are two mugs in there,' she said, urgently. 'Maybe Kate is here, Dan.'

Joining her, he saw a wooden tea tray on bare floorboards, and in front of the sofa were two abandoned mugs. He pressed his fist to the glass and rested his forehead on it. *Kate*, he urged, conjuring her face. *Please let me know you're OK*.

'We have to get inside.' Helen gripped the sleeve of his jacket. Letting go, she ran back to the door and pounded it with her fists. 'Mary, I know you're in there!'

Following, Dan caught her by the shoulders. 'For Christ's sake, Helen.' He felt an urge to shake her. 'You said yourself she's unhinged. Knowing you're here might push her over the edge.'

Helen wrenched out of his grasp. 'She's already over the edge, Dan.' Her eyes grew hard. 'She wants Kate's baby. *Your* baby.' She jabbed him hard with her finger. 'My *grandchild*,' she said, slapping her hand to her chest. 'We have to get in there right *now*.'

Seeing the fearless determination in her face, a thought struck Dan with diamond-bright clarity. He wanted to be the kind of parent Helen was, the sort who would do anything for her child.

Turning, he lifted his leg and karate-kicked the door. It didn't budge. He took a run and hurled himself at it with the full weight of his shoulder, reeling back as white-hot pain shot through him. 'It's not going to break.' He looked for a letterbox to shout through, but there wasn't one.

He cupped his hands round his mouth and bellowed, 'Kate!'

'Mary, I know you're in there!' Helen cried.

'Let me talk to my wife!' Dan couldn't seem to make his voice loud enough. He wasn't used to shouting. 'Kate, can you hear me?'

They waited. Dan pressed his ear to the door jamb, trying to breathe. A noise reached him – like a quickly stifled scream. 'Did you hear that?' he said.

Helen nodded, her eyes fixed to the door as if trying to burn through the wood. 'She must be in labour,' she said, her mouth wobbling around the words. 'She needs us, Dan.'

Chapter 25

Kate

Magda is out of the bathroom. 'Why did you lock me in?' Her voice is plaintive, as if she can't comprehend why I'm not cooperating. 'You shouldn't have done that, Kate. I was trying to help you.' She flicks on the light and comes round the bed, stepping over the suitcase, which has been zipped shut. I'm hunched over on the floor, panting through my contraction. 'What were you doing?' she says.

Somehow, I scrape some words past the dryness in my throat. 'Looking for the phone.'

She pulls it out of her pocket and looks at it, as if puzzled to find it there. 'What for?'

'I was going to call for an ambulance.'

She shoves it back and crouches in front of me, hugging her knees, and I think of an animal waiting to pounce. 'I've already told you we don't need one.' Her face is tightly clenched. 'Don't you trust me to look after you?'

'Of course, but . . .' I try to swallow. 'I don't want to do this here,' I say, tears flooding my eyes. 'I need Dan.'

'*Need* him?' She gives a grunt of disdain. 'I needed someone too once.' Her eyes become unfocused, as if she's looking at something else. 'He let me down, the bastard.'

Confusion swirls. 'Patrick?'

Her gaze clears. 'Of course not.' She lays a hand on my leg, butterfly light, and I try not to flinch away. 'My father,' she says briskly, standing up with a grimace. 'He wanted me to get rid of you.'

Not another one. I have a crazy urge to laugh. Did anyone actually want me, apart from Mum?

Magda holds her hands out and waggles them. 'Come on,' she says, her face relaxing. 'Let's get you back to bed, missy.'

Her moods are like quicksilver, and I curse myself for not noticing something wasn't right from the start. Mum must have seen it. That's why she took me, changed her name and never went back to Leeds.

But maybe Magda wouldn't be this desperate if she'd had a chance to raise me herself. If Patrick had joined us, and we'd been a proper family.

But even as I wonder how I'm going to face Mum, I long for her anxious presence. She'd find a way to get me out of here. She'd whisk me to hospital in her car, stay with me through the birth, and wouldn't let anything bad happen ever again.

'Come on.' Magda's hands are still waggling, but I'm pinned to the floor as another convulsion takes hold.

'I can't,' I manage, my voice stripped bare, wondering how long this is going to go on for. I've heard of women being in labour for days. *Please God, don't let me be one of them.* I don't want to have my baby here, but as long as I'm having contractions, I'm incapable of anything else. *Reason with her*, pipes a little voice. 'Magda,' I say, when the worst of the pain has subsided. 'You can come to the hospital with me. We don't even have to call Dan, or anyone else if you don't want to. I'd just rather be somewhere safe.'

Her face hardens and I realise my mistake. 'You're safe here.'

'What I mean is, they'll have all the right equipment at the hospital if anything goes wrong,' I say quickly. 'My blood pressure could drop, or shoot up, and the baby could get distressed.' I've been warned this could happen but haven't considered it might become a reality – that I'd be stuck somewhere with no means of help or escape. 'You'd feel awful if anything happened,' I try, more tears gathering in the corners of my eyes. The thought of my baby struggling into the world makes me want to scream. After monitoring his every kick, jab, roll and hiccup for the past eight months, after singing to him, talking to him, eating foods to nourish him, how can I let him down now? He's relying on me. I have to keep him safe, yet I've never felt more powerless. 'Magda, *please*,' I say on a sob.

'You're not giving me any credit, are you?' she says, unmoved. 'Do you think I haven't done this before? I used to be a midwife in a hospital.'

'Even if you were,' I say, 'you're hardly equipped for an emergency.'

'Nothing's going to go wrong; I won't let it.' She speaks more gently this time. It sounds like a promise, and I badly want to believe her, but knowing the lengths she's gone to already, how can I?

'Things happen,' I persist, levering myself off the floor by walking my hands up the wall behind me. My thighs protest and sparks of pain shoot round my belly, but I need to stand up and show her I'm not helpless, that she can't keep manipulating me. 'Please, Magda, let me have the phone.'

She heaves a great sigh and shakes her head, the movement causing more strands of hair to float free from their moorings. 'I didn't expect this,' she says and there's hurt in her eyes. 'Jane's had you all these years. I want to be with you for this one event and you're complaining.'

'I'm not complaining,' I say, sagging back against the wall, my thoughts a mushy stew. 'You *can* be with me. Just not here.'

She straightens suddenly, as if making her mind up about something. For a second, I think she's seen sense and is going to call for help, but instead she crosses to the desk, takes out a bottle and rattles it. 'I think half of one, to settle you down a bit,' she says, almost to herself, twisting the top off and shaking some pills into her hand.

'Magda, no!' A bubble of dread fills my throat. 'You can't keep sedating me; it's bad for the baby.'

'It won't do any harm at this stage.' She turns to smile at me, but the smile doesn't reach her eyes, and in the hard gleam of the bedroom light her irises look black. 'You could be in labour for quite a while yet.'

I start to edge towards the door, a taste of acid in my mouth.

'Now where are you going?' She sounds amused and I want to run at her and knock her to the floor, but she's got my arm in her grasp now, tugging me towards the bed. 'Come and lie down.'

'No!' I wrench free and grip the metal frame, head bowed, trying not to be sick.

'Stop fighting me,' she says in a reasonable voice. 'It's all going to be fine.' She seems so certain, but how can she be?

'What are you planning afterwards?' I turn my head to look at her. She's snapped one of the pills in half and is holding it out on her palm. 'What exactly do you think is going to happen once the baby's born?'

'We've talked enough,' she says. 'Now, take this, it'll make you feel better.'

'I don't want it.' I lash out and knock the pill from her hand. It skitters across the floor and Magda grabs hold of my wrist.

'Lie down,' she orders. When I stay still, she grips my upper arms and manoeuvres me around the side of the bed, like a bulky piece of furniture, and pushes me down. As I fall in an ungainly heap, she lifts my legs and swings them up onto the lumpy mattress.

I kick out at her, but the movement wrenches my belly and

I gasp in pain.

Shaking her head, she retrieves the other half of the pill and pushes it against my lips. I try to twist away, but she pinches my nose with her fingers, and I have no choice but to open my mouth and swallow. The pill's hard and dry and I start to choke. Magda darts out and returns with a cup of water. I gulp at it, eyes streaming, feeling a scratch in my throat as it goes down.

My belly's throbbing again, the beat expanding, and pain leaches through me. 'Oh God,' I moan, falling back onto the pillow.

'Let me put something under you, just in case,' says Magda, all smiles and business now she has me where she wants me again. She bustles out and back and somehow eases a towel underneath me, the rough feel of the fabric quickly eclipsed by the strength of my contraction. 'I should check to see how dilated you are,' she adds, giving me a critical look.

'No!' I don't want her anywhere near my private parts. I don't want her near me, full stop. I manage to wriggle across the bed, sweat breaking out on my face.

'You really are being incredibly difficult,' she snaps, her composure slipping. She's not using my name anymore. She's not calling me Lexi, either. And the way she's looking at me . . . it's as if she's distanced herself and I'm just the vessel for what she really wants. What she's really wanted all along.

As the contraction loses its grip, I wait for fuzziness to creep around the edges of my mind as the pill takes hold. Will it slow my contractions – affect my baby?

I imagine him emerging, fast asleep, his tiny thumb pushed inside his mouth. What if he's not sleeping? What if he's—

Cutting off the thought, I jab the back of my throat with my fingers and bring up a trail of foamy liquid. Seeing the partly dissolved pill, I feel weak with relief.

'You devious little bitch.' As Magda leans over me, a burning hatred spreads across my chest. Clenching my hand, I swing my arm in an arc, catching her jaw with my fist.

Caught unawares, she reels back from the bed, clutching the side of her face, her eyes wide with shock. *Good*, I think. *See how you like it.*

She stares for a second, then gives a sad, vague smile. Her gaze turns inwards, as if she's playing out a scenario in her head, and my burst of anger evaporates in a woolly haze. I'm wondering if she's planning her next move, and how I can stop it, when I hear someone shouting.

'Kate!'

It sounds like Dan, but it can't be. Magda doesn't even flinch.

Another shout: a woman this time, who sounds a lot like Mum, but Magda's still fixed on whatever scene is playing out in her mind, her mouth tilted in a weird smile, and I wonder if I've absorbed some of the pill and it's playing tricks with my mind.

A nightmarish throb begins in my belly, and I slump back down, wishing with all my heart Mum or Dan really were here, that they've found out where I am and have come to rescue me. I've always been good at taking care of myself, but this is beyond anything I've ever imagined.

I need help.

Chapter 26

Dan

Fury had erupted inside Dan. If Kate was having the baby, he had to be with her. 'Are any of the windows open?' he said to Helen.

They ran around the property, looking for a point of entry. Dan tugged at a couple of the sashes, but they were either painted shut or locked. At the back of the cottage were two patio doors, leading off one of the rooms, but they were locked too.

Spotting a wooden bench, he lifted it, arm sockets wrenching, and lobbed it at the door. The sound of shattering glass cut the air like a thousand alarm bells.

'You could have tried climbing up there,' hissed Helen behind him, pointing to a half-open window on the second floor.

'Bit late for that,' he snapped, glancing at the densely cladded wall. 'And I'm not a bloody gymnast.'

She followed him inside, their feet crunching and cracking the glittering shrapnel on the floor.

'If Mary comes to investigate,' Helen said in a whisper, 'I'll keep her talking while you go and find Kate.'

He knew it went against all her maternal instincts, that she was longing to rip through the house to wherever her daughter was, but she knew Mary. Or at least, she had. Maybe she'd be able to find the words to get through to the woman.

Dan groped the wall for a light switch and flooded the room with brightness. 'Hello?' he called, but his voice didn't seem to go anywhere, trapped between the walls and ceiling. The fact there was no response, after the awful noise they'd created, frightened him more than anything. The car outside was probably Magda's, and lights were on upstairs. Soft piano music was coming from another room and a perfumed scent lingered in the air. She was obviously here, so why was she ignoring them?

'Do you think she's hiding?' Helen's voice quivered with emotion. 'Hoping we'll give up and go.'

'Magda?' he shouted, moving down the shadowed hallway, which was lit by a shaft of light from another room. It looked badly in need of redecoration and for a crazy second he thought they'd got it wrong, that Kate had been invited for no other reason than to quote for a redesign and was now on her way home, and they'd broken into an innocent woman's house. A woman who was probably hiding, terrified for her life.

Even so, he kept moving stealthily forward.

The kitchen was empty, apart from a tortoiseshell cat curled up asleep on a rug in front of an empty grate. Music drifted from a transistor radio on the worktop. Helen moved past him and picked up a folder, shaking out the contents. 'This is her, holding Kate,' she said, showing him a photo with a trembling hand. Her skin was the colour of porridge. 'I can't believe she's kept it all this time.'

He tried to look at it but was distracted by a tote bag on the floor with a laptop poking out. 'That's Kate's bag,' he said slowly, feeling as if he'd stepped through a wormhole into a parallel universe. 'She wouldn't have left here without it.'

'Or those.' Helen was staring at a point behind him, and he turned to see Kate's sample books stacked neatly on a table by a fruit bowl.

'Shit.' Within seconds he was climbing the stairs, grabbing at the banister as his legs threatened to give way beneath him, Helen right behind.

The perfumed scent was stronger on the landing, steam drifting from a splintered doorway. He rushed inside, but although the bath was full of bubbly water, the room was empty, a folded towel lying on the toilet lid.

'It looks like someone was locked in here.' Helen pointed to the cracked wood around the broken lock, her eyes wide with horror. She crossed the landing, pushing at one of the other doors. 'Look at this,' she said, beckoning Dan.

He joined her, and they stared wordlessly at a perfectly decorated nursery. The sort of nursery he'd seen Kate poring over in magazines and online when she was planning theirs.

'I knew it,' Helen said flatly, as if all her emotions had been temporarily used up. 'She wants that baby.' Her words froze him. She turned away, as though she couldn't bear to look at the room a second longer. 'Mary, it's Jane,' she called, her face set. 'Come out and talk to me.'

For a second Dan thought she'd lost the plot. She was calling herself Jane.

'Kate!' he called, heart beating so forcefully he thought it might crack his ribcage. He wrenched open another door, but it was only an airing cupboard.

'Must be in that one,' Helen said, nodding at the room opposite. Her hair stood up in tufts and her eyes were wild and red-rimmed.

Dan approached the door just as a sound emerged: a moan that rose in pitch – a noise that couldn't be stopped, like an animal being tortured. A sound that closed his airways.

'That's her, that's Katie,' cried Helen, throwing herself at the door.

They both pushed and shoved at it, rattling the handle and calling out, until it became obvious they weren't going to be allowed in.

A throttled silence fell, then a hoarse voice emerged.

'Dan?'

'Kate!' His heart seized.

A sob wrenched out of Helen. 'Katie.'

'Dan, I—' Kate's voice was cut off and there was a sound like a scuffle, followed by a muffled groan.

'No, no, no, *no*!' Helen's words echoed Dan's own, her eyes screwed shut as her fist pounded the door. 'Please don't hurt her, Mary, I'll do anything.'

'We're going to get you out of there, Kate, hang on,' Dan yelled, trying to sound reassuring despite the bright white fear burning through him. 'Just hang on, babe, it's going to be all right.' He sometimes called her babe in an ironic way, knowing it made her smile. *When had he last made her smile?* 'I love you, Kate.' His voice caught. 'Just hang in there.'

He motioned for Helen to step back, preparing to break the lock. It was doable, judging by the state of the bathroom door.

'Hurry up,' Helen urged, her face twisted with fear, but before either of them could move there was the scrape of a key turning on the other side. The door opened a fraction and a slice of someone became visible in the gap.

'You're not taking her.' Dan recognised the voice as the one he'd spoken to on the phone. 'She's mine now.'

He shoved the door, but the woman behind it was strong.

'Don't try that again, or I'll hurt her,' she said, her words sending a sliver of ice down Dan's spine. She lifted a hand and he saw she was holding a knife.

'Please talk to me, Mary,' said Helen, and a distant part of Dan was impressed that her voice was calm and clear, even though her whole body was shaking.

'I'm not Mary anymore. And you're not Jane.'

'That's right, I'm not,' said Helen. She flashed Dan a look that urged him not to move, but every instinct was propelling him towards the room. He wished he could develop superpowers, step right through the wood and fly off into the night, Kate safe in his arms.

He forced himself to wait.

Chapter 27

Kate

When the terrible sound of shattering glass breaks the silence, I know I'm not imagining things. Someone is in the cottage.

Magda jerks into life. She creeps to the bed, her face white apart from the livid patch where I struck her.

'They're here,' she mutters, eyes darting madly. 'Jane's here.'

So, it *was* Mum I'd heard shouting. I start to shiver, great shudders convulsing my body. Maybe she shouldn't have come. What if her being here makes everything worse?

'Dan.' My voice is croaky and dehydrated and doesn't penetrate the walls, but Magda hears.

'What do you want him for?' She bends over me, fists pressing the mattress either side of my shoulders. Her eyes are pits of blackness and spit has gathered at the corners of her mouth. 'Men are useless creatures,' she says, grinding the words out. 'You don't need him; he'll let you down. I won't.'

'Patrick,' I manage. 'You still want him.'

'That's different.' She straightens and prowls the room, her knuckles pressed to her teeth. 'Once we're with him, everything will be different; you'll see.'

'After all these years?' It hits me how unbelievable it is, that she could simply reconnect with a man who walked out on her thirty years ago.

'This time, I'll have you and the baby,' she says, and I'm shaken again by how accurately she appears to be able to read my thoughts. 'We have a connection, you and I, don't we?' She drops to her knees by the bed, her face level with mine. 'I know you feel it, Lexi.' She strokes her fingertip down the side of my face and I fight the urge to recoil.

'My name's Kate.' It seems important I keep saying it; as if not correcting her, I might accidentally become someone else. I lift my head off the pillow. 'I'm Kate, and for better or worse I'm married to Dan, and I have a mother who loves me, no matter what happened in the past, and they're here and you have to talk to them.'

Spent, I drop my head.

'They're not getting in this room.' Magda's voice is shot through with defiance. 'Just let them try.'

'Please,' I say, on a sob. 'This is wrong, Magda.'

There's more noise. People moving downstairs.

I try to sit up again, but it's like pushing through concrete. 'Mum?' Again, my voice barely makes an impression on the air.

Magda pushes me down and presses a finger to my lips. I wrench them apart and bite her and she snatches her hand away. 'You little bitch,' she snaps, eyes sparking with anger.

'You wouldn't speak to me like that if you were my mother.'

'You bit me.' She grasps the offending finger with her other hand and her voice grows wheedling. 'I don't know why you're being so difficult when I've tried so hard, when I all I want is to spend time with my daughter, alone.'

She turns to the chest of drawers and pulls out some tights. 'I'm sorry to do this, Kate, but it's better if you don't try to fight me.'

I wriggle as she twists my arms up and ties my wrists to the bedstead.

'Am I supposed to feel guilty?' I say on a sob. It's as if she's forgotten the lengths she's gone to, or she thinks that her behaviour is acceptable. 'There's no way back from this, Magda, if you don't open that door.'

Another contraction grips me, faster and harder than the last one. I hear a terrible keening sound and realise it's coming from me. Raising my head, I wince as the nylon digs into my wrists. I feel a sharp pinch inside me, like something tearing, and wetness gushes between my legs. I peer down to see a spreading stain on the towel, darkening the whiteness to grey.

'Your waters have broken.'

Magda sounds amazed and pleased, as if she'd suspected it would never happen and I wish I could stop it, force it back, because it means I'm closer to giving birth and there's nothing I can do to prevent it.

My head falls as Magda crosses to the door. I hear the sound of a key turning in the lock, then she returns. 'You need to keep quiet,' she urges in a whisper. 'They'll soon go away if they think no one's here.'

I try to reply, but my words seem to melt before they leave my mouth. I grope for something to say. Maybe if I'm nice to her . . . I need to tell her she must let Dan in, that he'll understand and won't blame her, if he can just see his baby come into the world.

Pain drags me under like a tidal wave and I quickly lose focus. It's a different pain, lower down, bringing an urge to push.

'Keep panting,' says Magda, her breath tickling my ear, and I feel her hand on my cheek. Has she forgotten we're no longer alone in the cottage? 'Just hang on a little longer, sweetheart. She'll be here soon, and then I'll be gone, and you'll never see me again.'

Her words reach me through a blanket of pain, but don't make sense. I try to ask what she means, but only a tortured moan comes out.

'Magda . . .'

'Hush!' She turns, her expression dark with fury, all tenderness gone again. 'Don't make a sound,' she snaps, and I see a glint as she pulls something from the pocket of her dress. A knife.

Terror slips through me. I want to tell her it doesn't have to be like this, but I can't summon the energy and anyway there's no point. She's gone beyond listening to anything I might say. I strain for signs of movement outside the door and start to wonder whether this is all part of the same weird dream – if I am, in fact, unconscious – but the pain gathering at the base of my belly tells me otherwise.

My throat closes over a roar of agony. Conjuring what little strength I have, I fight the urge to push. *Just hang on a bit longer, baby, please.* I chant the words over and over in my head, like a mantra and, miraculously, the feeling passes.

'Maybe they've gone,' murmurs Magda, seeming oblivious to my presence once again. Putting down the knife, she crosses from the door to the bed, crouches down and drags something from underneath it. Keeping my eyes half-closed, I see a Moses basket, with a frilly white blanket inside.

She starts pulling things out of it, tossing them onto the bed: a shawl, two baby bottles, a tin of formula, a pack of nappies, a pale-pink dummy wrapped in cellophane.

I want to stay in the moment and work out what's going on, but everything's fading except the pain and another urge to push. Twisting my head to the window, I try to concentrate on the view of outlined treetops against the sky.

A creaking sound seeps into my consciousness. Someone's coming upstairs. I hear footsteps on the landing and the sound of doors banging.

I think I hear Mum shout something, and Dan calling me 'babe' and telling me to hang on, but I can't be sure I'm not hearing things through the red mist of pain that's descended. Swivelling my eyes, I see Magda open the door a fraction, the knife back in her hand.

'You're not taking her. She's mine now,' she says, and a distant part of me feels so sorry for Mum, having to hear that, because no matter what's happened in the past, she's been my mother for thirty years. Then tears of relief squeeze past my eyelids, because she's really here.

'Please talk to me, Mary.'

Mary?

'I'm not Mary anymore. And you're not Jane.'

Jane? Mum's middle name.

'That's right, I'm not.' Mum's voice is gentle. She doesn't sound scared at all. She sounds calmer than I've ever heard her. 'Let's talk about Patrick, Mary. I've tracked him down and spoken to him and we're worried about you. He asked me to tell you something; he has a plan. Please come out, so we can talk about it.'

Chapter 28

Dan

'Please come out,' Helen repeated, gently. 'It's been such a long time, Mary. We've got lots to talk about.'

She flapped her hand for Dan to move back from the door. He badly wanted to ignore her, but knew Magda had to come out before either of them could get in.

He shrank into the shadows by the landing window, every nerve end in his body jangling. While Helen talked soothingly, as if trying to coax a wild animal, he fumbled for his phone in his jacket pocket.

For all he knew, Bernard was back at the farm with his feet up and Saskia was at home in bed, but from the sounds he'd heard behind that door, Kate was either badly hurt or in labour and needed help.

He pressed 999, but there wasn't enough signal to connect.

'Shit.' About to try again, he noticed a text. Dry-mouthed, he opened it and read, Message understood. Maybe in another life. Zxx

His burst of relief that Zoe was no longer a problem was

short-lived. Why was Kate so quiet?

He moved back towards the door, just as it opened further, and the woman he'd seen on CCTV stepped out, gripping a knife, her expression a mix of cunning and wariness that chilled him.

Helen grabbed hold of her arm, catching her off-guard, and pulled her away from the door. 'Go!' she hissed at Dan, but he was already inside the room, tripping over a suitcase on the floor as he rushed to Kate, his mind taking snapshots as he reached her. She was sprawled on a narrow bed, legs bent, bare feet pressed into the mattress, and her dress was crumpled above her enormous belly, her head thrashing on the pillow. She was fastened by her wrists to the bars of the bed behind her.

'Oh my God, Kate.' Struggling with the knots, he managed to get them untied and slid his arms beneath her shoulders, drawing her awkwardly against him, pressing kisses on her forehead. She tasted of salt and smelled faintly of vomit, and her lips were dry and cracked. 'Kate, talk to me,' he pleaded. 'Are you OK?'

She opened her eyes and looked at him blankly before recognition dawned. 'Dan?' Her face contorted. 'Oh, Dan, the baby's coming,' she gasped, clawing at his shoulders. 'We have to get out of here.'

'I know.' Out on the landing, he heard the rise of Helen's voice, arguing with Magda.

Kate's eyes flickered to the door and widened. 'What's she doing?'

'Your mum's fine,' he lied, freeing one hand, and trying to tug Kate's dress down. He'd never seen her like this: dishevelled and helpless, her hair a knotted tangle, strands of it plastered to her cheeks.

'You don't understand,' Kate said, her grip tightening on his shoulders. 'She can't be here; it's not safe.'

That much was obvious, but all he cared about at that moment was Kate, his relief at finding her mingled with terror. What the hell had happened to her? Her pupils were dilated, like Calum's when he was high. And how could she be this close to giving birth, when two days ago she'd been fine? He knew babies came early, but there'd been nothing in her phone message, or Magda's call, to indicate this might happen – unless Magda had deliberately kept it from him.

'What has she done to you, Kate?'

A wail of sirens interrupted whatever she'd been about to say, and a flash of blue lights danced across the ceiling. *Thank Christ.* Police, or an ambulance, he didn't care. Help was on its way.

'Come on,' he said, attempting to lift Kate off the bed, but she struggled, pushing him away.

'Get Mum,' she said hoarsely. 'I need to talk to her.'

'Not now, Kate.' He attempted to tuck his arm underneath her knees, but she kept straightening her legs and he had no choice but to drop her back on the bed.

'Dan, listen to me.' Kate ran her tongue over her lips. Gripping his hands, she tugged him towards her. 'She says Mum's not my mum,' she said, her voice coming in snatches. 'She took me when I was a baby and now Magda wants our baby.'

'No.' Dan shook his head, as if denying her words would make them untrue. Despite his earlier fears, he couldn't believe it. And even if it was true, that woman wasn't fit to be any kind of mother to Kate.

'It's true, Dan.' Kate's voice grew faint. 'She's got photos and she talked about my father, Patrick. She wants me to meet him.'

'Let's focus on you for now, my love.' He wound his hand through her hair to cradle her head. 'We'll talk about everything else later,' he said, as she started to protest. 'We have to go now.'

'I don't think she'll let me.' Her gaze became fearful, moving beyond him to the doorway.

Glancing round, he saw the two women on the landing, locked in an embrace, or a struggle; he couldn't tell.

'Helen?' he called, voice cracking. Was she OK? He had to get both women out of there but couldn't do it on his own.

He turned to call out again, but as he opened his mouth a terrible cry split the air. Kate stiffened in his arms, and her eyes locked with his in a moment of mutual horror. A rush of movement lifted the hairs on the back of his neck, followed by the dull thud of someone falling downstairs.

As Kate emitted a noise from somewhere deep inside, someone hammered on the front door and there were shouts outside.

Dan felt his grip on reality loosen.

'Don't move,' he told Kate, unhooking his hands with difficulty. He didn't want to leave her but had no idea what had happened to Helen. 'I'll be right back.' The sight of Kate's crumpled, terrified face was almost too much to bear as he backed out of the room. He couldn't seem to catch his breath, and nearly stopped breathing altogether when he reached the top of the stairs and saw Helen and Magda lying at the bottom in a heap of limbs, neither of them moving. 'Helen!'

He flew down, but she was already stirring as he reached her.

'She tried to kill me.' Helen seemed dazed as she turned her head and registered the inert body beside her. 'When she realised I'd lied about contacting Patrick, she lunged at me with the knife. I shoved her off me and she fell, pulling me with her.' An odd expression flickered over her face, gone almost before Dan could register it. 'She wanted me dead.'

'Come here,' Dan said, heart thundering as he held out a hand to help Helen up. 'Are you OK?'

She flexed her arms and winced. 'I banged my head, and my wrist hurts a bit, but I'm fine.'

There was more knocking and shouting outside, but Dan couldn't stop looking at Magda, twisted on the carpet. Her legs were bent underneath her, and a trickle of blood seeped into her hair from a gash on her forehead. Her eyes were closed, her jaw slack. The knife was lying beside her.

'I don't think she's breathing,' he said to Helen, a nauseous panic rising. He stooped to lift Magda's wrist, and to his relief felt the flutter of her pulse. 'She's alive.'

'Pity.'

Helen's tone froze him. For a second, he couldn't speak. When he looked at her, she was flexing her arms again, rolling her head as if her neck was aching. 'She's a dangerous woman,' was all she said, in response to whatever she'd read in his expression. 'Is my daughter safe?'

Before he could answer, the hammering at the door increased, galvanising them into action. Helen ran up the stairs while Dan stepped over Magda's body to struggle with the front door. It was cluttered with bolts and chains, which explained why they hadn't been able to get in.

He finally wrenched it open, almost collapsing with relief at the sight of a burly paramedic on the porch, another behind him, holding a collapsible wheelchair. 'She's upstairs,' he said, but their gazes had slid past him to the figure on the floor. 'My wife's in labour,' he elaborated, pointing at the staircase as an agonised cry erupted from the bedroom. 'I think she's been drugged.' His panic was gaining traction with every passing second. He'd left Kate alone too long. Anything could be happening. 'Please, you have to help her.'

'OK, mate.' The man raised his eyebrows at his female colleague, and they pushed into the hall, filling the space with fast, efficient movements.

'What about her?' The woman nodded at Magda.

Dan turned to look, half expecting to see she'd sat up, ready to say she was fine and that there'd been a terrible mistake, but she hadn't moved. Shock rippled through him. She might not be dead but was clearly badly injured.

'She looks in a bad way,' the man said, bending to press capable fingertips to the skin on Magda's neck.

'She was keeping my wife here against her will, and she had a knife,' Dan said baldly, pointing to it. The sight of Kate on that lumpy bed, her tear-stained face convulsed with pain, replaced the one of Magda's twisted body. 'You have to help Kate *now*.'

Keeping his eyes on Dan, the male paramedic requested another ambulance into the crackling radio attached to his shirt. 'Police are on their way too,' he said, turning back to Dan. 'They'll have questions.'

'Not now.' Dan pushed the words through clenched teeth. 'I have to be with my wife.'

He took the stairs two at a time, and a hush fell as the paramedics hurried to the bed and examined Kate. Seeing the state of her, Dan felt as if his heart would burst. 'I'm sorry, I'm sorry,' he kept saying, but he didn't know if she could hear. Her eyes were shut, and she was whimpering, her face beaded with sweat. Helen was beside her, stroking Kate's hair and urging her to breathe, which might have been funny any other time.

'I know how to breathe, Mum,' he imagined Kate saying, rolling her eyes, but he was urging her to breathe too, to keep living, to deliver their baby, to forgive him, to come home. *Please get through this and I'll never let you down again.*

Watching Helen with her daughter, it suddenly seemed ridiculous to have thought for a moment she was anyone other than Kate's mother. He wanted to apologise to her too.

Voices and a crackle of radios rose from downstairs. A second ambulance had pulled up and the police had arrived. They'd want to know what had happened to Magda, but only Helen knew the answer to that – until Magda gave her side of the story.

Dan recalled the look on Helen's face when he told her Magda was alive. Had she really fallen, or did Helen push her? Could he blame her if she had – if Magda really had meant to harm Kate and take the baby?

Helen was only looking out for her daughter.

A groan from the bed stilled his spiralling thoughts. He was here now. He would spend the rest of his life making it up to Kate if he had to.

'Her BP's on the low side,' said the female paramedic, removing the cuff from Kate's arm, where it left a red indentation. 'Do we have any idea what she's taken?'

'Not taken,' Dan said, his voice thick with frustration. 'She wouldn't take anything of her own accord. She's been *given* something.'

'Found these next door.' He hadn't noticed her colleague leave the room. He was holding out his latex-gloved hands and the sight of the vials and pill bottles and blister packs he'd gathered made Dan's blood run cold. 'There's something herbal and some sleeping pills, and something else I've never heard of.'

'Oh God.' Helen gripped her mouth with her hand, her eyes wide with shock. 'She'd planned this all along.' Her voice sank to a whisper. 'She wanted the baby. I told you, Dan.'

Words rolled helplessly in his head. 'Do something,' was all he could muster, dragging his hands through his hair. He didn't want to listen to Helen's theories and didn't want Kate to hear them. The only thing that mattered was getting her out of here.

'Let's move her into the ambulance.' The paramedics indicated for Dan and Helen to stand back while they lifted Kate into the wheelchair. Dan wanted to help, or at least to touch her, and settled for gripping her hand.

'I love you so much; I'm sorry, Kate; it's going to be all right.' He prayed that it was, relieved when she squeezed his hand.

'Glad you came,' he thought she said, her lips so pale they merged with the rest of her face. Her eyes flickered open and found his. 'So glad you came.' Her mouth sketched a faint smile.

'I love you, and I love this baby,' he whispered, raising her hand to his lips and kissing her fingers. 'We're going to the hospital now.' He rested his other hand on her stomach, which felt as taut as a drum. 'Everything's going to be fine.' As her head lolled back and she began to groan, he turned to the paramedics. 'Haven't you got a stretcher?'

'This will be fine; don't worry.' The female offered a sympathetic smile, and he wondered briefly what she must make of them all. 'If you could wait downstairs, please.'

He didn't want Kate to see Magda, but when they emerged, she'd already been removed, and the house was swarming with officers. Through the open front door, he saw Bernard, craning his neck to get a better view of what was going on.

Kate's groan grew to a wail. She was trying to draw up her knees, her hands clutching at her belly. 'I need to push,' she cried, dropping her chin to her chest, her face reddening with effort. 'It's coming,' she panted, and he reached for her hand again. 'I can't stop it, Dan.'

Everything sped up after that. Brushing off a police officer, promising he'd talk to them later, he found himself in the back of the ambulance with Kate, being driven through the night to the hospital, while Helen followed in her car. The female paramedic – who told them her name was Jo and that she'd delivered several babies before – took charge, settling Kate on a stretcher-like bed, instructing her when to breathe and when to push.

As the siren shrieked and the miles rushed by, the world outside shrank to a pinprick, and everything fell away. It was just the three of them: Jo, encouraging and soothing, Kate gripping his hand as she yelled and pushed, Dan rubbing her back and urging her on until, twenty minutes later, in the back of the ambulance, his son burst into the world.

Chapter 29

Kate

I'm the mother of a six-pound baby boy. Possibly the most perfect baby in the world. He has a swirl of feather-soft brown hair, a rosebud mouth and dark blue eyes with spiky lashes, like Dan's.

The scent of him is already lodged in my memory, and although I'm more tired than I've ever been, I can't stop gazing at him.

I can hardly believe he's here.

The events leading up to his birth have become a blur, but some things are vivid in my mind. I remember being in the back of the ambulance with Dan and Jo, the bouncy paramedic with thick brown hair in a ponytail, who was patient and kind and reassuring. I remember the look on Dan's face as he tried to keep hold of my hand without losing his balance in the swaying vehicle – a blend of panic, fear and tenderness that told me far more about his feelings than words ever could. I remember clutching his fingers, the force of pain inside me bigger than anything I'd imagined, followed by unbearable pressure, then a slippery wetness between my thighs. A terrifying silence had been broken moments later by a mewling cry that cracked our faces into grins.

I thought my heart would explode with love.

'He's here.' Dan's voice had caught. 'It's a boy.' His face, damp with tears, had seemed to melt when Jo handed him our baby. He cradled him gently, one hand cupping his head, his face dipped close to his son's as he murmured hello, and in that moment, I knew it would be all right. He might not have known it, but Dan was ready to be a father.

When the ambulance pulled up at the hospital entrance, Mum had tried to clamber in but was reassured that all was well and told to meet us inside.

'It's a boy,' I told her, waves of exhaustion crashing over me. I was so tired, I felt delirious.

'Oh Kate, you did it,' she'd cried, running beside us to where a doctor and midwife were waiting to whisk us away. In spite of her tears, she'd looked so happy. Her hair was standing in tufts, and there was a rip at the cuff of her jacket, but she seemed more vital somehow – as if she'd been switched off and rebooted. I'd thought it odd after everything that had happened but figured it must be the transforming power of the baby. Everyone who looked at him smiled, apart from the doctor who greeted us. He must have been forewarned, because he took him away to be checked immediately, his face clenched with concern.

I remember the fraught, heart-stopping fear while we waited, and the shot of euphoria when we were both given the all clear.

We decided to name him Joe, after the paramedic who delivered him, and once I was allowed to breastfeed, Dan took photos on his phone then called his parents, and Saskia and Eric, to break the good news.

I remember telling Dan how sorry I was for storming out of the house that morning, and how he cupped my chin in his hand and looked into my eyes for what felt like the first time in months.

'I should have talked to you,' he said, brushing away my tears with his thumb. 'I'm the one who's sorry. I was an idiot. But you're safe now, Kate, and so is our baby, and I honestly couldn't be happier.'

Mum, who'd barely left my side, gave him a look of approval I'd never seen from her before, and it struck me they'd bonded somehow. They'd been thrown together in a way that would never have happened if I hadn't met Magda.

It's when I think of Magda that the memories falter. The drugs she gave me have reduced them to a murky haze, for which I'm mostly grateful, because if I think too hard about what happened – and what could have happened – I'm not sure I could bear it.

She'd had sleeping pills, luckily out of date and probably not that strong, and a herbal remedy meant to induce labour she'd laced my drinks with. More worryingly, some drops she'd put in water, which if taken undiluted can cause a heart attack.

The police think she must have got them from a dealer, and I realised then how little I knew her, and how ill she really was.

We've been told that she has a serious back injury from her fall and might never walk again. She's in a secure hospital and faces months of treatment and psychiatric reports.

All she's said since regaining consciousness is that she wanted her baby back, so she and Patrick could be together again. I almost felt sorry for her when I heard that, but then I remembered what she'd done and how close she'd been to harming my baby and me.

Her name's not really Magda. She's called Mary, and Mum knew her briefly a long time ago. Mary thought Mum had taken me, but things had got muddled up in her head.

'To be honest, I started to think your mum really might have kidnapped you,' Dan admitted when I cried to him, ashamed that I'd been taken in by Mary. 'It fitted with the way she was,' he said, taking a crying Joe from my arms and walking him up and down. 'Let's face it, she always seemed to be hiding something, or holding back, and she's overprotective.'

Grateful, I'd clung to his words, allowing myself to be reassured, but I'd worried it was more than that. That an alternative life to the one I'd had with Mum – one that included a longed-for father – had briefly seemed more attractive to me.

I haven't absorbed it all yet. I'm not surprised Mum kept such an important part of her past from me, and I understand she did it to protect me and can't really blame her for that. She suspected things hadn't ended when she left Leeds, and the feeling had persisted over the years. It's just as well, because if she hadn't been certain she'd seen Mary, or had the note pushed through her letterbox saying 'I know what you did', and Dan hadn't thought to check the CCTV, I dread to think what might have happened. Would the realisation my baby was a boy have pushed Mary over the edge?

No one's said it, but I'm sure Mum and Dan believe she might have killed me. I prefer to think she wanted to keep us both and would have tried to talk me into going to Vermont with the baby to meet Patrick. But occasionally, the image of the look on her face when she slapped me slides into my head, and I believe it too.

Some of the things she'd told me were true – about her father being a doctor and her doing medical training. She was a midwife for a bit, but took a baby from the hospital and was struck off. Her mother did die when she was young, but she didn't have a brother, so I don't know why she told me that, unless it was wishful thinking – or to draw me further in.

No one knows what happened to her baby. Medical checks show she did give birth, but the police think maybe the baby died, or maybe she killed it, but without a body there's no proof. I can't believe she'd be capable of that, but if she had severe post-natal depression, who knows what she might have done. Perhaps she couldn't live with her actions and preferred to think someone had taken her baby instead.

The police contacted Patrick Gilmore, but while he remembered Mary as an intense girl who had a crush on him at medical college, they only dated for a short while. He'd relocated to Canada soon after he ended their short relationship and hadn't wanted to be a father, had even doubted Mary was pregnant when she told him. He never saw her again.

Mum told me she'd called round to Mary's house by chance one day, looking for a work colleague who lived on the same street and thinks it was around that time Mary had given birth, and somehow Mum's face got fixed in her head, so when she saw Mum in the park that day with me, she convinced herself it was Mum who'd taken her baby.

'You didn't believe her, did you?' Mum asks. It's a week later and I'm finally home with Joe and Dan, marvelling at how everything looks the same, yet different. Mum's done her best to give us some time alone, but turned up this morning laden with baby outfits, and a one-eyed cat for Joe that used to be mine.

'What do you mean?' I say, though I know perfectly well what she means. It's the question I've been dreading but have somehow avoided so far.

'You didn't really believe that she was your mother?' Mum's looking at Joe, asleep peacefully in his Moses basket in the living room after a fractious night, but I know she's eager for my answer.

I remember Mary's voice, and the way her words wound through me, putting down roots, how plausible she'd been. A combination of her own belief in her story, according to the psychologist I spoke to at the hospital, and the sedative she'd laced my food and drink with, plus the photo of her and Mum. There'd almost been no reason *not* to believe her. Even so, I felt terrible that I'd taken her at her word – that something didn't kick in to tell me it wasn't true.

Now the drugs were out of my system, the whole story seemed ludicrous.

'Of course I didn't believe her,' I say, getting off the sofa to look more closely at Joe. His button nose is the same shape as Mum's, and his eyebrows are exactly like Dan's. I can't see anything of me yet, though Saskia insists he's got my chin. I suppose people see what they want to see. 'She was very convincing,' I add, 'though if we'd gone ahead with a DNA test, the truth would have come out.'

'I suppose, in her own mind, she believed it,' Mum says without bitterness. I cast her a look but can't tell if she believes that I wasn't taken in by Magda's story. Maybe it doesn't matter. Maybe it's enough that I'm here and safe.

'What did you say to her on the landing, before she fell?'

Mum meets my gaze. 'I told her that I would never forgive her for what she'd done to you; that's all. She guessed I hadn't spoken to Patrick and didn't take it well.'

Mum's looks rejuvenated these days. Her face, normally dragged down with worry, seems on the verge of smiling all the time. She's wearing a new top in a pale-blue shade that matches her eyes, and it feels like something more has happened than me being safe, and her becoming a grandmother. Maybe the fact that Mary's no longer a threat is a weight off her mind. She's even asked Dan for some motorcycle lessons.

Flashing back to the blood-curdling scream as Mary fell down the stairs, a shudder passes through me. It could so easily have been Mum lying broken at the foot of the stairs. We've been interviewed by the police – as were Bernard and Tomasz – and they're satisfied Magda's fall was an accident. Magda seems to have no memory of what happened, or so she says. She's been charged with kidnapping, drugging me and inducing my labour, but it will be a while before it comes to court – unless she pleads guilty.

I want to stay in the present now, to hold on to the happiness Joe's brought into our lives, which has spread like sunshine, casting out the shadows. I don't want these early days with him tainted by bad memories. I've let go of my anger with Magda and try not to worry that the drugs she gave me will affect Joe in the future.

'He was probably ready to come out anyway,' Saskia had said, turning up at the hospital in her pyjamas half an hour after Dan called her, her eyes red-rimmed from crying. 'Remember you'd been having back ache all week.'

She blamed herself for not knowing where I'd gone. 'You can't visit clients on your own anymore,' she'd said, wiping her eyes with the back of her hand, only for more tears to fall. 'I should have gone with you.'

'There was no way you could have known,' I told her, and Dan pointed out it was a good job she'd known how to access the surveillance footage.

'Massive fluke,' she said, but her tears finally slowed. 'Thank God your mum recognised the mad bitch.'

'Anyway, I won't be working for a while.' I'd looked at Joe in my arms, his dimpled fist curled against his cheek, and wondered how I could ever leave him again. 'You're going to be in charge from now on.'

'I'll need an assistant,' she said, with a flash of her old spirit.

I didn't argue. For once, I couldn't imagine my job being anywhere near as important as it had been.

I loop my arms around Mum from behind and rest my chin on her shoulder. 'I love you,' I whisper, and her hands come up to cover mine. We gaze at Joe sleeping for a while. His lips make little sucking movements, as if he's feeding in his sleep, and a fierce surge of protectiveness rises inside me. I want to scoop him against me and hold him there forever.

'It's overwhelming, isn't it?' Mum says, as if I've somehow communicated my feelings, and I realise it's always been this way. She's always had the ability to know what I'm thinking, even when I haven't spoken. 'We'd do anything to keep our children safe.'

She straightens and turns to face me, and reaching out she tucks a strand of hair behind my ear. 'I need to talk to you about something, Kate.'

Her voice is so serious my heart gives a little flip. Her expression is unfamiliar, both tentative and determined, as if whatever she wants to say is something she's been putting off, and I suddenly don't want to hear it. What if it's something I don't want to know? Like, she really *did* take me from Mary. But that's stupid, I know it is, and I can't understand why the thought even popped into my head.

'Kate?'

'Could you make some tea first, Mum?'

She nods, looking almost relieved, and heads for the kitchen. I cross to the window and look out at the garden. It's rained overnight and everything looks freshly washed. The grass is greener, the sky bluer. Everything's more sharply focused, but that's not surprising as my head's clear for almost the first time in a week.

I watch Dan getting out of the car, which the police retrieved from the garage at Little Acorn, where Mary hid it to stop me leaving and so no one would see it parked outside.

He's wearing a short-sleeved shirt I bought him for Christmas and heads up the path with a bounce in his step, swinging a bag of nappies from the supermarket.

He's shaved his beard off and looks like the man I fell in love with – the man I want to spend the rest of my life with. I still can't believe I thought he was having an affair with Zoe. Another side effect of the drugs, and possibly Mary leading me towards that conclusion to suit her own plans. I'm so glad I didn't mention it, especially now the band is breaking up. Eric's taking a job at his father's company, and Calum's apparently in love with a bridesmaid he met at the wedding gig and is hoping to join another band. I don't know what Zoe's doing and haven't asked.

I can't say I'm sorry. It'll be nice to have Dan home more. He's going to keep his hand in as a session player, and after seeing the beautiful crib he made for Joe, I know he'll never be short of work as a furniture maker.

As if sensing me watching, he raises his hand in a wave.

'It's not what you're thinking, Kate.'

Mum puts the tea down and plucks Joe from his Moses basket. She holds him against her shoulder, bobbing him up and down, and her actions look so natural that for the first time I see her as she might have been with me.

'So, what is it?'

'It's about your father.' Her words are so unexpected, I can only stare. For a second, it's as if I'm back at the cottage with Magda spinning her story, weaving me in.

'What are you talking about?'

'He found me, and he's been in touch.' Her gaze is unflinching. 'He wants to meet you, Kate.'

I take Joe from her and sink down on the sofa. 'All this time, you wouldn't talk about him.'

'I know and I'm sorry.' Her cheeks are flushed, eyes bright, hands clasped tightly in front of her. 'You have a right to know; I see that now.'

I cuddle Joe, still sleeping, and try to process her words.

'What's his name?' I don't know why that's the first thing I ask.

'Andrew.'

Andrew. My father. He wants to see me. 'I thought he was married.'

'He divorced his wife several years ago. He said he's never stopped thinking about us.'

She looked . . . *happy* when she mentioned his name, a flash of warmth in her eyes she couldn't disguise. Like Mary when she'd spoken of Patrick, who'd barely registered her existence.

Mum still loves my father. I can't begin to unravel this line of thought.

Dan comes in and opens the bag of nappies, ready for when Joe's been fed. He's proving very hands-on. His parents are coming at the weekend, and he can't wait to show off his son.

'What's going on?' he says, looking from me to Mum. She's sitting stiffly in the chair opposite, eyes on my face, and I think of Mary again, but this is a true story, and one I want to hear. One I've waited to hear all my life. One Mum should have told me a year ago, ten years ago, as soon as I was old enough to understand.

I want to be angry, but instead I feel sorry for her. Her life has been difficult. She lost all the people she loved the most but managed to love me anyway. She did her best. Isn't that all we can do?

Dan comes and sits next to me, placing an arm around my shoulders. We're touching again and it's good – as if there'd never been that period of estrangement.

Mum looks over at him and he nods, and I realise she's talked to him already and I'm glad, because it means he knows and he's OK with it. He didn't think it necessary to warn me; he's been waiting for her to tell me.

I lean into him, feeling his strength, knowing I'll need his support more than ever for whatever's coming, and rearrange Joe in my arms.

'Come here,' I say to Mum, patting the sofa beside us and she does. She takes my hand, and all the anxiety has left her face. She looks again like the woman I saw in the photo with Magda – the one full of hope for the future. 'You'd better start at the beginning.'

After

The woman boards the plane and walks down the aisle.

She doesn't look at the man in the seat next to hers but feels his eyes tracking her movements as she stuffs her bag in the luggage compartment. She's left most of her things behind. She won't be needing them now.

The landlord won't be happy about her abrupt departure, but once she'd made her mind up to go, she didn't want to hang around. Leaving feels like the only rational decision she's made in a long time.

Going home will be a fresh start, not the defeat she's envisaged so many times. She'll build bridges with her family, if they'll let her, and maybe get some counselling. It's not fair to keep blaming her mother for every failure in her life. She has to take responsibility.

Her mother's only ever done what she thinks is best, she can see that now. Has probably known it all along if she's finally being honest with herself. She's had plenty of time to think lately, and especially during the long wait at the airport, after the flight was delayed due to stormy weather.

If only her mother had been honest with her from the start. Admitted she'd stolen her all those years ago, and that was the reason she looked so different from anyone else in the family.

Once the confession had started it wouldn't stop, as if a tap had been turned on, the words flowing out of her mother like water. It turned out she'd heard a baby crying and crying, in a house in the street where she was living at the time. She'd been off work with the flu and was out walking as she recovered. On impulse, she'd knocked on the open door of the house, and receiving no reply had let herself in. There, she'd found a woman in an upstairs room, sleeping as though her baby hadn't been crying for ages, in a terrible state. She'd previously cut off her baby's hair, said the child – Lexi, she'd called her – was possessed and that's why she wouldn't stop crying.

Her mother had simply picked the baby up and walked out. She never went back to work. She told them there was an emergency at home and her family needed her. Then she used her savings and flew to America. She stayed with an old friend, saying the father of her baby had died and she needed a fresh start.

For her family, she concocted a story about an American boy getting her pregnant and dumping her, and by the time they came out to visit, she'd moved into a small apartment and no further questions were asked.

She'd been scared for a while that the woman would go to the police and report her baby missing, but nothing happened. All the same, she'd never dared return to England.

It had all been such a shock. Not just knowing her pretty, wholesome mother was capable of such an act, but that her birth mother hadn't cared about her.

'She was obviously ill,' her mother had sobbed. 'But I couldn't take the chance she would harm you.'

Her mother loved children, had wanted to be a teacher, but ended up working in an office before coming to America. With the help of her friend, she eventually retrained and worked in a primary school for years. She was a good woman, who loved her daughter dearly, and managed to convince herself most of the time that the child really was her own.

She hadn't bargained on her daughter being so different, on probing her about her 'dead father' as soon as she was old enough to ask, or constantly asking why she didn't look anything like her mother.

And when she found out the truth, it hadn't mattered that she'd had a happy childhood, with a mother and stepfather who adored her, and a younger brother and sister she got on well with.

She'd been abandoned. Her real mother had wanted her gone.

It became the thing that defined her.

She went off the rails after that, drinking too much, self-harming, getting in with the wrong crowd. She knew she'd been born in a town in England, and years later decided to move there. Partly to punish her mother, but mostly because she wanted to see the house she'd been stolen from. She decided her birth mother must still live there and was waiting for her to return. She dreamed they'd have an instant connection, form a bond, and live happily ever after.

When that didn't happen, she considered going to the papers or the local news and putting out a plea.

'Was your baby stolen from a house in Leeds thirty years ago? If so, here I am!'

But she knew it would only attract the wrong sort of attention.

She tortured herself with scenarios. Her birth mother was dead. She was married with a family of her own, a daughter better than the one she'd let go. She was anyone, and everyone. She lived in Australia, New Zealand, on the moon. She was nowhere.

She would never find her.

She could never ask her why.

She grew to accept it and was tired of looking, had ended up moving to Marlow after seeing an ad in a music magazine for a band looking for a lead singer, though she hadn't sung for a long time. For a while it had been enough. She accepted the money her mother kept sending to ease her guilty conscience and rented the most expensive apartment she could find.

Then she fell in love, and nothing else mattered.

The plane begins to taxi down the runway. She keeps her eyes on the view outside, as the man beside her fidgets. His shoulder brushes hers and she senses it's deliberate. She shifts slightly to leave a gap between them.

Outside, rain falls like needles, bouncing off the ground, but above the clouds she knows it will be sunny.

She shivers, thinking about how close she's come to destroying lives lately. Thank Christ she came to her senses before it was too late. She thought about breaking up his marriage, but in the end, she loved him too much and worried he would hate her.

She thinks of her adoptive mother, waiting at the airport to welcome her daughter home. A wave of relief washes over her, so intense tears flood her eyes. She absently scratches the faded scars on the underside of her arm, then stops when she realises the man beside her is watching.

Turning, she looks at him more closely. He has wide dark eyes and curly brown hair, and a dimple in his cheek when he smiles.

Her breath catches in her throat.

She turns away, and in the oval window briefly catches the glint of red at the roots of her parting. She's letting her hair go back to its natural shade after years of covering it up. She was bullied for a while at school because of the colour but wants to reclaim it. It seems fitting somehow – a tribute to her unknown parents.

She thinks she might take painting up again too, to complete the transformation. She can't imagine singing anymore. It made her feel like someone she no longer liked.

'I'm Mark.' The man beside her breaks into her thoughts, extending his hand towards her.

Inwardly, she sighs. It's a long flight to LA. She supposes it won't hurt to make small talk. She'll never see him again; she's sure of that. He reminds her too much of Dan.

'Hi, Mark.' She meets his gaze as she takes his hand. 'I'm Zoe.'

A Letter from Karen Clarke

Thank you so much for choosing to read *The Mother's Secret*. I hope you enjoyed it! If you did and would like to be the first to know about my new releases, you can follow me on my socials below.

I hope you loved *The Mother's Secret* and if you did, I would be so grateful if you would leave a review. I always love to hear what readers thought, and it helps new readers discover my books too.

Thanks,

Karen

Twitter/X: https://twitter.com/karenclarke123
Facebook: https://www.facebook.com/karen.clarke.5682
Website: https://www.karenclarkewriter.com/

My Best Friend's Secret

She knows her. But can she trust her?

When **Rose's** old friend **Elise** suddenly arrives on her doorstep having just escaped a controlling marriage, she offers her a place to stay.

But Elise wants more than a safe refuge, she wants Rose to help her get her daughter back, so that she can truly start afresh with five-year-old Daisy safely in her arms. Every little girl needs her mother, after all.

Ready to insert herself into Elise's old home, Rose gets a job as a teacher, home-schooling Daisy.

But when Rose is asked to take the little girl and bring her to Elise, she gets cold feet . . . Elise's behaviour is becoming increasingly erratic, and Daisy's father is far from the monster described . . .

Will Rose take Daisy and return her to her mother, or is the real danger closer to home?

Who should she trust?

My Husband's Secret

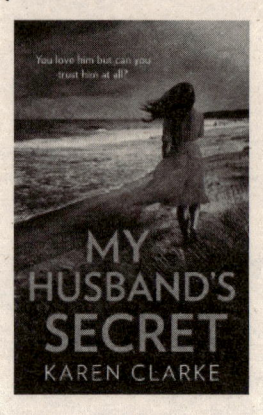

**His secret could destroy them, but her truth is
even harder to bear . . .**

One year ago, my husband Jack left. I've longed for the
moment he would walk through the door and tell me all he
ever wanted was to be with me.

Now he's back, but this isn't the reunion I had dreamed of . . .

Jack has been in a hit-and-run accident. He doesn't remember
we aren't together, has no clue about his other family, and no
recollection of the phone call he made before the crash – I made
a terrible mistake that I can't put right. All I can do is get out.

Jack is different to the man who walked out and I'm certain
he's hiding something too.

But I finally have my husband by my side, and with Jack
suffering from amnesia, surely the easiest thing would be to
stay quiet . . .

**But can you really trust a man who simply vanished from
your life? And should he even trust me?**

My Sister's Child

**I promised her I'd protect him ... and I'll do
anything to keep him safe.**

Five years ago, my sister Rachel left her baby boy on my doorstep. A little bundle wrapped in blankets. I loved him. I cared for him. I called him Noah and raised him as my own.

Rachel was full of secrets, and the truth about Noah was one we shared. A secret just between sisters.

Now, my sister is dead. The police say it was an accident ... But I'm convinced that's a lie.

I owe it to Rachel to uncover the truth ... Even if I risk losing the family I've fought so hard for.

Acknowledgements

I would like to thank the amazing team at HQ Stories, with special thanks to Audrey Linton for all her insight and guidance, and to my lovely new editor Seema Mitra. Thanks to Jon Appleton for a brilliant copyedit, Michelle Bullock for an eagle-eyed proofread and Anna Sikorska for another amazing cover. Thank you also to the marketing team.

I'm in awe of the readers, bloggers and reviewers who take time to spread the word and give lovely feedback, which makes all the hard work worthwhile – thank you.

As ever, a big thank you to my family and friends who manage to stay interested and always read my books, and to Amanda Brittany who reads the dodgy first draft and gives priceless feedback.

I couldn't do any of it without my husband who has somehow survived this process yet again. Once again, Tim, thank you.

Dear Reader,

We hope you enjoyed reading this book. If you did, we'd be so appreciative if you left a review. It really helps us and the author to bring more books like this to you.

Here at HQ Digital we are dedicated to publishing fiction that will keep you turning the pages into the early hours. Don't want to miss a thing? To find out more about our books, promotions, discover exclusive content and enter competitions you can keep in touch in the following ways:

JOIN OUR COMMUNITY:

Sign up to our new email newsletter: http://smarturl.it/SignUpHQ

Read our new blog www.hqstories.co.uk

🐦 https://twitter.com/HQStories

📘 www.facebook.com/HQStories

BUDDING WRITER?

We're also looking for authors to join the HQ Digital family!
Find out more here:

https://www.hqstories.co.uk/want-to-write-for-us/

Thanks for reading, from the HQ Digital team